To London
more than a
gathering to gossip
of the ton. *But the women of Lavender*
House share an uncommon gift that will
lead them to days filled with danger—
and nights of unquenchable desire.

With her smoldering glances and dazzling beauty, Ella St. James, Countess of Lanshire, could bewitch any man. But she isn't about to squander her unique attentions on the mundane task of finding a husband. After all, the perfect man is a mere fantasy, and she has more urgent worries. A close friend and fellow Lavender House lady has gone missing, and Ella is determined to find her. But everywhere she turns, she finds only the handsome, alluring, and troublemaking Thomas Donovan.

Thomas has secrets of his own, secrets that could destroy him, and his attraction to the tantalizing Ella is a terrible risk. Yet when her investigation leads her into mortal peril, Thomas cannot help but try to rescue her, love her, and devour her . . . for he has fallen under her spell.

By Lois Greiman

If You've Enjoyed This Book,
Be Sure to Read These Other
AVON ROMANTIC TREASURES

Coming Soon

UNDER YOUR SPELL

Lois Greiman

An Avon Romantic Treasure

AVON
An Imprint of HarperCollinsPublishers

AVON BOOKS
An Imprint of HarperCollins*Publishers*
10 East 53rd Street
New York, New York 10022-5299

Copyright © 2008 by Lois Greiman
ISBN 978-0-06-119136-7
www.avonromance.com

First Avon Books paperback printing: June 2008

Avon Trademark Reg. U.S. Pat. Off. and in Other Countries, Marca Registrada, Hecho en U.S.A.
HarperCollins® is a registered trademark of HarperCollins Publishers.

Printed in the U.S.A.

10 9 8 7 6 5 4 3

To Cary Bardell. Thanks for being a friend to me and to the lost children of the world. You are the kindest, most courageous woman I know.

Under Your Spell

Chapter 1

Elegance St. James, Countess of Lanshire, took a sip of champagne and glanced about the salon. Everyone with a title and two pence was present. But she seemed to be the only witch.

And that was just as well, for she was weary of witches. Tired of their conniving and plotting and spells. Tired of their spats and alliances, their triumphs and failures. It was time to be normal. Normal but irresistible, she thought, and carefully preened her aura. Tonight she was beautiful, at least to others.

Near a table spread with every conceivable delicacy, Lord Milton shoved a peach tart into his mouth, glanced her way, then glanced again, eyes widening with interest. The little baron was middle-aged, homely, and somewhat paunchy. Rumor suggested he was also financially unstable, which made him a perfectly suitable match. Ella gave him her best come-hither smile.

From near the doorway by the lead-glass windows, the Viscount of Cleftmore scrutinized her. He was tall, elegant, and wealthy. She granted him a cool nod, then turned back toward Milton, who was, even now, struggling through the mob toward her, jiggling between a potted palm and a liveried servant, then striding rapidly across the hardwood floor. Ella offered him an encouraging smile. Let the others battle for the charms of the handsome, well-placed suitors. Let them become besotted and bedded and wedded. She had done so. It was not for her.

"My lady." Lord Milton was panting rather heavily by the time he reached her side. He was balding slightly, she noticed happily, and was a fair bit shorter than she.

"My lord," she said, and tilting her head, gave him a coy glance through lowered lashes. As lashes went, hers were far from spectacular. In fact, nothing about her physical appearance was particularly noteworthy. Never had been. Her sister Maddy had inherited their father's dark, good looks, leaving Ella rather ordinary by comparison, with hair that could not quite decide whether it was brown or red and curves that would never quite . . . well . . . curve. She was tall. Some might say spindly. Indeed, some had said just that. But none would say so tonight, for tonight she had employed all her powers to make her appear dazzling. And her powers were considerable.

"You are looking quite . . ." Lord Milton's eyes were round, his face flushed. "Quite . . . dazzling."

"My lord," she breathed again, and raised the pale lace fan she'd brought just for this purpose. She couldn't say why men found it appealing when women peered at them from above fans like so many peeping cockatiels, but apparently they did. "You flatter me."

"Flattery. No. No." He was perspiring a little above his upper lip, which was considerably larger than his lower. "Not at all. You are beauty itself. Like a beacon that . . ." From across the room, Miss May Anglican laughed. She was flirting. And by the sound of it, her chosen companion was either relatively attractive or extremely wealthy. Either was acceptable to May, though, in actuality, she flirted only to make Lord Gershwin jealous. After all, a mistress who could not make her lover envious might just as well be a wife.

But Milton seemed to notice neither the flirtatious tone of their hostess's laughter nor the burgeoning crowd. "Like a beacon that . . ." he re-iterated, but his words faltered again. Ella stifled an impatient urge to tap her toe, gave him a hope-ful smile over the top of her ridiculous fan, and visualized the word *shines*. It did no good whatso-ever. "That . . ." He floundered.

Miss Anglican, or Merry May, to those bold enough to know her well, was making her way through the crowd toward them. It was impos-sible to miss her. For while most posh ladies of the *ton* dressed in muted pastels and free-flowing gowns that fell like water from their nipples to their slippers, May wore anything she damned well pleased. And today tight-fitting, garish red seemed to please her tremendously.

"A beacon that, umm . . ."

"Ella!" said May, shattering Milton's concentra-tion and ruining any hope of a quickly concluded compliment. "I am so glad you have come." May was small and dimpled, with the demure person-ality of a beleaguered terrier. And if she was not quite beautiful, it hardly mattered. For she was Merry May, siren of every soiree, belle of every ball. Not Ella's usual type of friend, but then Ella had changed, hadn't she? Had left her life of dark concentration behind.

"Miss Anglican," Ella said, giving the other a

4

courteous smile and carefully maintaining propriety lest she scare off her potbellied prey. "I wouldn't have missed one of your gatherings for all the world. Indeed London is blessed to have—"

"Oh pish," May said, and taking Ella's arm, steered her aside. "If you'll excuse us, Lord Milton, I fear I need a word with . . ." Her eyes were shining with mischief and humor. "Your beacon."

With that, they left poor Milton in the rear.

"Listen, May—" Ella began, but May stopped her immediately.

"What the deuce do you think you're doing?"

Ella stifled a scowl, remembering to keep her expression pleasant, to keep her image obtuse. It was one of the more difficult tasks in her dealings with the *ton*. "I'm simply enjoying your fine party," she said, and glanced over May's shoulder at the little lord. He seemed to still be wrestling the kinks out of a few stunning similes.

"*Milt?*" said May, voice rye-toast dry. "You're considering Milt?"

"I'm sure I've no idea what you're talking—"

"She would have teeth like a picket fence."

Ella smiled at a passing dowager. Her skin was rice-powder white. Her hair was piled blue and high, reminiscent of days she seemed not quite ready to leave behind. "You haven't gotten into the blue ruin again, have you, May?"

"Do you want your daughter to be bald?"

"I don't have a daughter."

"And you're not about to. Not with the likes of Milton at any rate," she said, steering Ella through the crowd toward the gardens.

"Lord Milton happens to be—"

"A drunken lecher who is half your height and, so far as we know, entirely incapable of siring children of any sort, bald, snaggletoothed, or ugly as sin."

Ella opened her mouth, ready to disagree, but changed course at the last second. Lord Milton *did* have a tendency to stare at her chest, even when it was modestly garbed, which, by the by, was not the case this evening.

Her sheer muslin frock barely covered her bosom. Pale as a mint julep, it was topped with a delicate Austrian lace that showcased her modest cleavage to its greatest advantage. Tiny embroidered vines twined beneath the lace, crept along the cuffs of the close-fitting sleeves, and highlighted the hem that just brushed the toes of her delicate dancing slippers. Dancing slippers that showed her ankles to perfection when she performed the quadrille. Not all her spells were cast with potions and incantations, after all. Some were as simple as the sight of a well-turned ankle, a scent, a glance over the top of a ridiculously frilly fan.

"I knew I shouldn't have confided in you," Ella said.

"Of course you should have," May countered. "How else would I talk you out of your imbecilic plans."

"Having a child is hardly imbecilic."

"Well, having a child out of wedlock is—"

"Perfectly acceptable. And you very well know it. I could name a dozen well-placed ladies right now who have illegitimate children. Upper nobility notably included. And no one thinks the worse of any of them."

"But nary a one is Lord Milt's by-blow, is she?"

Lady Shirling glided past on her doddering husband's arm, ears all but reaching for them. Ella gave her a carefully trimmed smile.

"I won't be married again," Ella said from the corner of her mouth, and Merry May laughed.

"Married? What nonsense. Who said anything of marriage?"

Near the beverage table, Lord Finley's wife was becoming noisily inebriated. His mistress, however, looked to be perfectly sober.

"I believe *you* did," Ella said. "Something about your being more comfortable if your friends were safely wed."

May waved a dismissive hand. "That was before I realized what an unmitigated disaster your first union was."

Ella nodded her thanks to a passing servant, took a fresh flute of wine, and didn't bother to respond.

"What went so wrong, by the by?" May pressed.

Ella scanned the crowd. Gowns of every muted hue fluttered like butterfly wings. Laughter and curses melded easily with the sound of the be-wigged orchestra. "I didn't say anything went wrong."

"But if your marriage was happy, you would surely wish to wed again."

"Unless, of course, I couldn't bear to defile my dear departed's cherished memory by inviting another into my life," Ella suggested.

May scowled dramatically. "Very well then, don't confide in me, your best and most interesting friend, but if you're going to have an affair, at least make certain it is with someone who is not . . ." She glanced toward Lord Milton, who still seemed to be struggling mightily with his prose.

Either that or he was suffering from a rather severe bout of indigestion. "Repugnant," she said.

"There are far more important things to consider than one's appearance," Ella said, carefully maintaining her magical allure.

"Ahh, so it's his wit you find irresistible?"

"That's just the thing," Ella said, and spared poor Milton a glance. He seemed to be mouthing something to no one in particular. "I've no desire to be attracted at all."

May snared two flutes from a passing waiter dressed in scarlet livery, realized Ella already held a glass, and kept both for herself. "So your former husband was a handsome devil, was he?"

"I didn't say as much."

"I know," May said, and grinned impishly.

Ella stifled a scowl. Men didn't like it when women scowled. It was dreadfully unrefined. Come to that, they weren't all that fond of having their feminine counterparts think either. "It simply doesn't matter how the man looks," she said.

"Well . . ." May took a sip of her drink. "You certainly have the right fellow for the job, then."

"My thoughts exactly."

"But if you're not going to be saddled with the man for a lifetime, why not choose someone who will . . ." She trilled her hand in the air for a second. "Set your world afire."

"Because I've no desire to be scorched."

"You know exactly what I . . . Oh . . ." May said, then narrowed her eyes in thoughtful consideration. "What about Mr. Simpton? I've heard he's the devil himself between the sheets."

Ella turned toward the man in question. He was fair-haired, unrepugnant, and aloof. "I know this is going to surprise you, but I don't want a devil. Between the sheets or elsewhere." Taking a sip of champagne, she slipped into the crowd, but May followed her.

"Why ever not? As you've said yourself, you're not looking for ownership, just a bit of time on your back . . . or your hands and knees. Or . . . if you're really adventurous—"

"Miss Anglican," Ella said, and stopped so abruptly, the other was forced to lift her drinks high to avoid crashing them into Ella's barely covered bosom. "All I want is—"

"The lieutenant," murmured May. Ella scowled down at her, but the other failed to notice, for she was staring intently across the crowded room, expression a strange mix between dreamy and concussed.

"What on earth are you talking about?" Ella

asked, but glancing across the dance floor, she saw him. Dressed in a dark cutaway coat, snug buff breeches, and black riding boots, he was bowing over Mrs. Bumfry's hand, but in a moment he unbent to military straightness, standing tall above the milling crowd. Like a lighthouse on a rocky shore, his hair shone blue-black in the flickering gaslight. His skin had been tanned to a pecan hue by the sun. His nose was slightly bowed and his countenance stern, as if he'd faced a hundred enemies, had faced them and found them lacking. No pale fop was he. No preening dandy. He was steel in a field of daisies. A shark in a sea of—

"Sir Drake," May said, "newly returned from the battle of Grand Port. Good saints, he's like a shark amidst guppies."

"Exactly," Ella breathed.

"What?" May asked, but the other was just able to shake herself from her foolishness.

"Exactly what I don't want," she said coolly, and turned away.

"What in blazes are you talking about?" May asked, striding after her. "He's poetry."

"And ego."

"And excitement."

"And . . ." Ella cast another glance over her

11

shoulder. He was scanning the crowd, eyes like a hunting osprey. "And anger."

"But what does it matter? You're only borrowing him. Yes?"

"Look, May," Ella said, stopping near a relatively quiet corner. "I want a baby. *My* baby. Not someone else's. And certainly not his."

"Why ever not?" May asked, watching the lieutenant again.

"Because he's far too . . ." Ella spared him one more glance. She felt her stomach tumble gracelessly as his gaze met hers, then pulled her attention deliberately away, heart working overtime. "Everything."

"I'm going to tell you something, Elegance, and I mean it in the nicest possible manner," May said, and took Ella's arm in a tight hold. "I believe you might very well be deranged."

Ella's steps faltered, and suddenly she was somewhere distant, somewhere dark, where hope was only a glimmer, an almost forgotten memory where happiness dared not tread. La Hopital, it was called. A place of healing for the mentally disturbed. But torture was the order of the day.

"Ella?" May said, but the darkness had risen, threatening to drown her, to choke her. Voices whispered from sightless corners. Laughter echoed from bottomless pits. "Elegance!" Fingers tightened on Ella's arm. "What's wrong?" May's worried voice broke through the murky haze, sweeping aside the tattered memories.

"Nothing," Ella said, and drew herself from the morass with clawing determination. "It's just a bit close in here. I believe I'll get some air, if you don't mind."

"I'm sorry," May said, and took her arm again, but gently now, carefully, as if it might crumble beneath her grasp.

Ella glanced into her eyes, and there was something in them. A knowing that should not have been. An understanding where there should have been confusion. Could it be that she was not the only witch in the assemblage? But no, she was seeing ghosts where there were only shadows.

"I'm fine," Ella said, and made it so, smoothing the fraying edges of her carefully maintained image, brightening her smile. She had long ago become the mistress of her circumstances, and she would not falter now.

"I'm sorry," May repeated earnestly.

"And well you should be, Merry May. There is nothing so disturbing as being charged with a condition obviously present in one's accuser."

May stared at her a second, then smiled hesitantly, eyes still apologetic.

"Go back to the other lunatics," Ella said. Her tone was mildly scoffing, lightly teasing. She had been carefully tutored, after all, and knew that a well-phrased lie was not enough. One must match the words to one's expressions, speech patterns, movements. "Before bedlam breaks out," she added, and tugging away, made her way through the crowd. Lord Milton tried to catch her attention, but Ella was no longer in the mood, regardless of her careful self-control. Yes, she longed for normal, for peace, for a child, a baby to replace the hope she had lost in La Hopital, the tiny seed that had kept her sane amid insanity for the duration of its short development. Maybe the miscarriage had driven her truly mad, just as Verrill had accused. But whatever the case, she was now ready to repair her life, to make it full, to have someone to nurture and teach and cherish. Perhaps Merry May was right, though. Perhaps Lord Milton wasn't proper paternal material. Maybe a somewhat more imposing lord would be a better choice. Or maybe she should broaden her search, look outside her social circle. A manservant or merchant or . . .

The hostler at the livery stable came abruptly to

mind. He had lovely arms. Once upon a time she had seen him roll up his sleeves to brush a gray cob. The morning sun had slanted kindly through the open door to shine with reverent reflection on his flexing biceps. And when he had bent to retrieve a fallen crouper, his breeches had stretched tight across his—

But none of that mattered, she reminded herself. She simply wanted a child. One to call her own, to give what she had not been given herself.

Still, the hostler had . . .

Oh, what the devil was wrong with her? The hostler was probably all of eighteen. Nearly a baby himself, and even she wasn't that desperate. Perhaps.

The air outside felt cool and rejuvenating against her face. A light mist was falling, obscuring the globed lanterns that scattered light across the damp, cobbled walkway, caressing the roses that nodded beside the footpath. Reaching out, she stroked a velvet petal.

And then she felt it, something out of place. Something dark. Something sinister.

Evil. As sharp as a needle in her side. And it had taken residence in the garden.

Chapter 2

Ella's breath stopped in her throat. Someone was out there. Someone was in danger.

Thunder rumbled in the distance, a low, ominous warning.

She took a step toward the garden without volition, without thought, tugged along by sheer instinct. But good sense flooded in, forcing her to a halt. She wasn't that person anymore. Not the one who interfered in the lives of hapless strangers and ill-fated passersby. Not the one who schemed and trained and labored, only to fail in the end. That was behind her. And she would not invite the pain of that failure again. Not today. Not ever.

But just then a gasp of pain filtered through the ight and shivered against her tingling senses. he tightened her fists, willing herself to turn away, to escape before she was pulled back into the dark maelstrom. But she could not.

And suddenly she found herself in the middle of the garden, peering through the rising mists. Three shapes were outlined against the pale stone fence. Three shapes, but only two desired to be there.

It was not difficult to move closer and remain unseen, even though cloaking was not her gift. The fog held a veiling magic of its own, hiding her just as it hid the trio.

"A tanner? That's all y' got on y'?" growled the tallest of the three.

"I fear I am rather rolled up." The voice that answered was cultured, educated, and drunk beyond any hope of good sense. "But if you will allow me to return to my—"

"Shut yer trap," snarled the second brigand, holding the victim's arms tight behind his back, "before I tear yer tongue from outta yer 'ead."

The young dandy stared in befuddled uncertainty for a moment, then convulsed, bent forward, and heaved forth the contents of his traitorous stomach onto his tormentor's footwear.

Cursing soundly, the fellow behind dropped the boy's arms and jigged back a few steps.

The hacking stopped gradually. Silence settled in, then: "Y' just 'urled on me good shoes."

"I am terrible sorry." The gentleman sounded quite sincere, and though he might be drunk out of his mind, he wasn't so inebriated that he couldn't recognize the venom in the other's voice. "I shall buy you—"

"I'll kill y' for that," snarled the first. His eyes were shadowed beneath his battered hat, but his narrow lips were visible, curled with derision and cruelty as he reached into his coat. But in that instant, the gent seemed to come to his senses with a start. Lurching sideways, he careened down the footpath toward Ella.

For a drunken fool, he was fair fast and made it all of twenty strides before they caught him, snagging him by his coat and spinning him about.

He sputtered something, the words inarticulate, but the frantic meaning clear. Mercy. He begged for mercy, but there would be none. Ella felt it in her soul.

They were close now. So close she could all but feel the blow that crashed into the boy's belly. Could see his face, pale as snow, with eyes as round as a hunter's moon.

And it was the damned eyes that always snared her.

An image began almost unbidden in her mind. She could feel the power of it rising steadily within her, could feel the force washing over her senses, and when she spoke, the voice was not her own.

"Who goes there?" she rumbled.

The nearer thief cursed, but the other only straightened, still holding his prey by his shirt-front as he squinted through the mist at her.

"'Oo are you?" he demanded.

"I'm Constable Everett of the watch," she said. She kept the officer's image steady in her mind, but dared not venture closer lest her rapidly cobbled illusion faltered. She hadn't planned for the sop to approach so rapidly, and time was the very essence of magic. Time and concentration, even for the simplest spell. "Release that gentleman."

Silence echoed in the garden, then: "We was just 'elpin' the gent 'ere back to the 'ouse. Seems 'e took a nasty—"

"Release him, I say," she demanded, voice ringing in the darkness.

The scoundrel did as ordered, opening his hand so that the boy dropped to his knees, then fell leisurely to his side, prone and still.

"Leave now and I shan't—" she began, but suddenly the villains sprang toward her.

Fear came with them, bursting in her soul, but magic was the very air she breathed. Reaching into her deepest resources, she snatched out an incantation.

"Aduro!" she rasped. Fire flared from her fingertips. The closest man's sleeve burst into flame. He skidded to a halt, squeaked in fear, then dropped to the ground, rolling madly. But the other leaped at her. No time for flames now. He slashed at her, slicing his blade across her sleeve. She trembled in response and felt the constable's image flicker.

"'Oo the devil are you?" hissed the villain, but even as he spoke, she whirled and kicked. Her timing was shaky. Nevertheless, her heel struck him in the chest, crashing him backward, where he teetered, breathing hard. "She's naught but a dollymop, Ned," he grunted as his friend scrambled to his feet. "Grab 'er and we'll 'ave us some fun."

"No fun here, Ned," she snarled, not shifting her attention from the taller of the two. "Not unless you enjoy bonfires."

Ned remained where he was, but the other attacked again. Fast. So fast. And deadly as a snake. The knife sang toward her. She swept her right arm across his, thrusting the blade aside, then slammed the heel of her other hand into his face. He staggered back, but suddenly Ned was behind her. He grabbed her, squeezing her arms against her sides.

"She broke m' nose." The tall man's voice was muffled through his fingers. "Broke me bleedin' nose," he moaned, and lowering his hand, stumbled toward her. "Damn you, stupid cow, I'll make y' sorry y' messed with the likes of Leonard Shay."

Fear was curling in her gut, freezing her senses. Nevertheless, she spoke, flippant and steady. "Who?"

He paused, seething. "Shay," he hissed. "Remember the name 'cuz you're gonna want to be pleading with me when you die." He was advancing again, head bent low, eyes shining madly in the darkness.

Terror bubbled up, but she fought against it, brought forth the training, the endless hours of defense, the innate abilities that had saved her a hundred times. "You don't want to do this, Leonard," she crooned. He stopped for a moment, but Ned was behind her, unaffected.

"What you scared of?" he snarled, and tightened his grip across her breasts. Pain squeezed through her, bending her concentration, and in that moment Shay lurched toward her. She waited as long as she could, praying, biding her time, then yanked her feet from the ground and kicked forward with all her strength. Shay's cheekbone crunched beneath her heel. He staggered backward and collapsed. Behind her, Ned toppled to the ground, bearing her with him. They landed in a heap. His arms loosened, and in that instant, she rolled to the side and slammed her elbow across his throat. Rattling gasps issued from his gaping mouth.

Ella sprang to her feet, ready, wary, but there was no more danger. Only Shay staggering upright, hands covering his face. Only Ned still struggling for breath and—

Dammit! Someone else! Near the gate. Why hadn't she sensed him earlier?

"What the hell's going on?" a voice growled from the mist.

Ella snapped her gaze to the left.

Lieutenant Drake! What the devil was he doing there?

A dozen possible lies flitted through her mind like fireflies. She snatched up the most logical of the swarm and staggered toward him.

"Sir!" she rasped, blocking his path to the would-be thieves, delaying him as long as possible. With a bit of luck, the hapless villains would gather their floundering wits and escape before they felt a need to share the foolish notion that they'd just been bested by a woman. "Thank God you've come." She caught the front of the gentleman's cutaway coat, dragging a little as if she might fall.

Drake grasped her wrists in both hands, supporting her easily as he peered over her shoulder at her attackers. But she didn't turn. Instead she listened gratefully to the scuttling sound of stumbling feet, the grunts as the two hoisted themselves over the wall and away.

"What happened?" Drake asked, pulling his gaze from the rapidly retreating forms. His voice was a low, deadly burr, just as she knew it would be. This was not a man to be trifled with. Dammit.

"I'm. . ." She wilted a little more, but he did not lift her into his arms as surely any well-versed gentleman should. "I'm not entirely certain." She made her voice wispy, her hands shaky against his coat. "I came into the garden for a bit of air, never thinking . . . I mean to say, what is this world coming to? Scoundrels accosting—"

"You came out alone?"

"I never dreamed—"

A moan interrupted her lies.

"What was that?" snarled Drake. Grasping both her wrists in one hand, he pulled her to the side and stepped out in front, shielding her from the downed gentleman she had very nearly forgotten.

The rush of fear and excitement was easing away, and she was not quite certain if she should be insulted or flattered by her would-be savior's high-handed behavior.

But the moan sounded again, putting a halt to her debate. Drake stepped toward the source, and she trailed along in his wake, keeping her footfalls unsteady.

"It must be the gentleman who saved me from those horrid thugs," she said, and grasped the back of Drake's coat, making sure he could feel the shudder she so artfully performed.

"Saved you?" he asked, coming to a halt and staring down at her supposed rescuer. The drunken imbecile seemed to be unconscious, the smell of liquor and vomit strong enough to knock them back half a pace.

She resisted covering her nose with her palm. "Yes. Two men came at me." She made a fluttery motion with one hand and stepped up beside Drake so that the finer nuances of her performance would not go unappreciated. "I was terrified, scared straight out of my wits, but this gentleman appeared from nowhere and came to my rescue like a hero from days of yore."

They shifted their gazes and stared down at the wrinkled heap of humanity in thoughtful unison. Ella managed not to scowl.

"Are you certain?" Drake asked.

"Yes, I'm certain," she said, then softened her tone and tried again. "Of course. Of course I'm certain." Kneeling beside the downed sot, she closed her eyes against the stench and shook him gently by the arm. "Sir, please, do awaken. Please. I must thank you."

He didn't so much as stir an inebriated finger.

"The lady said to wake up," Drake rumbled, and squatting, smacked the fellow's face with a stinging slap.

The boy came to with a start. "Fiend seize it! I've not seen that bit of muslin before in my life. The side-slip's not—" He stopped and blinked, seeming to take in his surroundings, head rolling, neck rubbery in his bed of delicate columbine. "Who are you?"

"What did he say?" Drake asked.

Drunken colloquial nonsense, Ella thought, and tightening her grip in the gent's sleeve, launched into her own version of the truth. "You saved me, my lord. Masterfully rescued me from two heathens who attacked me in Merry May's—"

"Thunder an' turf! The blowens! Are they

gone?" He sat up abruptly, eyes wide and white-limned in his moon-pale face. Thunder grumbled again, closer at hand.

"Yes," she said, peeved by the interruption to her performance. Acting was not necessarily her forte, and when she was doing well she didn't like to be distracted, but she soldiered on. "You frightened them off with your bravery and your manly strength. How can I ever thank you for coming to my—"

"Bloody hell!" he rasped, and grabbing her arm in both hands, staggered raggedly to his feet. "I thought the bastards were going to kill me. I was a bit tap-hackled, I don't mind saying. Not properly shot in the neck by a stretch, but a mite foxed. So I ambled out here for a snatch of air and—"

"And glad I am you came along when you did, good sir," Ella interrupted. "For you surely saved my life."

"I did?" He turned toward her, staggering unsteadily and seeming to truly notice her for the first time.

"Yes."

"Are you certain?"

Moron. Perhaps she should have let the thieves beat a bit of sense into him after all. "Why yes. Surely you remember. You were quite a dashing figure as you valiantly fought for my honor." She tried to imbue her tone with breathless admiration, but truth be told, she was a bit miffed by this turn of events. At least at Lavender House she had been able to spill the facts, compare notes with the rest of the coven, and even, if circumstances warranted, boast of her efforts.

"Oh. Well . . ." The sot tried to bow, stumbled back a pace, and managed a lopsided grin. "That'll teach them to mess with their betters, what?

"Edward Shellum, at your service, my lady. Always . . ." he began, then rolled his eyes up into his head and flopped back into the columbine, dead to the world.

Chapter 3

Sir Drake remained absolutely silent. His parents had named him Thomas Donovan, but years ago on some leaking tub he longed to forget, the crew had compared him rather unfavorably to a scoter, and the epithet had stuck. Which was just as well, for he had little desire to claim kinship with his father. A man so cold he could resist his gentle wife's impassioned pleas to allow their son to remain with them just a few years longer.

Drake stood in silence now, staring down at the unconscious Mr. Shellum. The lady beside him did the same. She was tall for a woman. Tall and willowy and as beautiful as a descending angel, fire-bright hair loosed about her narrow shoulders, eyes shining like priceless gems in her moon-shadowed face.

As for Shellum, it was difficult to discern

whether he was tall or willowy or angelic, for he seemed to be snoring, his breath gently rustling the herbage near their feet.

"Just how did he rescue you exactly?" Drake asked, and turned back toward her, but for a moment the brilliance of her beauty stole his senses. He steadied himself, remembering that he had survived a score of battles. Not well, certainly not bravely, but he had survived, so surely he could face this one slim maid without faltering.

She didn't glance up immediately, which was just as well, for her delay afforded him an opportunity to study her unobserved. And he would need all his wits about him, for there was something strange afoot here. Something not quite what it seemed.

"It was quite astounding really," she said, but continued to watch the downed fellow as though expecting him to rise like Lazarus at any given moment.

"Did it have something to do with his breath?" he asked doubtfully.

She glanced up at him, eyes wide in the darkness, full lips quirked, and for a moment he actually thought she might laugh, but that would hardly be appropriate for a maid who had just endured such a horrid trauma. Then again, there was something about the way she stood, the way she moved that did not seem quite appropriate either. A confident elegance, for lack of a better term.

"I'm not entirely certain what happened," she said instead. "I was terribly frightened, you know. What with—"

"Were you?" he asked.

Her golden brows dipped a little. "What's that?"

"Were you frightened?" he asked, and taking her arm in a careful grasp, led her through the friendly mist to stand beneath a hanging lantern that illuminated a silvery circle. She felt solid and steady beneath his fingertips despite her ethereal grace.

"Of course," she said, and lifted one hand to her breast, splaying her fingers helplessly across her bosom. "Of course I was. What woman would not be?"

He ignored her question, though in truth he had wondered the same himself. "There's blood on your gown," he said instead.

"Oh!" she gasped, looking down.

"But it's not yours."

"What?"

"You've not been wounded."

30

"How do you know?"

"Have you?"

"Well I . . ." She touched her arm where the sleeve had been severed, but the edges of the fabric were clean. "The blood must be poor young Mr. Shellum's then."

He shook his head. Perhaps it was the military training that made him certain. Or maybe his own memories of world-shattering pain gave him some insight into the situation, for even in the darkness he could tell she was unhurt. Likewise, he could see that Shellum bore no serious wounds, other than his stupidly self-inflicted inebriation. "He was not bleeding either," he informed her.

She blinked at him, almost angry. "Well, then it must be from the thugs," she deduced. "When my hero—"

"Your hero?" He tried to keep the dubious tone from his voice, but it was no simple task. The lad looked as dangerous as a barnacle.

A friendly mist had begun to fall.

She scowled. "My hero . . ." she said, emphasizing the words as she nodded toward the snoring sot. "When he saved me he must have wounded the thugs, who subsequently got blood on my frock when they grabbed me."

"They grabbed you?" The thought disturbed

31

him, awakened something in him that he had thought might well have died, might have been killed in some distant battle he could barely recall. So many dead, so many wounded. Friends, comrades, rivals. Little more than lads fresh from their mothers' arms. The memory sent an aching throb through his right thigh.

Silence slipped between them, soft and elongated, then: "I am sorry," she said.

He brought himself back to the moment at hand. A moment of peace. An instant of beauty. "For what?" he asked.

Her expression was thoughtful, her tone the same. "The war."

He narrowed his eyes. Who was she? What did she know of him? And was she as enigmatic as she seemed, or was it just the moonlight? "May I ask your name?" he said.

"I am Lady Lanshire, but you may call me Elegance if you like."

"Elegance?" He could not quite help but smile.

She raised a brow at him. "Or Ella, if you're the lazy sort."

"Lady Lanshire," he said, and sketched a bow. "How did you know I was in the war?"

She smiled a little. "Merry May is a friend of mine."

He narrowed his eyes, watching her. Aye, she was a bonny thing, a glimmer of beauty in the moonlit shadows, but there was more to her than eagerly met the eye. There was an intellect, a graceful pattern of thought and speech that intrigued and enlightened.

"She is quite enamored with tall men with handsome physiques and stately faces. Indeed, she often feels the need to point them out to me," she explained.

He thought about that for an instant, then gave her a shallow nod. "Firstly, my thanks. I believe that was a compliment. Secondly, you are most probably not entirely to blame for the war."

Her face was solemn, her eyes entrancing, and when she spoke, her voice was singsong. *"For things like that, you know, must be, after a famous victory."*

He couldn't help but be surprised both by her lyrical tone and the verse she chose. "You read Southey."

"Well . . ." She shrugged and gave him a sidelong glance through her lashes. "I cannot spend all my time chasing inebriated young gentlemen into dark gardens."

Her eyes sparkled, as verdant as the first leaves of spring in the overhead light. In some way they reminded him of his sister's, though he could not have said why. Sarah had been very young when he had last seen her. Too young to exhibit this kind of depth, for there was wisdom beneath Lady Lanshire's laughter. And perhaps pain beneath that. But maybe Sarah had learned wisdom too, in the long years since his exodus. He hoped now, belatedly perhaps, that she had not learned of pain. But what did he know of her really? He had been gone too long. Had just recently learned of her death, in fact.

"So you were giving chase," he said.

"Aren't we all? In one way or another?"

"Perhaps. But most of us are not chasing him," he said, and tilted his head toward the peacefully snoozing Shellum.

"Why ever not?" she asked.

He thought about that, the inconsistencies, the oddities. "I can think of several reasons," he said, and raised a hand toward a nearby bench. She hesitated for an instant, then, flowing regally in that direction, took a seat with a graceful sweep of her skirt. He sat beside her, easing out his right leg, willing away the pain.

"Name one reason," she challenged.

"Well . . ." He considered how best to phrase his words for a moment, watching her. She refused to look away, but met his gaze full on as if she were entirely unafraid. Entirely nonplussed. Who was she? And what was she hiding? Had she possibly encountered the thugs alone? Might she have sent them running? But no. She was tall, not stout; intelligent, but not foolhardy. "A woman of your quality seems unlikely to have to chase any man."

The night went silent for a moment, filled with the kind of thoughtful quiet that only a mist-shrouded garden can grant. "Firstly, thank you," she said. "I believe that was a compliment, and secondly. . ." Her lips quirked up into an intriguing bow. "Perhaps I am quite desperate."

He watched her face, bright-eyed, animated, mesmerizing. "I would rather doubt it."

"Then you would be mistaken," she said, but her expression was as serene as Sunday.

"Desperate, are you?"

"Quite."

"For . . ."

She shrugged. "A man, of course."

He watched her. She possessed a supple grace that could neither be taught nor practiced. "For what purpose exactly?"

Her eyes were laughing again. She didn't bother to lower them, to look away, to act coy. "The usual, I suspect."

Her words sent a trill of warm arousal through him, and that in itself was near miraculous, for he had not been entirely certain he would ever be aroused again. Not since Grand Port. The battle had been ugly. The pain had been unimaginable. And the ship's surgeon, when he could be convinced to set aside his rum, had seemed undisturbed when he'd informed Drake that he would never walk again, much less sire a child. "Might the usual entail saddling mounts and hoisting heavy loads?" he asked. "Or something more intimate?"

"Heavy loads? Oh heavens no," she said, and laughed. Her narrow hands were curled demurely in her lap. "I already have a man for that sort of thing."

"Do you?"

"Yes indeed. His name is Winslow. A fine fellow. Built like an ox."

"I see. Then I shall have to assume we speak of something more personal."

"Personal?" She canted her head, seeming to consider not only his words, but his nuances. "I suppose one might say as much."

Desire coursed through him. Amazing, really. He was still surprised to find himself alive, much less . . . *alive*. "Does it involve sharing a bed?"

Her mouth slanted up provocatively. "If you're unimaginative."

He stared at her a moment, then laughed, feeling life flow through him like a swelling tide. "In that case, my lady, I would like to offer my services."

"You?" She seemed surprised. He wondered vaguely if he should be insulted.

"Why not?"

"Because you'd never do."

He sat back, thinking, then nodded his head toward the besotted oaf. "But he would?"

"Perfectly."

"Might I ask why?"

She was watching him closely, face scrunched a little as if in deep thought. "You don't look the type to become inebriated at all."

"You're looking for a sot?"

"Well . . ." She sat back, still watching. "Not necessarily someone who will be unconscious every minute of the day, but someone who will not become . . . overly involved."

"With . . ."

From the house, laughter roared. Shellum snorted and rolled onto his back, but Drake barely noticed. The lady's face was a study of emotions. A picture of intelligent intensity.

"Me," she said.

"You don't want him to be overly involved with you."

"That is correct."

"Shall I assume you've been married before?"

She laughed. "An astute guess."

"And it did not go well?"

"Perhaps it could have been better."

"And you're bitter."

"No. No," she said, almost seeming surprised to find it was true. "Simply wise enough to learn from my mistakes."

"And marriage is a mistake."

She shrugged.

"While sharing a bed—"

"If you recall, you were the one who mentioned a bed."

He narrowed his eyes, thinking of his past encounters, which had been, by the by, lamentably few. "It seems so much more comfortable than the alternatives."

"See there." She shrugged. "Yet another reason you would never do."

"You despise comfort?"

"I despise tedium. And I've been widowed for a host of years."

He almost laughed, but she seemed so sincere.

"I doubt you're much beyond a score and two even now."

She cocked her head, eyes gleaming. "I didn't take you for the flattering sort, Sir Drake."

"Generally I am not, but I'm hoping you haven't entirely given up on the idea of a bed."

Her laugh was like warm rum, intoxicating and smooth.

"Well, I am flattered, but I'm afraid—"

"I rather doubt that."

She looked at him straight on. "What do you doubt?"

"That you're flattered . . ." He paused, watching her, mesmerized. "Or afraid."

Her smile was a strange, earthy magic, silvered by mist, shadowed by darkness.

"You're wrong," she said, and suddenly she seemed almost serious. Almost honest. "I am both, on quite a regular basis."

"But not tonight."

"One," she said, "but not the other."

"And it is my task to decipher the mystery of which is which?"

"Not at all," she countered. "I am hardly mysterious."

"You jest."

"My good sir," she said, "have I not admitted

that I came here to seduce the very man who lays inebriated at our feet?"

"That you did."

"A man that, I admit, I've not yet had the pleasure of meeting. Surely that depletes the mystery a bit."

He watched her, thinking it should be true. "I doubt it's even possible where you are concerned," he said.

She canted her head, studying him as if he were an odd new species. "Tell me, Sir Drake, might you be smitten by me?"

"If I told you, would that not deplete *my* mystery?"

"Absolutely. But I do so wish to inform Merry May that I've netted the dark lieutenant who intrigued her so."

He bowed his head. "Then far be it from me to deprive you of such pleasure. You may tell her that I've been netted, speared, and nicely sautéed."

"Oh dear. It sounds quite gruesome."

"Is love not supposed to be?" he asked, remembering a hundred poems he had read aboard ship while boredom and melancholy washed over him in waves. He had not been meant for the sea. Indeed, at one time he had rather fancied himself a poet, though the idea seemed laughable now.

"Love?" She chuckled musically. "I hadn't dared hope your feelings had gone so far as all that."

"Surely you did not expect otherwise."

"On the contrary, sir, we've only just met."

From the darkness, Shellum snorted and twitched.

"Though the circumstances *are* a bit unorthodox," she added.

"Are they?"

"It is not every day that I am attacked in a friend's garden if that is what you mean."

"I thought perhaps it was," he said. "I thought perhaps you were attacked and duly fought off your aggressors regular as clockwork."

Her brows lifted in concert with the corners of her mouth. "Surely you don't believe a mere woman bested those horrible thugs."

He watched her. Beauty wrapped in intrigue. "Such an assumption would indeed be foolish," he said.

She delayed a moment, studying him. "Absolutely," she agreed finally and rose to her feet. "Well, I'd best be—"

"But many things are," he said, and rising beside her, pulled her into his arms and kissed her.

Her lips were warm and sweet. Her breasts

were soft as midnight dreams against his chest, and her fingers, where they curled into his hair, felt strong and urgent, tugging him nearer, pulling him close. His hale thigh settled between hers, and for several seconds she did not resist. But suddenly she pushed away.

Gone was the lady of composure and grace. "Good Lord!" she said.

"Good indeed."

"I must go."

"To find a bed?"

"To find my chastity belt," she said, and rushing from the garden, disappeared into the new-falling rain.

Chapter 4

Elegance opened her eyes. The house was dark, silent, fraught with shapeless shadows that leaned against her bedroom wall, heavy-shouldered and belligerent. The moon had given up the battle for dominance in the beleaguered sky, but she knew the truth; she was not alone. She tensed, studied the feelings, tested the air, and smiled.

"So you've returned," she said aloud.

"Oh, deuce it," Madeline cursed, letting out her breath in a rush. "Someday I shall pounce on you from the doorway and scare you from your very wits."

Ella closed her eyes and said a silent prayer of thanksgiving before schooling her features into a contented smile and sitting up. "It will never happen. Your thoughts are as loud as a herd of pachyderms." Besides, it seemed all but impossible for others to use magic against her, just as it was difficult for her to use her powers against others who were gifted. Somehow, in her case at any rate, conflicting powers tended to wash each other out, dilute the effects. Reaching to the side, she passed her palm slowly over a nearby candle. It flickered to life, casting light across her sister's lovely countenance. Ella studied each perfect feature, the aquiline nose, the cat-slanted eyes, the bounty of midnight hair cascading down the back of her velvet traveling suit. "You're safe?"

"Of course," she said, and pulling off her damp gloves, tossed them flippantly onto the nearby wardrobe.

But few things were as they seemed. Ella had learned that early on, hence she examined the other's face in silence. It was unscarred certainly. Some would say unchanged. But some would be wrong. There was a bit of difference in her sister's emerald eyes. "What happened?"

"Nothing. All went as planned."

"Don't lie to me," she ordered, but Madeline laughed as she plopped onto the bed.

"Oh Josette, you sound like Jasper."

"I do not," Ella said, but perhaps the tiniest bit of petulant childishness had crept into her tone.

"Yes you do. So stern. Like a nasty schoolmaster. As if I've been a naughty girl caught stealing crumpets before tea."

But Madeline was a little girl. Three years her junior, she was Ella's only living relative.

Maddy's fingers felt cold beneath her own. "What happened?" Ella asked.

Emotion flashed through Madeline's soul, but she smiled, a tilting of her ruby lips if not a lightening of her mind. "You know I cannot say."

"Secrets," Ella said. She was angry suddenly. "Always secrets." Pulling her feet from beneath the soft warmth of her counterpane, she dropped them quickly to the floor. Rummaging through her wardrobe, she tugged a night rail from a pile and tossed it onto her sister's lap. "Jasper always did like to be the only one with all the puzzle pieces."

"You're being unfair, Jos," Madeline said, fiddling with the gown.

"Get out of those wet clothes," Ella ordered, and rummaged again for stockings.

"Sometimes I almost think—" she began, and stopped.

"What?" Ella said, still searching.

"Sometimes I almost think you're in love with him," she said.

"What?" Ella turned with a start, but Madeline wasn't laughing. Instead she sat staring up at her with wide, solemn eyes.

"Are you?"

Ella puffed a breath of surprise. "In love?"

She nodded.

"With Jasper Reeves?"

The room went silent.

"You can admit it," Madeline said, but Ella continued to stare, unable to speak. "I mean . . ." She plucked a loose thread from the borrowed nightgown. "He saved your life. It would only make sense."

Closing her mouth with a snap, Ella walked over and placed her palm on her sister's brow, but Madeline turned her head sharply away.

"I'm not ill."

"Maybe just a touch of fever," Ella said, and laughed, but Maddy pushed her hand away.

"I am quite serious."

"Then it's just as I always suspected. *You're* the one who is mad."

Maddy scowled. "Neither of us is mad."

Sighing, Ella plopped down beside her. Pulling her bare legs up beneath her gown, she crossed her arms atop her knees. "I fear there are a host of people who would disagree on that count."

"But none we cannot turn into toads," Madeline whispered, and they laughed, remembering back. Past the good times, past the bad times, to the beginning, when they had thought they could do all things. Right all wrongs.

The tension was gone from Maddy's soul. "So you're still busy gadding about London?"

"I am not gadding about," Ella said. "I have a serious and important task to perform."

"Oh yes. That's right. Breeding."

Reaching out, Ella whacked her sister on the back of the head. "Choosing the father of your future niece," she corrected.

"Breeding," she repeated.

"Really Maddy, your language! Mother would turn over in her grave."

She laughed. "And she'd have no trouble whatsoever with her firstborn planning to give birth out of wedlock?"

"Better that than brewing stinky potions while plotting to topple kings and principalities in the bowels of Lavender House."

Maddy's lips were still tilted, but her thoughts seemed far away, "In truth, I think she'd approve," she mused.

"How can you even guess?" Ella murmured. She had died so young. Well before they were ready to let her go. Before they could subsist on the sparse dribblings of their father's love. Before they had learned to judge a man's heart. To stand on their own, to survive.

"I wish you'd come back, Jos."

"Come back?" she said, and shook her head. Nervous suddenly. Jittery. "It's you who must leave, Maddy. Before it's too late."

"Too late for what?"

Ella drew in a careful breath, trying not to remember. "He won't protect you, you know." Her voice had dropped low, though she didn't know why. She had few servants. There was Winslow, who was, in fact, built like an ox, but was mostly deaf. And Amherst and Cecelia, who were well past the age of listening at keyholes.

"You're being unfair," Madeline said.

"He's got his own agenda, his own plans. He's obsessed with them, in fact. If circumstances turn against you, he'll not stand with you."

"We know that. Have known it all along."

"Maybe it's different to know it and to experience it."

Maddy scowled. "You're still angry."

"Angry!" Ella stood, paced, rounding the four-poster. "Of course I'm angry. It was senseless. Stupid."

"But not his fault."

She stopped. "No." She squeezed her hands together, crunching her fingers in her own grip, hurting her knuckles. "The fault was mine. All—"

But Madeline stopped her. She was up in a second, gripping her arms. "You're wrong. It was no one's fault."

"No one's . . ." Ella huffed a laugh. "How can you still be so naïve? After all you've seen. After all—"

"Very well then, it was Grey's fault."

The air left her lungs.

"It wasn't you, Ella." Maddy's grip tightened on her sister's arms. "You did everything you could."

"Did I?" She searched her sister's eyes. Madeline was the compassionate one. The good one. Perhaps Maddy was right. Or perhaps she saw what she wanted to see. What she needed to see to remain sane. To remain happy.

"You did everything," Maddy repeated slowly.

"And yet she died," Ella murmured. She shook her head. Remembered. "What if it had been you?"

"It wasn't."

"She had so much talent. So much potential."

"Not as much as you."

Ella drew a careful breath, steadying herself. Perhaps Madeline was right again. Maddy had inherited the major portion of good sense, of logical practicality, of optimism, while Elegance had received the lion's share of the magical powers.

She'd give it all up for a buttonhook and a nice pair of dancing slippers.

"Well . . ." She shrugged and tried a smile, though there was little point. Maddy was her sister. She would know her thoughts. "That's all in my past. From here on in, it's parties all the time."

Maddy smiled, though her own expression was no more convincing. "So who is the potential lover of the moment?"

A dark face from just hours before flashed through Ella's mind. A lean form sauntered into her thoughts. A low Celtic burr shivered along her memory.

Madeline raised an eyebrow, but Ella set the disturbing images aside before they were dragged out for examination.

"I'm considering Lord Milton," she said.

"Lord . . ." Maddy began, then widened her eyes and blinked. "Milton?"

"Yes."

"The short baron?"

"In truth, Madeline, I really don't care how tall my child is."

"The short, paunchy baron who couldn't string together two coherent words if you spoke them in his mind and moved his lips for him?"

"Now you're being cruel."

"Not as cruel as it would be to condemn my lovely niece to being incoherent, bald, and short."

"It could be a boy."

"I thought you wanted a daughter."

"Well, I do." She smiled a little. "But I'm not a witch, you know. It could be either."

Maddy grinned and tightened her grip on her sister's arms.

"I worry about you."

"Me?" Ella said. "Whatever for?"

"It's unnatural, you avoiding the coven. It's been nearly two months now since you've been to Lavender House. And years that you've been living here alone like some . . . like some nasty old crone."

"I'm practicing for the future. Besides, the coven survived a couple centuries before I came along. I'm certain Les Chausettes will endure without my esteemed presence for a few more years." Indeed, perhaps they were safer. She had planned to help Sarah, after all. To teach her to hone her

51

craft, to protect herself, to remain unnoticed in a world that abhorred the inexplicable. But things had gone horribly wrong. She *had* been noticed. Had been seduced. Not unlike Ella a lifetime before. She should have been able to predict it, to save her, she thought, but Maddy spoke.

"Faye bested Shaleena."

"What?" Ella turned toward her, drawn from her dark reverie. "Not in hand-to-hand."

"Yes," Maddy said, and grinned. Shaleena had been a nettle in their drawers since they had first arrived in London seven long years before. Haughty, beautiful, and as gifted as any, she had lorded it over the two battered waifs from an unknown village near Marseille. "Just last week. Slammed her to the floor. Wouldn't let her up. I thought Shaleena would die long before she'd admit defeat."

"Shaleena," Ella scoffed. "What kind of a foolish name is that anyway?"

"Probably entirely fabricated," Madeline agreed. "Not at all like Elegance."

"Watch yourself, or I won't take you to Lord and Lady Bowles's soiree."

"How ever will I survive?" Maddy quipped, but there was worry in her eyes again. Worry and fatigue. Ella could help with that, could brew up a potion that . . . But she no longer did those things. Normal. She was normal. An everyday widow woman who enjoyed flowers, dancing, and poetry read before a nice fire. A fire over which she could concoct a potion . . .

"I'm going to sleep," she said.

"As am I," Maddy agreed, and pacing to the far side of the bed, flipped back the covers.

"Not in my bed."

"It's already warm," Maddy said, and before Ella could drag her out, she'd bunched the pillow beneath her head and fallen asleep.

Chapter 5

"Lady Redcomb," said Milton. "You look quite . . ."

Ella and Madeline smiled in helpful unison, waiting for the little lord to continue, but he seemed to be blocked again.

"Quite . . ."

"Ravishing," said Merry May, coming up from behind.

"Yes, quite ravishing."

"I haven't seen you in ages." Today May wore blue. Not a soft powder hue. But a blue so bright it all but hurt the eyes. "Have you been abroad, Lady Redcomb?"

"I do so wish." Maddy sighed. "How I long to see the sun rise over the River Seine. But I fear travel is unsafe these days. At least until *le petit caporal* quits his incessant foolishness."

"Foolishness? Is that what you call the devastation of all of Europe?" May asked.

"Oh please," Madeline begged piteously. "No politics. Not when I am yet mourning my enforced banishment from Paris's wondrous chocolate shops."

Ella watched her sister turn the conversation effortlessly aside. As if she had not a thought in her head but the memory of the sweets served in France's best cafes.

"I fear there is nowhere like it in all of Britain," she said. "And I have searched."

Merry May laughed. "Is that what you have been up to, then, ferreting out the best chocolate houses in our fair kingdom?"

"Nothing so interesting as all of that, I fear," Madeline said. "'Twas naught but an extended stay in the country. My dearest aunt is aging, and I felt compelled to spend some time with her."

She rambled amicably on about the country air, the birth of new spring calves, the deplorable roads. But it was all a lie. They had no aunt. No country estate. It mattered little though, for Les Chausettes were taught to weave fabrications from the very moment they set foot inside Lavender House. They were thought of as a cluster of bluestockings, brought together at Lavender

House, where they discussed the latest news and literature over blackberry scones. But they were so much more—a cluster of gifted women, some badly bruised by the world, all who were offered a chance to hone their gifts and better their circumstances, who were given orders from some unknown official and expected to conduct their lives as ordered.

Lie. Lie well and lie often. For the lives of the others may well depend on your ability to deceive, Jasper Reeves had said.

In fact, their entire identities were untruths. Their titles had been mysteriously bestowed on them by means Ella refused to contemplate. Their histories were a sham, their very appearances were products of hard work and clever deception. From the moment the sisters had sailed into English waters, they had become someone else. Someone different, until their very essence was left behind, lost in the dark annals of their past. Indeed, in the eyes of the *ton* they were not even sisters, for Reeves had no desire for any to make the connection between the ragged urchins he had wrenched from the screaming maw of Marseille.

No, they would not return to France no matter how splendid the chocolate, Ella thought, and steadied the tremor in her hands.

"Hello."

She turned at the sound of an almost familiar voice, only to find a handsome, well-groomed young man standing before her. It took a moment to recognize him as Edward Shellum, for he looked entirely different upright. His silver-shot waistcoat was adorned with purple buttons and topped with a snowy white cravat. His frock coat was long, his breeches fashionably snug, and though it was clear he had imbibed, he was not so drunk as he had been the previous night, as evidenced by his apparent consciousness.

"Good evening," Ella said, and shutting out dark, hovering thoughts, kept her tone carefully vague. She had been rather hoping she would never again have to face Shellum, but luck was a fickle friend.

Merry May cocked a brow. "You two are acquainted?"

Ella gritted her teeth against this bad fortune and smiled. No good could come of the truth, but she would feel her way carefully. "I believe we are. Mr. Shellum, isn't it?"

He looked a bit bemused, but covered himself with some aplomb. More evidence that he was not yet pickled. But the night was still young. "Yes. Yes, you look quite familiar, but lawks!" He bowed and managed to keep from falling face-first onto the floorboards. "My deepest apologies. I cannot quite seem to remember where."

She smiled. All hail to strong spirits.

"I believe I had the pleasure of meeting you some months past," she said. "On St. Martin's Lane, wasn't it? You were ordering buttons, I believe." Messrs. William and Sons were known for their unique, if ridiculously expensive, fasteners. She was willing to bet, by his ostentatious vest, that he was one of their patrons. "These are particularly appealing," she said, gazing at the row of buttons that ran down his flat chest. "Amethyst, aren't they?"

"Why yes." He glanced down. "Aren't they all the crack?"

"They're quite lovely."

"And what of the waistcoat?" He fondled the garment lovingly. "My father thought I was spending the bustle a bit too freely, but I found the fabric irresistible."

Ella deciphered as best she could. "I'm certain they're well worth the money. You look quite marvelous. Don't you think, Lady Redcomb?"

"Absolutely," agreed Maddy, but gave her sister an odd glance from the corner of her soul.

"You met while shopping?" May asked.

"Where all good things happen," Ella said,

sticking to her story and studiously avoiding the tale of the night before. Chances were good Mr. Shellum had been as drunk as an Irishman while shopping on St. Martin's at one time or another. No reason to believe he would remember every encounter. "It was a lovely day. You do recall, don't you, Mr. Shellum? You were wearing your black Hessians." Every gentleman worth his snuff owned a pair of black Hessians.

"My . . . Oh yes, lovely boots. Very nice. I was fairly flush in the pockets then and could not pass them up. Though they pinched a bit in the toe. And I was never quite sure of the—"

Ella tried to focus on the inane chatter. If her luck held, he would assume the woman he met on the previous night was someone else entirely. After all, she had not been so foolish as to give him her name. But in that instant, her attention was snared by another. She turned to the left.

Drake's gaze caught her like a hapless hare. His hair shone darkly in the gas lamplight, and his eyes . . . She felt her breath leave her throat, felt her composure crumble. Shifting her attention back to Shellum, she tried to look enraptured, but Drake was already heading toward her, strides long and sure, eyes like a raptor's. She could feel his approach in her itchy palms but did her best to ignore it, nodding attentively at the meandering tale of cravats and kid gloves.

"Lady Lanshire," Drake said quietly from beside her. For a moment she actually considered ignoring him, but of course that would never do. Especially since Shellum's soliloquy had stopped. His brows raised in question.

"Sir Drake," she said, turning slightly.

"You're recovered, I hope."

Dammit! She should have told the truth from the start, but dark thoughts of France had shaken her good sense. "Of course. Never better."

"Why would she not be?" May asked, but Shellum was already bursting into the conversation.

"Fiend seize it! You were there, sir."

Drake turned toward him with slow consideration, dark eyes giving nothing away.

"In Miss Anglican's garden," Shellum said, but with a little less certainty.

"In my—" May began.

"After I bested those demmed Bristol men."

"Bristol men?" Milton said, scurrying into the conversation.

"There was a strawchipper." Shellum shifted his bauble-bright gaze uncertainly to Ella. "She was set upon in the garden. But I saved her. Quite heroically, I might add."

"You saved her?" May asked.

"Why yes." His brows dipped a little in thought. "Though I admit things were a mite befogged. It was quite dark. And I may have been half sprung."

"Who was she?" May asked.

"What?"

"Whoever did you save?"

Ella cursed in silence.

"I thought . . ." Shellum paused, scowled. "In truth, I'm not quite certain. It was all a bit blurry what with the fisticuffs and whatnot."

"There was a fight?"

"I planted a facer on the largest of the mob and they set to."

"You fought for some lady's honor?" Milton piped in.

"Well . . ." Shellum puffed a little. "One can hardly allow the riffraff of the street to molest our ladies fair. What?"

"Indeed not," Milton said.

"Who was this lady?" May asked.

"Well . . . that's . . ." Shellum paused. "It was bloody dark, as I've said, but . . ." He turned toward Drake. "My apologies." He bowed. Almost steady. "I don't believe we've been properly introduced. I am Edward Shellum."

Introductions were made all around.

"Sir Drake," Shellum said. "Correct me if I'm befogged yet again, but you were . . . were you not, in the garden last night?"

Drake never so much as shifted his gaze to Ella, but nodded solemnly. "A very impressive display of manliness."

Sarcasm. Ella ground her teeth. She should have simply told the others of her attack-in-the-garden debacle immediately. Should have stumbled back into Merry May's house, breathless and distraught, instead of whiling away her time with some dark stranger who could spill the story later on. Henceforth everything she did would seem suspect. After all, what kind of woman would not have mentioned such a fright at the time of the incident? Who but a carefully trained government witch who—

"Your roses are quite spectacular, Miss Anglican," Drake said.

Ella turned toward him, brows lowered. What the hell was he doing? Why hadn't he spouted the tale?

"Thank you," said May, "but it seems there were thieves on the grounds."

He didn't shift his eyes from May. "So I am told, but in truth, I fear I came a bit late to the excitement."

"But there was a lady there," May said.

"Yes." He nodded, sounding uncertain. "I believe there was."

"Who was she?" asked May and Milton in unison, but he was already shaking his head.

"It was quite dark and . . . *befogging*, as Mr. Shellum here has said. And I'm new to the city. I fear I didn't ascertain her name."

"'Tis the same with me," Shellum said. "But I believe she looked rather—"

"Shaken," Drake said. "As you can well expect. She went straight home after the incident."

"Of course she would," Maddy said, speaking for the first time.

"Can you describe her?" May asked.

"The mist was beginning to thicken and I had no wish to intrude on her privacy, but she was wearing a light-colored gown, I believe. Don't you agree, Mr. Shellum?"

"Well . . . yes." He scowled judiciously. "Yes. Quite light."

What the devil was he playing at? Ella wondered. Should she tell the truth even now before circumstances worsened, or should she continue with this ridiculous charade?

"Not much help there at all," Milton said. "That could be any of a hundred ladies."

"Perhaps I was a bit nervous. I admit, I was not expecting trouble in such a fine neighborhood as yours," Drake said.

"One must be ever vigilant," said Shellum.

"Indeed," agreed Ella, and refrained from slapping him upside the head.

"Not all of us can be as brave as Mr. Shellum here," Drake said. "Don't you agree, Lady Lanshire?"

Likewise, she refrained from hitting *him*. Surely she deserved some sort of award for such restraint. "I hope you were not hurt, Mr. Shellum," she said.

"My cheek is yet a bit tender," Shellum confided, touching a bruise under his left eye. "From when they struck me."

Or from when he'd fallen face-first into the flowering columbine.

"Good show I've been doing a bit of boxing down at Gentleman Jackson's Saloon," Shellum said.

"Have you indeed?" Milton asked. "I've been thinking of doing the same myself. How did you find it?"

"Well . . . were it not for that gentleman's training, I daren't think what might have happened to the lady last night."

Maddy made a breathy sound in her throat and tsked.

May glanced at Ella curiously, then shook her head. "You were very brave, Mr. Shellum. Whoever the mystery lady was, I am sure she is quite grateful."

He smiled at her, bowed, recovered. "Thank you. You are terrible kind."

Behind them, the orchestra was playing the haunting strains of the opening minuet.

"Might I have this dance?" Shellum asked.

"Certainly," May said, and reaching out, laid her hand on his arm.

The others watched them go.

"Horrible," Milton said, shivering as he turned toward Drake. "And you say you have no idea who the poor woman was?"

"I should have been more astute."

"I'm surprised you weren't," Milton said. "Being a military man as you are."

Drake turned his gaze on the little man. For a moment the world seemed quiet, then: "My apologies to all and sundry," he said, and bowed. "Now, Lady Lanshire, if you've no objections . . ." His eyes were dark, laughing at her. "I'd like to ask your friend here for a dance. Lady . . ."

"Redcomb," Maddy said.

"Redcomb . . ." He reached out his hand. "Would you do me the honor?"

Madeline's brows rose in surprise. "I'd be delighted," she said, and grasped his fingers, leaving Ella alone with the stumpy little baron.

Chapter 6

"**W**here were you wounded?" Lady Redcomb's voice was low and soft when they were reunited sometime during the minuet. She was pretty, dark-skinned, and quietly alluring.

He looked into her eyes. They were wide and bonny. But they were not as green as the endless hills of his homeland. Not filled with a humor and sorrow so deeply ingrained that a man could not extract himself. Not like the beguiling Ella's. But it was more than Ella's eyes that drew him. It was everything about her, the way her lips quirked up in an almost smile of mystery and allure, the way she lifted her hand, or turned, or walked, as graceful as a swallow.

But why the devil hadn't she admitted her role in the drama of the previous night? In his admittedly limited experience, ladies of the *ton* reveled in being the center of attention. And the attack on her person would make a fine tale.

"Is it so obvious as that?" he asked.

Lady Redcomb smiled a little. "You dance very well, despite the injury."

The memories were bitter, scalding. He pushed them into the dark compartment he kept for such things. He had not loved the sea, was not seduced by the swelling waves as some men were. But he'd had little say in the matter. "I was fortunate," he said.

"Were you?" she asked.

"There were those who thought I would succumb to my injuries." Captain Fowler for one, though he had seemed neither surprised nor notably disappointed at the thought of his "mongrel" lieutenant losing a leg.

Ensign Stewart's impassioned tale of Drake's heroics, however, had made a lasting impression. Perhaps it was the scrawny little ensign's dramatization of Drake's efforts to drag Fowler's unconscious body from beneath the falling battle debris that had changed the captain's mind. Perhaps the tale had convinced Fowler that even a mutt Irishman might be more valuable with two legs than one. Either way, it was probably best that young Stewart had neglected the portion of the tale that told how Drake had planned to do the opposite. Had planned to toss the bastard's dead weight over the quarter while the crew was scurrying to escape the unexpected ferocity of the wounded French *Bellone*.

"I'm sorry." Her words brought him back to the moment at hand. The moment with no squalls. No lightning storms in the midst of blackness, no bellowing cannons.

It was the second time in two days that a beautiful woman had apologized to him. Conditions were improving considerably. "That I lived?" he asked.

She smiled. "That you were injured."

"As was I," he admitted.

"But no more?"

He glanced over her head. The little lord named Milton was leading Lady Lanshire toward the dance floor. She wore a silver-blue gown that flowed around her like silken waves. Her hair was upswept, kept in place by some kind of magic only women understood, and adorned with long, golden pins from which a small string of beads swayed with her movement.

Milton's stout form was garbed in mismatched yellows and opulent green. It was like pairing a Thoroughbred with a wild ass. Wrong on so many levels. The lady was made for dancing, as lovely as a dove in flight, as elegant as a swan. But there was more, something that made it impossible for him to look away. Who the devil was she? "Had it not been for the injury I would still be on the *Sea Witch*," he said.

Lady Redcomb raised her brows. "I sincerely hope that was the name of your ship," she said, and he couldn't help but laugh.

Her mouth quirked up a little, reminding him of Ella, and though he knew the comparison was caused by foolish infatuation, he couldn't help but inquire about their relationship.

"How well do you know Lady Lanshire?" he asked. It wasn't as if the two women looked alike, but they had adopted similar mannerisms. How far back did their relationship go? he wondered, and searched the crowd for her, but his partner's peeved tone snagged his attention.

"Sir Drake, have you been at sea so long as all that?"

"I'm not certain what you mean."

"It's quite unfashionable to be so obvious about your interest in one woman while you are dancing with another."

He chuckled. They parted, reeling away with different partners. "My apologies," he said upon meeting her again.

"I should think so." She fell silent for a moment as they spun. "She's not looking for a husband, you know."

"Oh?"

A quirk of irritation twitched her lips, but whether it was real or performed for his entertainment, he couldn't be certain. "A *gentleman* would have said, 'Are *you?*'"

He really had deplorable social skills, but neither had he been a shining example of naval excellence. Indeed, he had advanced through the ranks mostly by the grace of attrition and the luck of misunderstandings, some of which were accidental. Still, he had been suited for little else and had nowhere else to go since his mother's death and his estranged father's move to London. Thus he had remained at sea for years on end. "Which is exactly what I would have said next, of course, had your charms not driven my manners clear out of my head."

"Much better," she said, and laughed. The sound was light and musical. He couldn't help but wonder if Lady Lanshire heard it.

"Have you never been married, Sir Drake?"

"I fear I've spent too much time in the company of the *Witch* and her like," he said.

A question flared in her eyes, but understanding dawned in an instant. "Ahh, your ship."

"Is there another witch about?"

"I see you've not met Lady Hamilton," she said.

From across the room, Lady Lanshire was laughing, but he reminded himself not to glance her way. Not all strategy was staged at sea, after all. "Perhaps she only seems disagreeable in comparison to your pleasing temperament," he said.

She gave him an approving nod. "Much, much better," she said, and smiled. "You learn quickly for a military man."

"It must be your irresistible presence."

"Quite impressive indeed," she said.

Lady Lanshire laughed again. He resisted the frown that threatened, but couldn't quite manage to squelch the question. "Is it too early to ask how you first met her?"

"It most certainly is," Lady Redcomb said, and gave him a disapproving glance as they walked a slow circle. "Hence I might just as well tell you so you don't shame me by asking. As it happened, we met over a spirited game of whist some years ago."

"Spirited," he said. "Is that another term for *dangerous*?"

She scowled a little as if thinking back. "Threats may, in fact, have been issued. In the end I lost a small fortune and my dignity, but we became fast friends. We were, after all, both new to this country. Both widowed young."

"She's widowed?" She had said as much, but in truth, he had no idea what to believe. Lady Lanshire was lying about other things. Why did that intrigue him more than disturb him?

"For some years," she said.

"What was he like?"

She gave him another tilted look from beneath her lashes. "Tell me, Sir Drake, don't you wish to know if she's sinfully wealthy?"

"Only a fool or a rich man would not."

"And which one might you be?"

"I fear I'm not wealthy," he said.

She smiled. "So honestly, why did you not ask *her* to dance?"

They twirled. "I thought that was what she anticipated."

"And . . ."

"Surely you've heard of war tactics, Lady Redcomb."

"Indeed I have. I've just never seen them employed on the dance floor."

"I doubt that's true."

She looked at him, canting her head and concentrating. What would she see? A bitter man, hard used and bone weary? Or the less likely image of the elegant, newly knighted hero he hoped to project?

"So you're planning a surprise attack," she said.

"I'm still strategizing."

"I believe she's off her guard now."

"You think so?"

She glanced to the right. "She's speaking with Lord Milton. The most tiresome man in Christendom. She's most probably out of her mind with boredom."

"Just what I was hoping for," he said.

The song came to an end. They bowed in unison.

"Go talk to her," she said.

"Perhaps I'm shy."

"Perhaps you're a liar."

"Perhaps."

She laughed. The sound was a bit louder and more flirtatious than seemed natural. He lifted an eyebrow in question.

"It's for Lady Lanshire's benefit," she explained. "She's watching."

He turned to find his quarry, but his partner stopped him with a tight grip on his biceps.

"Don't look," she hissed.

"My mistake."

"I should say it is," she said, then stretching up on her toes, whispered, "War tactics indeed, Sir Drake. 'Tis little wonder you were wounded."

"If only you had been there to instruct me."

"And defend you."

"Are you so dangerous?"

"I can spread some wicked *on dit*," she said, and linking her arm through his, gazed admiringly into his eyes as she led him back toward the object of his fascination.

"I've no idea what half the populace of this city are talking about most of the time," he murmured.

"Just follow my lead," she said, still smiling as Lord Milton scurried into the crowd. Lady Lanshire glanced up, eyes widening before she jerked her gaze toward the little lord as if hoping to draw him magically back.

"Damn," Lady Redcomb whispered, smile tightening a bit.

"What is it?" Drake asked.

"Harrison Sutter approaching from the starboard side."

"Sutter?" He glanced casually to the right. "The man with the perfect nose?"

"I think he's quite enamored with her."

He failed to stop his frown. "What are her feelings for him?"

She glanced up, smiling flirtatiously. "I'm surprised you lasted a day at sea."

"I was too pathetic to dump overboard." They were drawing close. He could feel her nearness in the very air she breathed. As if it had somehow been energized.

"I'll get rid of him," she murmured.

"I've got nothing against the man, of course," he said, remembering the perfect nose. His own had been broken. Twice. Once by a loosed jib and once by an ensign. The same one who had so dramatically portrayed the saving of Captain Fowler, in fact. "But if you feel the need to kill him I'll help you be rid of the body."

"Good Lord," she murmured, then turned with a smile to the man with the perfect profile. "Mr. Sutter, how good it is to see you."

"Lady Redcomb, you look resplendent."

"As do you."

It was true. He wore the costume of the *ton* as if he'd been born to it. The perfect match for Lady Lanshire's mind-tingling elegance.

But the introductions were beginning. Drake gave Sutter a nod, but Lady Redcomb was already reaching for the other's hand.

"A waltz," she said. "How lovely. Will you favor me with this dance, Mr. Sutter?"

Sutter delayed an instant before bowing with elegant grace. "I would be delighted," he said, and escorted her back onto the floor.

Drake clasped his hands behind his back and watched them go. "On the grand scale of things, how obvious was that ploy?"

"Ridiculously," Ella said, not bothering to glance at him.

He nodded, agreeing. "Why did you not tell the others about your troubles in the garden?"

Milton was bobbling through the crowd toward them. Neither turned to watch, but he was certain she was aware.

"Are you intending to ask me to dance or not?" she asked.

Still watching Lady Redcomb, he canted his head the slightest degree toward Milton. "I thought *he* was your chosen one."

"I said I wanted to sleep with him. Not talk to him."

"You saw my efforts."

She gave him a tilted glance from the corner of her eye.

"On the dance floor," he explained. "If you still wish to accompany me, you must be rather desperate."

"I've seen worse attempts."

"You are kind," he said, and thrust out an elbow.

"Not generally," she said, and took it.

The lilting waltz flowed on. Thank God for the scandalous Viennese, he thought, and took her in his arms.

There was almost a glow about her. An illumination he could neither quite substantiate nor dismiss, but it seemed to cast everyone around her in muted darkness. Perhaps she was not beautiful. He couldn't quite tell, for she was enchanting.

"The truth is," she said, "I have yet to decide whether I wish to sleep with Shellum," she said.

He focused on her words, but it did little good. "I'm not certain I understand."

"If my contemporaries know he saved me from those fiends in the garden . . ." She shivered a little. "They will surely expect me to be grateful."

He thought about that as they spun across the dance floor. "Grateful enough to sleep with him."

She gave him an abbreviated nod. "Especially once I become promiscuous."

"Which you've yet to do?"

She scowled. "In truth, I've been quite busy. But I shall get around to it soon enough."

"Might *soon* mean tonight?" he asked, and raised a brow.

She lowered hers. "Don't look so hopeful."

"Procrastination is one of the seven deadly sins."

"No it's not."

"But its status might be elevated at any moment so—"

"I'm not going to sleep with you, Sir Drake."

She was mesmerizing. "Even if I plead."

She cocked her head at him. "Pleading might be interesting."

How easy it would be to become lost in her eyes. "Please," he said.

She waited, looking expectant, then disappointed, then downright peeved. "That, my good sir, is the most pathetic pleading I've ever heard."

"My apologies." They twirled again. His leg throbbed, but it could hardly compete with the thrill of holding her. "So you don't want people to know he saved you lest they expect you to share his bed."

"Exactly."

"Perhaps you could simply tell them you're not attracted to him."

She scowled. "Since I have every intention of

79

sleeping with Milton, I hardly think that will make a great deal of sense to them."

He chanced a glance over her shoulder. The little man was watching them, brows lowered like a burrowing rodent's. "And why was that again?"

"Some might think him less attractive than—"

"I meant to say, why are you planning to sleep with him."

"Oh. Because I am quite certain I won't get attached."

"Of course." He spun her past an aging couple. Her neck arched gracefully with the motion. Her gown flared like the tail of a falling star, but he caught her gaze and held it. "And why, my lady, are you pretending Shellum saved you instead of the other way around?"

Chapter 7

Ella held his gaze. Smiled a little. Remained calm. That was, after all, what she had been trained to do.

"Tell me, Sir Drake, might you have been eating Hull cheese?" she asked.

He scowled.

"The *ton's* jargon," she explained, "for drinking."

"Ahh. Only of your beauty," he said.

She raised a skeptical brow.

His features remained perfectly schooled, but his coffee-dark eyes were smiling. "Lady Red-comb suggested that I may have better luck if I were a bit more . . . flowery."

"Did she also say you should refrain from sounding like an idiot?"

And now his eyes laughed, though his lips remained unbowed. "She may have failed to mention that."

"Then let me be the first to inform you, Sir Drake, you should also refrain from—"

"Why did you lie about last night?" he asked again.

She kept her gaze absolutely steady. "You might also refrain from accusing a lady of fabricating a story for no particular reason."

"'Twas not an accusation." They spun across the dance floor. She was like magic in his arms, like a kite on a silken string, filled with promise, with freedom. "Simply a question. Why would you say Shellum bested the bastards?"

"Perhaps this will surprise you after your long years at sea, sir, but ladies of quality do not go about trouncing thugs."

"If I may be so bold . . ." he began, and twirled her again, making her think, perhaps, he would be so bold as to do anything he pleased. "Neither do men who are so inebriated they cannot tell their head from their arse."

"Then perhaps I should sleep with Shellum after all."

He stared at her, hypnotic eyes questioning.

"Since he is obviously a very talented man."

"Able to trounce a pair of thugs while remaining absolutely unconscious?"

She tilted her head. "What makes you think there were two?"

"You are quite a remarkable woman," he said. "But I doubt you could have stood against three."

She laughed. "I admit, Sir Drake, I am rather impressed by your imagination."

He tugged her an inch closer as the song flowed to an end. His eyes burned her. His burr deepened. "Does that mean you will share me bed?"

"That means, good sir, that I am leaving," she said, and pulling from his arms, curtsied sweetly. "Thank you ever so for the dance."

He released her, returned the bow, eyes sparking. "The pleasure was mine, my lady."

"Perhaps," she said, and left with all due decorum, but her heart was banging overtime against her ribs. Foolishness. All foolishness. Reeves would disapprove if he knew. And he would know. One glimpse of her face would tell him.

You are panting like a draft horse, Josette. Do you want others to die because you cannot control your own breath?

"Lady Lanshire," called a cultured voice.

Ella found the place of quiet in her soul and

turned, face placid, heartbeat slowing. Lord and Lady Bowles were plump and middle-aged. Happy in that way that she doubted she would ever understand. In that way that made her ache inside, for they had built a life, shared a family that laughed and cried and cared. "My lord, my lady, what a lovely gathering. Thank you for the invitation."

"You're not leaving so soon, surely," said her hostess.

"I fear I must. I hope to ride to the hounds first thing in the morning." Who was this Sir Drake and why was he so interested in thugs and gardens and who had trounced whom? "The two of you should accompany us."

"Riding," said Lord Bowles, and faked a dramatic shiver. "Perched atop one of those temperamental beasts like a cricket ball on a stile?"

"It's not so horrible as it sounds."

"No. I imagine 'tis far worse. Give me a nice brougham with a pair of placid nags or let me stay home with a blackberry cordial and the *Times*."

"We are not much for equestrian sports, I fear," explained Lady Bowles.

"But we are devils on the dance floor," said her husband, and taking his wife's hand, swirled her once before dipping her toward the carpet.

She giggled.

Smiling, Ella said her farewells and stepped outside.

It was quieter out of doors. She took a careful waft of night air and motioned to Winslow. He might have been all but deaf, but he kept a sharp eye, and in a moment had urged Dancer to draw her carriage up to the cobbled walkway. The gelding bobbed his head, ready to be off, and they soon were, trotting rhythmically down the rough-paved street.

Berryhill was not far from the Bowleses' impressive manse, but it was humble by comparison. Located in the south of Camden, it had a tilting roofline and crumbling mortar. Nevertheless, it looked much as it must have a hundred years before. Winslow stopped the cob near her arched front door and dismounted to hand her down.

Impatience beat at her. She wanted nothing better than to bolt for the privacy of her property, but propriety was everything. England's very existence seemed to hinge on a lady's ability to wheedle away the hours, to gamble and dance and giggle behind her fan.

"Thank you, Winslow," she said, and made her way up the meandering walkway. Her feet were silent on the cool, smooth stones, for she had abandoned her slippers while in the carriage and carried them hidden in the folds of her skirt. No one met her at the door. Perhaps she flouted society too much in this case. Perhaps crowns would topple because she hung her own cloak on the brass hook that was anchored beside the door, but this was her home, and here she allowed herself a modicum of herself.

Her journey up the stairs was quiet, the product of long years of training. Or perhaps, more correctly, it was the product of fear. There had been a time, a seemingly endless period of darkness, that she wanted nothing more than to disappear, to remain unseen, unnoticed.

"And who are you today, my dear?" He was there again, peering at her, watery eyes bright and ungodly eager. He called himself Dr. Frank. But she knew him as Satan.

"I am myself," she said, but her voice sounded raspy, broken, beyond terror, beyond hope. Her unborn child was dead. Her husband had betrayed her. There was little reason to live. And yet she did. "Just myself, Josette de Moreau."

"And the demons? What of the demons?" he hissed.

Ella gripped the handrail in fingers turned to claws, felt the wood scrape beneath her nails, and remembered to calm herself.

All was well. She was safe. Home. Free. As was her sister.

But she had best think more clearly in the future. She'd made an error in judgment. She should not have spoken to Drake in the garden. Should certainly not have flirted so outrageously. Indeed, hindsight suggested that she should have returned posthaste to Merry May's ballroom. Should have told her story with drama and flair. Maybe even should have swooned. But she had not. Instead she had allowed herself to be seduced by the humor and wit in an unknown man's mesmerizing eyes.

Foolish. Idiotic. She knew better. Far better. Verrill too had had mesmerizing eyes. Mesmerizing eyes and a lying tongue. He had vowed to love her forever, when, in fact he had loved nothing so much as her inheritance. But that no longer mattered. None of it mattered. Not anymore, for those years were far behind her, left shackled in a dark, fetid cell.

The problems at hand were all there was to consider. What should she do now? Admit to the *ton* that she had, in fact, been the woman in the garden? The woman Shellum was proclaiming to have saved? Or let the story play itself out? The gentry, after all, were easily bored. Surely the tale would soon grow old.

Or perhaps, she thought . . . But suddenly her breath caught tight in her throat. Something was wrong. Something was different. Her palms tingled. Her bedchamber door was closed as it should be. No sinister shadows played upon her walls. All was quiet.

Yet there was an intruder in her house. She was certain of it. Reaching up, she slipped a pin from her hair and removed the tiny cap from its end. There was a fluid inside. A special liquid. The spike would slice through skin like a needle, would deposit the fluid deep inside. And all would go quiet.

Taking a deep breath, she visualized her room in her mind. It was large. All but empty save for a few pieces of furniture. Against the far wall was a lone window, tall and narrow. It was locked from the inside. There were those who could open that lock. But only a few.

She drew a deep breath, forced herself to relax, and stepped inside, senses searching. The other's identity came to her with immediate clarity, and her voice was steady when she spoke.

"Good evening, Jasper."

He would be beside the door, hidden until she closed it. She turned to do just that, but he spoke first from the other side.

"You are becoming rusty, Josette."

Her heart tripped in her chest. She calmed it, turned. Moonlight flowed through the window, glistening on her weapon.

"Am I?"

He saw the pin. She knew it. But neither spoke of it.

"What would happen if I intended you harm?"

She capped the weapon. "Do you?"

Perhaps there was the slightest irritation in his voice. "That is hardly the point."

Replacing the pin in her hair, she took a step forward, past him, to pull the drapes shut. Darkness fell around them, soft and complete.

"I don't have your gifts, Josette," he said.

He had told her as much a host of times. It was a reprimand of sorts, reminding her that there were powers she had not yet tapped, abilities of which even she was, as of yet, unaware. Which did he refer to now?

"Do you think I can see in the dark, Jasper?" she asked.

She could sense his irritation. Or maybe she *could* see it, in a way that could not quite be explained.

"Regardless, a little light would be appreciated."

"So you don't like to be in the dark either, I take it."

He was quiet for a second, then: "You're being childish."

It was true. She was. "Perhaps I'm allowed," she said. "Because I am so wonderfully gifted." Passing a candle, she swept her palm above the wick. It flared to life, illuminating the sharp planes of his face. He was barely taller than she, but there was something about him that had always made him seem larger than life. Still, it was his eyes that captured one's attention. They were old, as old as death itself. And just as secret.

"Perhaps you have obligations," he said, "because of those gifts."

"Still afraid you haven't gotten your money's worth, Jasper?"

"No." He took the room's one chair. "You were a fine investment. Everyone agrees."

"Everyone?" She had long suspected that the humorless Earl of Moore was intimately involved with the workings of Les Chausettes, but truth to tell, she no longer cared what great powers pulled the coven's invisible strings. Not anymore. She had ceased to be one of the government's secret pawns, ceased to be involved in the espionage, the crimes, the failings.

He ignored the question, as she knew he would. "I've been asked to request that you come back to Lavender House."

"By whom?"

Perhaps he was frustrated, but he would not show it. No pacing or swearing for Jasper Reeves. No emotion whatsoever, in fact. He did what he must. If people died, they died.

And they had.

"A child is—"

"No!" She pivoted toward him, stopping his words before she heard more. Before she was sucked in, drawn under, drowned. "Don't say it."

"Elizabeth is—"

"I said no!"

"It wouldn't be difficult. Not for you."

Anger flared in her soul, set a-kindle by seething frustration and the deep etching of pain. "It shouldn't have been difficult with Sarah."

Tension swallowed the room. He rose to his feet, but the movement was smooth. Controlled. She should have stabbed him with the damned pin just to get a reaction.

"I am sorry about her."

"Are you?"

He paused for a second, then: "It wasn't your fault."

She almost took a step back. Was she so obvious that even Jasper Reeves could read her? "I never said it was."

Another pause. "Lady Redcomb suggested you might blame yourself."

Madeline? Why? Why was Maddy talking about her at all? And why did he always refer to her sister by her title, while Ella was only Josette? A scared, scarred woman-child from another land. Then again, why did she care? He had never been anything but her employer . . . and her savior. For it had been he who Maddy had told of her sister's powers and subsequent incarceration. He who had found a way to secret Ella from the hideous bowels of La Hopital.

But she squelched the thought. The anger. The gratitude.

"Actually . . ." She dropped her slippers, sat down on the bed. "I blame you for Sarah's death."

He watched her in silence. "She wasn't a Chausette. There was nothing—"

"She was a person!" she snapped, and found that she was standing again, facing him, anger seething from every pore.

"I can barely protect your—" He stopped himself. Firelight flashed across his eyes.

She watched, surprised by his passion, but perhaps she shouldn't have been, for he *did* protect. He kept them safe from all outside forces so he might decide how best to spend their lives.

"She had already revealed herself to Grey," he said, his voice perfectly level once again. "She couldn't be trusted with the secrets of Les Chausettes. No matter how gifted she may have been."

"So you allowed her to die." Her voice was filled with venom. Rancid with time and bitterness. Perhaps she was being unfair. And perhaps she didn't care.

"I had no way of knowing it would come to that."

"The truth is, you didn't think her worth the trouble."

"She didn't have your gifts, it's true."

"You have no idea what her gifts were. She was young. Untrained."

"She was a wild card and a show-off."

"As was I."

He remained silent for a moment, letting her think. "Maybe once," he said finally.

And he was right. By the time he had found Ella, chained and battered and filthy, she had been little more than an empty shell. Wanting nothing more than to hide. To be left undisturbed with her madness. If she had powers, she would not show them, not to anyone, no matter if they swore to love her always. That much she had vowed. But in the end, those same powers that had damned her, had saved her. For it seemed there were those who were looking for women with her gifts.

"Sarah could have been trained," she said.

"We could not afford to become involved. You know that. It could have compromised the—"

"Damn the program!" she snapped. "You simply didn't think her worth your time."

His eyes aged yet again. "You're right," he said, and she felt herself wilt, her anger melting toward bitterness.

"Get out, Jasper," she said, but he remained as he was, silent, watching her.

"I think we may have been wrong," he said finally.

She turned away with a snort. "I shall alert the *Times*."

"About Grey," he added.

She glanced back, stiff, breathless. "What are you talking about?"

"We have reason to believe his was not the body found in the fire."

A thousand questions leaped through her mind. She kept them at bay, sifted carefully through them. "The house was rented to him."

"Yes."

"His belongings were inside. The items she . . . the items he forced her to steal."

"Some of them, at least."

Silence stole in, dark, stifling. "You think he's still alive," she breathed.

"Yes," he said.

And outside the window, quiet as a secret thought, evil smiled at the night.

Chapter 8

Who was this Grey? What had he done to Sarah? How had he done it? And perhaps even more importantly, could he do it again? To someone else? Someone Ella loved.

Beneath Ella, her blood bay mare trotted rhythmically along. Perhaps it was not perfectly acceptable for her to ride alone down the wending streets of London, though her status as a wealthy, titled widow allowed her nearly as much leniency as her own flaunted eccentricities. But just now she cared little for the social mores of the day; Madeline's image dominated her mind, and with it came a dozen errant memories. Memories of them playing together on a distant riverbank, discovering secrets, awed by fledgling powers they dared not admit. Memories of them wrapped in a faded counterpane, bare toes tucked beneath white nightgowns as they whispered into the night about hopes and dreams and promises.

Promises to care, to protect, to guard their secrets with their very lives.

But Ella had failed. Had failed and had paid. She would not be so foolish again.

Wisdom was needed. Wisdom and power. Thus she went to the one person she had gone to for years. The world called her Lady Beauton, but the women of Lavender House knew her simply as Vision.

The old woman's cottage was covered in ivy, her garden riotous, her walkway uneven. Dismounting unaided, Ella turned toward the aging man who shambled toward her. His face was as black as mistreated shoe leather, his belly as round as a pumpkin, straining the buttons of his scarlet livery. He was, and always had been, strangely proud of his portly form.

"It is good to see you, my lady," he said, and took Silk's reins in one broad hand.

"I can barely see you at all, Gets," she said. "With you becoming as thin as a reed."

He chuckled. The sound was deep and melodious. "Don't you know it is a sin to lie, my lady?"

"Tantamount to gluttony, I believe," she said,

and he laughed as she made her way toward the front door. It opened before she reached it. A long, narrow face and faded blue eyes greeted her from beneath a tilted mobcap.

"Lady Lanshire, we've not seen you for some time." There was a reprimand in the woman's voice. The kind that can only be found in servants who have been faithful for years beyond count.

"My apologies," Ella said, and stepped inside. "I've been quite busy."

"Well . . ." She closed the door and strode briskly away, leading into the interior of the house. "I suppose the regent's foolish doings seem important to some. More important than an old woman's loneliness."

"Aldora." A scratchy voice came through the doorway from the parlor. "Are you making my guests feel guilty again?" The voice was followed by an old woman in a large-wheeled chair. "Ella." Her smile urged a hundred new wrinkles into her parchment features. "Welcome."

Ella bent, hugged her. She was thin, faded, spring-blossom fragile. "Lady Beauton, you look well."

"Ach . . ." She waved a blue-veined hand. The movement almost seemed more than she could manage, but her eyes were bright. "I look a fright.

Gets would barely help me into my chair, I look that hideous. I fear they'll leave me abed until I die of tedium one of these days."

Ella switched her gaze to the servant. Worry skipped through Aldora's eyes, but she snorted, dismissive. "You're too much trouble by half when you're wheeling about. Can barely find you to fetch you your tea."

Lady Beauton chuckled, but her face contorted with pain for a second, then calmed, brought under control by sheer force of will. "I suspect I should apologize for the difficulties I cause."

"You'll do no such thing," Ella said. "Instead, we shall sit in the parlor and make them serve us crumpets and jam as if we were at court with Princess Caroline."

"Do you mind, Aldora?" asked the old woman.

"I'm only a servant," she grumbled, but she gave Ella a grateful glance before she hurried away.

Ella took the handles of the chair and pushed the aging dowager back into the parlor. The sun was bright there, a shaft of gold that lit the old woman's remaining treasures: a vase from New Delhi, a mirror from Peking. Souvenirs from her days with Les Chausettes. Her dead legs were yet another memento. A keepsake from four years before, during her time in Madrid. She had gone to visit a friend, or so said the official story. The truth was far different. That much Ella knew; Napoleon had been about to march through Spain on his way to Lisbon. Vision's presence there at the same time had not been a coincidence.

Leaving her to face the window, Ella rounded the wheelchair and sat on the settee. The old woman took her hand, folding it in her own. The aging skin felt as cool and dry as parchment.

"I'm well," Ella said. She was not quite sure if a question had been voiced aloud. But that was the way with Lady Beauton, who had not a drop of nobility, unless one acknowledged the royal blood of the Gypsies that flowed hot and wild through her aging veins.

"And the rest of the lassies?" Her voice was soft, raspy. "What of them?"

"Everyone is well. Doing splendidly, in fact."

"Shaleena's not causing too much trouble, I hope."

"No. Everyone's—" Ella began, but the old woman touched a finger to her lips. Still it seemed like a full minute before Aldora reappeared, bearing two cups and a teapot on a silver platter. She set it beside them on a low table.

"Thank you, Aldora," said her mistress.

"I suspect you can manage to pour," said the other, looking down her nose at Ella.

"Aldora," the old woman scolded, but Ella was already lifting the teapot.

The servant bustled away.

Tea mist curled above the delicate cup. Ella handed it over, steadying it for a moment as the old woman took it in an uneasy hand and raised it to her lips. She took a sip, lowered the cup, smiled.

"Shaleena is gifted," she said. "Indeed . . ." Her eyes were distant. "She reminds me of another."

Ella knew she spoke of Leila. For there was none to match her. Even now, four years after her death, her name was whispered in connection with the rise and fall of nations. She had been Lady Beauton's Spanish counterpart, an unacknowledged adviser to the king. If rumors were true, she had been found dead before Vision could warn her of Bonaparte's impending march. "Same shrewd cunning. Same vanity." She grinned wistfully. "I did not think I would miss her, but had she lived . . ." She glanced up suddenly, as if just remembering Ella's presence.

"One would think me too old to spill state secrets now," she said.

Those same secrets had somehow involved Vision. The woman who could see so much could not have foreseen the loss of her legs. Some said she had battled with the very man who had killed Leila. Some said that was nonsense. They had, after all, hated each other.

"None could argue that you've served your country well," Ella said.

"None who knows, perhaps." She smiled. "But what of you, Josette?"

Ella shook her head. "I fear I have neither your courage nor your gifts."

"Pish," said the old woman. "I've never seen another more gifted."

Ella didn't bother to hide her surprise. Vision was not the sort to fawn. "Thank you, my lady, but—"

"But you've not come for compliments."

"I never turn one aside if it happens—"

"What's wrong?" The old woman's tone had become very businesslike. Reminiscent of the early days, when she had lived at Lavender House. When she had tutored and protected and scolded.

"Is it a sin to visit my most respected mentor?" Ella asked, and forced herself to take a drink.

"Not at all." Vision took a sip, all the while

watching Ella over the faded gold rim of her cup. "But as Gets said, it is a sin to lie."

"Since when?" Ella asked, not surprised by the old lady's knowledge of the conversation. Secret knowledge was her business, after all.

"If Jasper heard me say so, he'd give me a scolding, wouldn't he?" Vision asked, and set her cup down, face somber. "You've left the coven," she said.

"I—" Ella began.

"You've left them," she said quietly. "And the guilt consumes you."

Ella couldn't quite look up. "You know how disconcerting it is when you look into my mind."

The old woman chuckled, touched Ella's hair, smoothing it back from her forehead. "You could do the same if you liked. Scares folks something terrible." A bit of Rom dialect had crept into her tone. When she let down her guard, her Gypsy ancestry shone through like the sun in the south window.

"It's not leaving that bothers me most," Ella admitted. "It's . . ."

"Sarah's death."

Regardless of the past, of her knowledge of the old woman's gifts, she was surprised. Generally, Vision's powers grew more precise with proximity, but she hadn't visited for some months. Perhaps shame *had*, in fact, kept her away. "You knew about her?"

The aged face contorted, but whether from pain or empathy, it was impossible to say. "Not until this moment." Her eyelids drifted, almost closing.

"I shouldn't bother you with this," Ella said.

"Jasper's right." The old eyes snapped open suddenly, bright with intensity, wide with worry. "He's not dead."

Silence echoed in the room.

"Grey?" Ella hissed.

Vision's eyes remained immobile, looking past, looking through. "That's not his name."

"What is it then? Where is—"

But the old woman's face contorted again, twitching madly.

"Vision!" Ella grabbed her hand. "Lady Beauton, I'm sorry."

The frail body jerked, spasmed. Her eyes rolled back, her lax legs bucked twice, then went limp, slumping her in the chair.

"Aldora," Ella called, panic seizing her.

But Vision came to in a moment, hand tightening as she raised her head with a weary effort. "Don't make her worry," she said. Only the left half of her mouth moved. "Everyone worries so."

"Are you well?"

"Well?" She attempted a smile. The right side twitched lethargically. "No, my dear. I am dying."

"No. You—"

"Yes." Her smile was brighter now, her grip stronger.

"I'm sorry," Ella whispered, and the other sighed, nodded.

"As am I. I wish I could say it was otherwise. That I was happy to go. That I feel I've done my part, but . . ." She shrugged, little more than a shift of a bony shoulder. "Tell me more of your world, Josette. Who was this Sarah?"

Ella wanted to run for help, to see the old woman abed, to pamper her. But it was not Vision's way to allow such foolishness. "She was a friend," she said. "A young woman I met just over a year ago."

"Gifted?"

"Yes."

The old woman nodded. "We are often drawn together, those of us who are different."

"I could feel it in her," Ella said. "The strangeness. The powers. And I worried. She had no one to speak to of it."

"'Tis why Les Chausettes was formed at the outset so long ago. To give us a place to come together."

"And to harness our power."

Vision's glance was sharp. "You blame Jasper."

"No." Ella pulled her hand away, reached for the teacup, wanting space, wishing, almost, that she had not come. "No, I just . . ."

"You think he should have protected her."

She glanced up. "He could have."

"How? As he protected you?"

Ella said nothing, *could* say nothing, for her mouth felt suddenly dry, her throat constricted.

"You blame him for that as well," murmured the old woman.

Ella glanced toward the window, swallowed.

"You cannot blame him for doing and for not doing, Josette."

She lowered her eyes. "I fear that is not entirely true."

Reaching out, Vision cupped Ella's face with a weathered hand. "You expect too much of others, child, just as you expect too much of yourself."

"Did Jasper kill him?" she asked suddenly, surprising even herself.

For a moment, she thought the other might ask

whom she spoke of, but she did not. "Your husband was—"

"Did he kill him?" she asked again.

The gazes met. "No."

For a moment Ella felt relief sear her, but it was cheap and short-lived. She knew the game better than that. "Did he order his death?" she asked.

There was an eternity of silence, then: "The man was evil, Josette. Heartless. Soulless. Filled with greed and trickery. You know that better than any. Jasper feared he would find you and—"

"And tear apart his empire?" she snapped.

"And return you to the hell he had condemned you—" Vision began, but her face twitched again.

Ella fell to her knees. "I'm sorry, Lady Beauton. I'm sorry. Please forgive me."

"No." She closed her too-old eyes for an instant, patted Ella's hand. "Love should not, must not, be apologized for, no matter how misguided. No matter how dangerous."

"I don't love him," Ella rasped. "Not now at least. Not after La Hopital. Not after what he did. How could I?"

"Some men have a kind of magic, my dear. Not our kind, not the kind that can be honed and controlled. A magic of their own. Inexplicable. Inescapable."

"But I *have* escaped," she said.

"For a time."

"What do you mean?"

The old woman smiled. "You were meant to love, Josette. To love and be loved."

"A nice thought."

"It is the truth."

"I think, perhaps, this one time you are wrong," Ella said, but her thoughts were straying. If Grey was yet alive, there were things that could be done, *must* be done.

"Never tell an old lady she is wrong."

"I apologize."

"As well you should," Vision said, and smiled. "For that and the fact that you need to be off."

For a moment Ella almost argued, but there was little point. "I think it quite rude of you to read my mind."

"This time I am but reading your body, my dear."

Ella scowled.

"You are fidgeting like a tree squirrel. I thought we taught you better."

Drawing a deep breath, Ella tried to relax. "The truth is . . ."

"*Now* I am reading your mind. And I see that you have not gotten that for which you came."

Ella held her gaze. "I don't mean to trouble you."

The old woman smiled, an expression reminiscent of times long past. "It is only hair," she said. "It seems unlikely that I will need it in the afterlife."

Chapter 9

The day was dark. Thunder rumbled over the city. Rain fell in tiny droplets, trickling silently from a slate-gray sky. But Ella's bedchamber was warm. A blaze danced inside the immense blackened-brick fireplace.

Three years ago she had moved out of Lavender House and purchased Berryhill, this ancient home in Bloomsbury. It had touched her even then with its peaked roof and climbing ivy. But it was the master bedchamber that had inspired her most. It was large and open, overlooking unruly gardens and rough cobbled streets, granting her a feeling of quiet harmony in this half-forgotten piece of London. Built well before the advent of gas lighting, it blended aged practicality and mellowing grace. In fact, a rod was still imbedded into the stone floor of the fireplace. A rod that held a perpendicular arm that could be swiveled outward. It was that rod that Ella now employed. From it, she hung a cast-iron pot. Darkened by years and countless uses, it was as round and fat as a witch's cauldron. In fact . . .

Ella smiled as she chanted. True, she had vowed to cast no more spells, to mix no more potions, but Grey might yet be alive, and Madeline had not seemed her usual bright-eyed self. She'd looked tired and worried. Why? True, all of Europe was stewing in the fever of war, and Les Chausettes would forever agonize over the troubles of the world, but it seemed almost that Maddy's worries were not so all-encompassing as the matters of wars and rumors of war. It seemed almost as if it were something personal, something close to her heart. Something like a man that she could not quite get out of her head.

Ella added three strands of Vision's silver hair to the cauldron. "Bless her with the wisdom of age." Ella stirred the concoction with a wooden spoon. The sauce bubbled up to greet her, steaming in the early morning air. Lifting a few leaves from the floor, she tore them to bits. Even dried they would increase the recipient's knowledge, but fresh they were threefold more potent. "Healing and strength with the power of sage." A sprig of mugwort was added. "Artemis herb to keep her well." Of course, it was also known to increase one's sexual allure, but she would let Madeline worry about that. "All good fortune with the fragrant harebell."

Ella stirred the concoction again, then left it to brew. 'Twas a dying art, this ancient alchemy. Dying but not dead, secreted among her kind, given to those they loved . . . or hated . . . or feared . . . depending on the ingredients, the chanted words, the intention. For intention alone was ever-powerful among her own.

But she had intended to help Sarah, hadn't she? Had given her a potion, in fact, that was little different from the tonic she prepared now. But it had done little good.

Why? The mugwort had been dried, but it was pure. She had not used Vision's hair, but had added the bloom of an iris for wisdom. Nearly a full year ago, she had consecrated the fat, amber bottle by the light of the full moon and solemnly given it to the girl. Ella had believed the other had understood its importance, had believed in its merit. Yes, its scent was pleasing, but its true value lay in its intrinsic, inexplicable powers.

But they had failed. *She* had failed. And Sarah had died.

Rain beat harder against Ella's window. Shivering despite the warmth of the room, Ella rose to her feet. Leaving the potion to boil, she stripped off her clothes and stood silent and straight in the center of her bedchamber. *Sky-clad* was the term of the ancients, but naked was what she was, and she preferred to train that way.

Drawing in a few full breaths, she cleared her thoughts. Magic was an element of the mind, of the soul, an integral part of her most private self, but it was encompassed in the body, ever held in that fragile earthly vessel. So the vessel must be strong, but not inflexible. Hard, but not brittle. Trained, but not exhausted. And so she took a few initial movements, bending her knees, balancing on the balls of her feet, stretching until she was ready. And then, bowing to an invisible enemy, she attacked, twisting, turning, striking. Sinews stretched, muscles contracted, lungs heaved until her breath came hard and her skin gleamed with perspiration. Still, she pushed herself, sometimes a rhythmic dance, sometimes a fierce onslaught, pressing every muscle until she had defeated the demons within.

By the time Ella was cleansed and dressed, dusk had settled upon the city. Little darker than the preceding day, it lay like a soft blanket over steeple and stoop. Thunder rumbled plaintively in a bumpy sky, but weather was forever Ella's friend. She gloried in the dark feel of it, the thrill of electricity in the air as she strode, energized and ready toward the humble stable behind her house.

Winslow had already saddled Silk, but turned grumpily as she entered the barn. The mare stood quietly, one hind leg cocked, its full stocking perfectly matching the other three.

"Unfit weather." Winslow's words were muttered. So soft, in fact, that she was quite sure he could not hear himself. But he was not the type to shout. If one heard him, he heard, if not, it was his loss.

"All will be well," she said, looking into his eyes. She would not wound his pride by raising her voice, for he could gather her meaning well enough if he watched her lips. "I am but going to Miss Anglican's for a bit of whist and conversation. You needn't worry."

Lies had been her constant companion for as long as she could recall. Ever present but oft unwanted. Winslow's scowl deepened, but she could not concern herself with his worries. Not just now. Sighing silently, she mounted her mare and rode into the night.

Beneath her, the hot-blooded little barb arched her fine neck and strutted down the boulevard. Her hooves made a staccato rhythm in the quieting city. Gaslight flickered and gleamed in long streaks of gold on the damp cobbles, the mare's sable coat, the black mane.

Ella's riding habit was just as dark, draped elegantly over her cocked leg and single stirrup. The lady's saddle was a foolish thing, perching her atop her steed's withers like a praying mantis, hooking one knee high. But fashion dictated, at least in the polite world. The polite world was not her own, however. Not really.

She belonged to the night, to the quiet, to the deeds that were not spoken of in the light of day. Deeds such as the one she was planning even now, for she could not give up her darkling ways, not completely. Not until the world was safe from Grey. The world and her only sister.

It did not take long to leave Bloomsbury's beige respectability behind. Darkness had fallen in earnest by the time she reached East End, but she knew the landscape well, had studied it often, for one never knew when such knowledge might save one's life. Neither did one know when she might need all her balance and savvy. Having left the gas-lit boulevards far behind,

Ella unhooked her leg from the pommel and rode astride.

The city darkened further, both in light and in tone. Beyond the glittering grandeur of London proper, East End stretched grim and dangerous, seething with secrets and well-kept misery.

Here was where Sarah had died. Here, amid the squalor and hopelessness. The alleys became narrow, the streets rutted and muddy.

Silk tossed her heavy mane and snorted. Fear shifted in a stealthy inch, and Ella let it swell over her. For fear was only a hard-edged element of wisdom. Fear was caution, and she had long ago learned to use it. To control it, to let it sharpen her senses, guide her movements.

It was nearly full dark when she cued her mare onto Gallows Road. Memories reared their belligerent heads. Ella had been here before. Had come, in fact, to take Sarah to Lavender House, against Jasper's wishes, against his advisement.

Thunder rumbled in the distance. Dampness clung like dank spiderwebs, wetting her hair, wilting her clothes.

The hovel where she stopped was little more than a shell, burned from the inside. Even in the darkness, Ella could see the sooty stains that marred the tilted bricks. The door stood ajar.

Six weeks before, Sarah had opened it herself. Memories came again, sharp enough to cut. It had been dark, little different than now. But it had been chill then, the kind of cold that sliced clean to the bone. Ella had debated waiting until morning, informing the others, but fear or something like it had warned her that there was little time to spare. And when the door had opened, she had known she was right, for Sarah had changed. Her face, usually so bright with intellect, was devoid of expression, her eyes flat and shallow. As if her spirit were otherwise occupied. As if her body were empty.

Ella had planned to be conversational, to be casual, as though she wasn't certain Sarah's very life was somehow at risk, but the sight of the girl's soulless eyes changed everything. There was no time for frivolity. She had insisted that they leave together, had been adamant, had used every bit of mental persuasion she could conjure, and finally Sarah had nodded distractedly and turned away.

Ella remembered her burgeoning feelings of relief. She had won. There was hope, but suddenly, as if possessed by some wild demon, the girl had snatched a poker from the fireplace and flung herself across the distance, swinging wildly.

The weapon had struck Ella in the chest, slamming her backward, scattering her wits. Sarah swung again, slicing the heavy tip across Ella's arm. Pain and fear had brought her to her senses. She had fought then with primeval inelegance, trying nothing more than to stay alive, until finally she had seen an opportunity. A kick to the other's midsection, had slammed the girl backward.

She'd flown like a doll of rags, striking the stone hearth behind her.

Sarah's heather-green eyes had gone wide for an instant, as if just then, in that one startling instant, she had found herself. She opened her mouth as if to speak, and then she fell, dropping with liquid grace to the floor.

Ella remembered staggering forward, remembered bending down to touch the girl's hollow cheek.

Then came the roar of anger. She had lifted her head like one in a dream. A figure was flying toward her, arm drawn back, knife gleaming in the candlelight. She'd had no strength, mental or physical, to control her spell. Indeed, she had cast it in desperation though she knew better, had been taught better.

Flame had struck the figure like a wall, but he had kept coming, his face already blistered.

He'd slammed into her, catapulting her backward. She remembered pain, ripping, slicing agony. She remembered fear and regret, and then nothing. Blackness.

Sometime later she had awakened in Lavender House. Her lungs felt raw. Her head ached where it had been sliced open on something she could no longer recall. Her feet were bandaged where the fire had scorched them, but it was the news of Sarah's death that hurt the most. The fact that she herself had been the cause. Not the man who had taken her. Not the girl's own foolishness. But herself.

Chasing the thoughts impatiently from her mind, Ella glanced about. The street was silent. No one was near, no sinister shadows hovered beside the blackened remains, no evil shapes hid in the lee of the building. Hence she spoke a quiet word and urged her mare closer. Silk hesitated only a moment before mincing carefully up the stone steps. The doorway was narrow, but they squeezed inside where the elegant mount could not be easily seen.

Dismounting quickly, Ella removed her skirt and hung it over the saddle. It was little more than a single piece of fabric, after all, nothing but a shill that covered the breeches she wore beneath, the breeches that would aid in her manly disguise if need be.

For an instant Ella considered changing her image immediately, but she quickly discarded the idea. For now she would remain as she was, for the change oft threatened to overcome her natural psyche, muddling her sense of self, her own awareness. Just now she needed her woman's gifts . . . her intuition, her empathy, and maybe even her fear.

Silk, unimpressed by her internal debate, nudged her impatiently, and Ella acquiesced, pulling a dried piece of apple from her pocket. She had no magic over the beasts of the field, only a primal understanding of their honest, earthy ways. Lipping the treat from her hand, the mare bobbed her head, silent agreement to remain where she was, at least so long as the mood suited her.

Unbuttoning her shoes, Ella set them beside the door with her stockings inside. The earthen floor felt solid beneath her feet, but there was far more to it than that, for she had forever been intrinsically connected to touch, to the earth. Through the soles of her feet, she sensed anger and fear and confusion. The feelings were almost infinitesimal, so subtle and shifting, they might be disregarded as insignificant by another. And though discerning these latent emotions was not her greatest gift, Rosamond had helped her sharpen her skills. Indeed, the witches of Lavender House had taught her much: when to harvest each herb, how to control her thoughts and so control her body. How to survive . . . to keep breathing, when the world weighed in on you like a thousand sun-baked bricks.

Pulling a candle from her pocket, Ella wedged it into a brass holder, breathed on a flame, and prayed she would need no disguise this night, that she would find what she needed without interference. Then she went to work, silently sifting through the rubble.

Sarah had lived here. Had died here. There would be a clue to why. Some fragment of the past to tell the story of why she had left her home where she had been safe, if not content.

They had first met while riding the daily promenade around Mayfair. The girl had been shyly flirting with a penniless count. Flirting and smiling, but her hands had shown her abilities. They held the reins firmly but gently and reached often to stroke the arched crest of her handsome gray.

And in those first moments, Ella had felt the girl's inexplicable power. They'd introduced themselves and soon realized they had much in common.

But in eight months the situation had already begun to change. Sarah sold her beloved gelding, saying she planned to go abroad, to travel. And something in Ella's gut had clenched.

Wandering down a hallway, Ella moved quietly, absorbing every nuance. The house here was mostly intact. The ceiling was complete, casting her in darkness but for the wavering flame that melded shadows and stains on the too-close walls.

A door stood open to the left. A mattress lay on the floor. Flames had devoured the center, eating a black hole in the striped ticking. The charred horsehair stuffing lay exposed like painful memories, stifling and stagnant.

Had Sarah shared this room with the man named Grey? Had they lain together on that mattress?

There had been a feverish light in the girl's eyes the day she'd first mentioned him, an avid excitement in her tone as she spoke of his kindness, his wit. She'd known him for some months, she'd said, and the fearful niggling in Ella's gut grew worse, escalating to a quiver in her soul, a tingling in the palms of her hands.

But she'd reprimanded herself.

Jealousy, after all, felt much the same. She was accustomed to its pangs . . . the gnawing grind of envy as milkmaids and fishwives wandered past, fat babies propped with unfussy pride upon their outslung hips. The aching emptiness as fine ladies displayed their frilly daughters. And the dull, undeniable resentment at young brides' blushing admissions that they would soon be lying in. She had missed it all. Had mourned it in silence, so there was no reason to assume her feelings had been aught but the growling pangs of jealousy. A fretfulness for the maternal happiness that had eluded her.

After all, she had not been unlike Sarah once upon a time. Indeed, she had been just as awed by her own inexplicable gifts. Gifts she could share. That she could boast about . . . just as Sarah had.

But time and Verrill's duplicity had taught her better. Had taught her to warn those in similar situations, but the cautionary words had sounded cheap and spiteful to her own ears.

Lifting the candle, Ella scanned the floor around the mattress, then bent to examine a splash of red among the ashes. Digging through the satiny soot, she came away with nothing but a scrap of cloth. The garment it had once been had burned beyond recognition. She closed her eyes, letting the feelings take her, but there was little to be gained, only a melancholy weariness.

Opening her eyes, Ella glanced about again, realizing for the first time that there were no clothes left intact. No trunks, no personal items. Nothing.

Why? Had the house been vandalized since its destruction, or had Grey never brought his personal belongings here?

Scowling, Ella wandered into the only remaining room, but still there was nothing. Only ashes, loss, the clinging stench of smoke that choked her lungs and her spirit, that whispered of guilt and shame and mistakes realized too late.

She should have come sooner, before others had picked the place as clean as old bones. But perhaps that wasn't the case at all. Perhaps there had been nothing at the outset. Perhaps Sarah had not brought the consecrated little bottle with her. Perhaps Grey had somehow realized its purpose and demanded that she leave it behind. That would explain its lack of effectiveness, of course, but perhaps it had arrived here in this little hovel. If so, however, where was it now? The fire would not have destroyed it, but neither would others have easily noticed it, for it had been imbued with unique powers made for Sarah alone. Powers that had failed her.

Guilt washed in on a raw wave, but guilt was as worthless as weakness and just as unacceptable. Indeed, she thought, but just then a feeling whispered through the soles of her feet.

Ella straightened, heart thumping. Was someone near? Had he seen her light?

Hooves scraped erratically against the dirt floor near the door. Someone hissed an inaudible warning, then: "Catch 'er 'ead, you daft blighter."

Silk had been found!

Setting the candleholder on the floor, Ella turned, creeping through the darkened hall, mind churning. She reached the corner, flattened herself against the charred wall, and glanced past.

Three men had entered the house. One carried a lantern. One held Silk's reins. The smallest of the three gripped a knife in his grubby right hand. Its rusty blade shone dully in the flickering light, but he was not the only one who was armed. A bone handle protruded from the waistband of the bearded fellow who carried the lantern; a thick cudgel dangled from the wrist of the other.

Dammit! The odds were against her. Even if she could convince them she was a constable, she doubted she could hold the image. Maybe for one, but not all three, and certainly not if she were close to the light. The illusion would be too much of a stretch from her natural self.

Easing back, she considered her options and inadvertently scraped her foot against a half-burned timber. It bumped against the wall, loud as a cannon shot.

"I 'eard something," a voice hissed.

She swore in silence, heart beating heavy.

There was a hushed listening, then, "Find 'im."

Perhaps she could steal away, could sneak from one of the broken windows, she thought, but the truth was obvious; she would not leave Silk. Thus she closed her eyes, thinking, concentrating hard, cloaking herself in an image she had seen only days before in Merry May's garden. An image with a tattered brown coat, a bent hat, a swaggering Cockney accent. An image of Leonard Shay.

The change came gradually. She felt herself shift, her self-awareness swell with masculine virility, her sense of danger diminish. Why the hell was she hiding in this hovel like a cornered rat? There were only three of them. Haughty and belligerent, she swaggered into the flickering lantern light.

"And what the 'ell might you be doin' then?" she asked.

The trio started in unison, jerking toward her, faces grim with dirt and suspicion.

"Who are you?"

She strode forward, careful to keep Shay's aggressive nature at bay. She must not get too close. The shadows were deep and friendly, but her voice was forever more certain than her shape. Though that was good too, strong tonight. Leonard Shay was a force to be reckoned with. Her black riding jacket would resemble his tattered, dark coat. Her bonnet would appear as a battered hat. She had tipped her hat low, hiding her face, though that too would appear different, thin-lipped and deadly.

For one tilting moment, she considered introducing herself as Shay, but the risks were great. "They calls me York," she said, and sauntered a couple of steps closer. "'Ow 'bout you?"

The shortest of the three tilted up his chin as if testing the breeze, eyes narrowed like a ferret's. "Them what survive the meeting calls me Roth." He fingered his blade affectionately. "And the leader of this 'ere band of murderous free traders."

She nodded. "And what might you be doin' with me mare, Rot?"

127

"That's *Roth*!" spouted the bearded fellow, but their commander held up a hand and swaggered forward, cocky as a bantam.

"You a girl then?" he asked.

She nearly jerked at his words. Could he see through her disguise, past her barriers? But no. She calmed herself, found Shay's rapidly crafted psyche. The stunted brigand meant the words as an insult, nothing more. "You've a nerve, laddie," she crooned.

"Yeah? And you've a fookin' lady's saddle on yonder mount." He jerked his head toward Silk. "Ridin' askew 'cuz you ain't got no balls, aye, *laddie*?"

She smiled, knowing exactly how the expression would look in the slanting moonlight. "Or because me stones be so big there ain't no room against the leather."

Roth snorted, and Ella shrugged.

"Then again, could be the mare ain't been mine for so very long."

"Yeah?" The self-proclaimed leader's mouth twitched into the semblance of a flickering grin. "Body still warm, is it?" he asked, and fidgeted restlessly. The two behind him grinned. Evil shone in their expressions. But Ella kept her thoughts steady. For tonight she was one of them, a member of the countless leagues of cutthroats and rogues. Class made her hungry. Hunger made her dangerous. "Cold," she said. "Icy cold. And sinkin' fast. Just like you blokes is gonna do if y' don't leave 'old of the mare."

Roth grinned, eyes narrowed. "I see you got you some balls after all."

"Big as summer melons," she said.

"That's unfortunate for you, 'cuz this 'ere's our turf," he countered, and turned the knife slowly in his hand. It gleamed nastily in the erratic light of the lantern. "And we don't care much for interlopers, do we, lads?"

"Not much," said Beard. His eyes were wide, popping, bright with excitement. He licked his lips, nervous, anticipating. She'd found their weak link.

"You must be 'ard up," Ella said, nodding toward her surroundings. "Looks like you took everything but the ashes." She glanced casually about, as if there was no reason to keep her attention glued to him. As if she feared nothing from her own kind.

"Weren't nothin' 'ere at the outset," Beard said.

The tallest of the three still held Silk's bridle. He was missing a pair of teeth. One upper right, one lower left, making his face appear oddly lopsided in the uncertain light.

"Shut yer trap," said the leader, then to her: "What might you be wantin' 'ere?"

She shrugged. "Answers."

Roth tilted his head, mind racing behind his narrow eyes. He was small, smart, and dangerous as the devil. "You a Redbreast, then?"

She laughed, but not too hard. She would not overplay her hand, for he was close enough to the truth. She was not one of the mounted patrol who watched the city, of course, but she worked for the government just the same. Or at least, she had. "Do I look like a damned horse's arse to you, Rot?"

"A bit."

She grinned. "The lady I just met . . ." She nodded toward Silk. "She was more polite than you. But she died bloody just the same."

"You stick 'er?" Beard asked. A dollop of spittle oozed from his lips.

Ella's stomach coiled. She snarled a smile, canted her head. Attitude. It was all that stood between her and death. "What'd you know 'bout the gent what lived 'ere?" she asked.

"Which one?" Beard asked.

Ella's mind snagged on his words. There was more than one?

"Didn't I tell you to shut your hole?" Roth snapped.

Silk champed her snaffle and shuffled iron-shod hooves.

Ella kept her tone even. "Word is 'e died in the fire. You set the blaze?" she asked.

Roth chuckled. "Could be. Why you want to know?"

"Maybe I want to know 'oo to thank."

"And maybe you 'ope to stick me like ye did 'er mistress." Roth nodded toward Silk.

"Maybe," she agreed. "You know the bloke named Grey?"

"Never 'eard of 'im."

"'Ow 'bout you?" she asked Beard.

"Never 'eard of 'im," he echoed, but where Roth's tone had been challenging, his was matter-of-fact.

"Who 'ave you 'eard of?" she asked.

"I 'eard of Roth," Roth said, and shifted closer. "'Eard 'e's gettin' tired of conversing."

She shifted her gaze from Beard and speared the other with a glare.

"'Ow about livin'? You tired of that too, Rot?"

He stopped.

Roth," corrected Beard.

She smiled. "What do you know 'bout the bunter what lived 'ere?"

"The girl? I know she 'ad 'er some titties," Roth

131

said. Beard chuckled. Toothless said nothing.

Despite her altered image, anger splashed through Ella. Maybe it was her own. Maybe it was Leonard's. Sometimes it was impossible to differentiate. "You've never seen a pair before, I 'spect," Ella said.

"I seen me my share."

"Yeah?" Shay was becoming restive. "'Ow much you 'ave to pay?"

Roth shifted his blade to his opposite hand, shuffled his feet. "Least I don't swive no corpses."

Ella felt her blood heat, felt murderous intent well up inside her, but she took a firm hold of her psyche. "What the devil are you talking about?"

He chuckled. "Truth is, I'm getting fair tired of talking."

"Me too," Beard said.

"I 'eard she died in the fire," Ella said.

"She never come out of the 'ouse," Beard said. "Never come to the window. Only the gents. The pretty one and the—"

"Shut up," warned Roth. "Listen, York." He licked his lips, smiled a little. "I'm just 'ere 'cuz a fine 'orse is worth a good bit, but if you get dead in the process, I ain't likely to shed no tears."

Shay shifted inside her, swaggering a little. "I don't die so easy as you might think, friend."

"We'll see."

"I'll tell you what," she said, shoving Shay back a careful inch. "You give me back the bottle and I'll let you go on your merry, free and clear."

"What bottle?" Beard asked.

"I give the orders 'ere," Roth said, bristling.

"A cut-glass container," she said, ignoring the leader, speaking to Beard. "Brownish in color. Could be most full of cologne."

"I didn't see no bottle," Beard said, and turned narrowed eyes to Roth. "You 'oldin' back on me?"

"Shut up."

"It's worth a fair bit," Ella said, addressing the bearded member. "Ain't 'ardly fair . . . Roth getting the entire take."

"You already sell it?" Beard asked.

"He's playin' with you," snarled the leader.

"I want my share," Beard growled.

"Shut up."

It happened so fast. Faster than Ella was prepared for. But suddenly Beard slammed into Roth. They went down in a flutter of arms and legs. She watched for one stunned second, then, seeing Toothless's attention was diverted, she launched herself in his direction. He turned toward her a

133

moment before her shoulder hooked into his rib cage. But too late. He staggered backward even as she sprang for Silk's saddle.

The mare leaped toward the doorway. Ella teetered into the saddle, but the entrance was narrow, slowing their progress. Ella's leg scraped against the jamb. She gritted her teeth against the pain as they crashed down the stairs. Silk pivoted to the right, skidding in the mud, ready to flee, but suddenly Toothless was there, latching onto Ella's leg. She tried to kick him aside, but he held tight, and suddenly she was falling, tumbling toward the ground. Air exploded from her lungs. She jerked to her knees, gasping, but it was already too late. Three grim faces surrounded her in the darkness.

"Well now." Roth was breathing hard, fingering his blade. "I don't much like it when outsiders cause trouble betwixt me and mine."

Air rasped rustily down Ella's throat. She gasped, trying to breathe, to think, to hold fast to Shay's faltering image. At least the lantern and the candle had been left inside. It was as dark as hell on the street. Dark as hell with no help in sight and her chest burning like fire.

"Pick 'im up," Roth ordered.

Beard leaned in. He smelled rancid and unkempt. Taking a handful of coat, he hauled Ella to her feet. She struggled against him. Fear and disorientation made it difficult to hold the image. She felt it fading. Felt her own frailties return on a wave of weakness, but she murmured a fortifying incantation, holding on tight. The words whispered eerily in the night.

"What'd 'e say, Roth?" Beard asked.

"'E said you're a bleedin' idiot. Now get behind 'im and 'old 'im steady."

He did as told.

Ella felt an arm encircle her neck. She struggled for breath, for calm.

"Now . . ." Roth stepped close, fingering his blade. "Yer gonna tell me why you're 'ere, or you're gonna die wishin' y' 'ad."

Terror. Rage. Confusion. They brewed like toxins in her soul, stirring up Shay's restless image. She felt it swell in her once again, felt his raw energy consume her.

"Damn you to hell," she snarled, and Roth smiled as he put the knife to her throat.

Chapter 10

"Let her go," Drake ordered, and watched as the dark trio jerked toward him. He'd arrived only moments before and wished like hell he'd not left his mount down the street, but he'd only meant to see his sister's last residence once again. He hadn't planned to find trouble. But the light in the shattered windows had pulled him down the street like a wayward lamb.

He'd rounded the corner just as the woman's steed had skittered past, and now he stood, unarmed and unprepared, facing a ragged band of miscreants who looked in no mood to bargain.

"'Oo are you?" asked the man called Roth.

"Naught but a concerned citizen," Drake said. "But I suggest you do as I say."

"Oh?" The villain drew the knife from the girl's throat, but the other, the bearded fellow with the wide, popping eyes, remained as he was, holding her arms. "And why's that?"

Excellent question. "Because sometimes concerned citizens shoot street vermin through the heart. Me, on the other hand . . ." He raised his arm, hoping like hell the other couldn't see that he held nothing but a stick in his hand. "I like to aim for the eyeball. The left eyeball. I have excellent vision. Yours is clear as the dawn."

There was a moment of silence, then: "Yer lying."

Drake smiled a little, wishing like hell he'd brought a blunderbuss. Or a damned cannon. "The last fellow who thought so lived almost a full day." His voice was steady. So all those years dealing with drunken captains and dull-headed commodores hadn't been a complete waste. "Of course he would have been blind anyway, what with the missing eye."

"Damn you!" Roth snarled, but his tone was less than certain.

"Tell your hairy friend to let her go and I may let you keep yours."

"*Her*?" Roth asked.

But Drake refused to be distracted, either by his

own billowing fear or the other's obvious confusion. Apparently commodores weren't the only sorry bastards who were crazy. "Let her go," he repeated.

Roth delayed a moment, then stepped closer. "I'm thinking your eyesight ain't maybe so good as you think it is."

Dammit. "You willing to bet your eyes on that?" he asked.

Roth stopped for a second, then: "Yeah," he said, and in that instant, he launched forward. Drake jumped back. The blade cleared his cheek by inches. From the darkness, someone yelped, but it was all he could do to fight his own battle now, to stay alive. The knife swept at him again. He leaped back a second time, but his leg was already weakening.

Dammit all, he should have stayed astride. The knife again, but this time Drake lunged toward his adversary instead of away. They went down hard. Pain rattled through his thigh like a death-blow. He sucked in air, trying to remain lucid. But in that instant, Roth slammed something against Drake's ear. The world spun crazily, but he managed to roll sideways. It took him a moment to realize Roth was scrambling away, which meant only one thing; the bloody bastard had lost his knife, and if he found it . . .

And in that second he did.

Roth lurched to his feet and turned with a snarl.

Drake skittered backward on hands and feet. But too late. The other was already attacking, swinging wildly. The knife swept downward, cutting through the fabric of his breeches.

Drake roared in pain and kicked desperately. His foot connected with bone and Roth flew backward, allowing the other to lurch to his feet, ready to battle, to die.

But somebody's shout bit into the madness. "Get on!"

Drake spun about. A horse was bearing down on him, thundering toward him through the darkness. He didn't think, didn't wait. Reaching up, he grabbed hold of anything he could catch and swung aboard. For a moment he lost his footing. Looking down, he scrambled for purchase. The earth raced beneath him. Dizziness flooded in. But he tightened his grip, half on, half off, gritting his teeth as they raced into the night. There were curses and shrieks from behind, but in moments they faded in the fleeing darkness.

The woman spoke something incoherent, tone soothing, and the horse slowed. Drake dropped to his feet, fought for his footing, found his balance. His leg was screaming in pain.

"Are you hurt?" she asked.

Stupid damned question. Hell yes, he was hurt. His bloody leg felt like it had been ripped out of his hip. "I'm fine."

"No you're not." She was beside him suddenly, though for the life of him, he hadn't seen her dismount.

Her fingertips touched his ear. "Do you have a mount nearby?"

He gritted his teeth, fought for lucidness. "Not far back. Around the corner and—" He stopped suddenly, memory jostling as her features became clear in the uncertain light. "Lady Lanshire?"

He felt her surprise. Felt her draw back. Perhaps she hadn't recognized him in the melee either.

"Sir Drake?"

"What the devil are you doing here?"

"I . . ." She paused, seeming momentarily shaken, but not nearly shaken enough. What the hell was she doing in East End in the dark of the night? What the hell was she thinking? "You're bleeding."

He touched his skull, winced. "Sometimes that happens when people hit you in the head with a damned rock. Why are you—"

"I think it was a brick."

"What?" He stared at her, trying to sort things out, but it was no easy task. His head was spinning and his leg throbbed like the devil's heartbeat.

"I have excellent eyesight too."

He snorted. But a noise from behind jerked their attention to the rear.

"We'd best recover your mount," she said. "Before someone else does."

"Are you uninjured?"

"Yes. I . . ." Her voice shook a little. "Thank you."

"For what?"

She looked momentarily perplexed. "For so gallantly coming to my rescue."

He tried to reason out the problem with that statement. But another noise issued from behind. Their admirers seemed to be following. "I'll give you a leg up," he said, and cupped his hands.

Her foot was bare against his palm. What the devil was going on? he wondered. But she was already aboard, as quick and light as a fairy. He wondered rather dismally if he could do as well. It took him only a moment to realize he couldn't, but finally he struggled aboard and settled in behind her, head spinning dizzily. He swayed against the motion.

"Are *you* well?" She turned toward him in the darkness. The scent of lavender filled his head.

"Yes. Fine."

"You'd best hold on to me."

He considered arguing, defending his manhood, but he liked to think he wasn't entirely daft; he wrapped his arms about her waist. It was small and tight beneath the velvet jacket.

Leaning forward slightly, Elegance pressed the mare into a rocking canter. The movement pushed him closer to her back, doing nothing to disturb her balance. But in a matter of minutes they had reached his mount. The tall sorrel stood tied to a nearby elm and nickered low when he sensed their approach.

Drake glanced at the beast. The gentlemanly thing to do would be to dismount and ride his own animal, of course. On the other hand, passing out was rarely considered genteel.

Bending down, he untied his reins and straightened.

Ella glanced quizzically over her shoulder at him.

"Wounded," he reminded her. "In your defense."

"Ahh. Where do you live?"

"Clerkenwell. Warstock Street," he said, for he

could not quite think of Hawkspur as his home. He had inherited the estate upon his father's death a year and a half earlier, but had never stepped inside the house since that day.

Kendrick Donovan had made his fortune some years after sending his only son to sea, and had subsequently moved to London shortly after. Drake had never again seen his mother. Indeed, she had died in childbirth months before he knew she was expecting. The short, wilted missive he had received from his father had said little but that a daughter had been born . . . and a mother had been lost.

Ella pressed her mare into a high-stepping walk. The night was quiet but for the rhythmic clip of their horses' hooves. The mist was heavy around them, closing them in, feeling like a silver blanket against his back, as if there was not another soul in the universe.

But that was hardly the case. There were others. Others who lived. Who died. Others who tried to brain concerned citizens with rocks.

"So, lass . . ." He paused, touched his fingers to his aching skull. Maybe the bastard *had* been wielding a brick. Maybe she *did* have excellent eyesight. "Are you going to tell me?"

She glanced back again. Her profile was muted

by the darkness, but there was still something about her that moved him, emotionally . . . and otherwise. Amazing. "Tell you what?"

"Why you were there, in one of the most notorious parts of London in the dark of night."

She trembled gently beneath his hands. "In truth, I'd rather not, sir."

What the hell had she been doing near Grey's house, yards from where Sarah had died? How was she connected to his sister's death?

"I think, perhaps, I deserve a bit of explanation," he said, "since I was wounded in your defense."

"Let us remember that I did not ask you to come by." She paused, letting him think about that. "By the by, what was *your* purpose in being there?"

For a moment he was almost tempted to share the truth, but he had learned the value of fabrications long ago. A small boy alone on a ship of lecherous drunkards found it prudent to lie well and lie often. Better by far to keep her guessing, for there was much he had yet to learn.

"I had business in Ratcliff. I was on my way home when I heard a scuffle."

"Business?" Her tone sounded doubtful.

"Yes."

"In Ratcliff."

"Yes." Always stick with a story, but don't elaborate unless absolutely necessary. Any fabrication could be believed so long as you didn't vary. "And what of you?"

She faced forward, straightening her back a little. "I believe I told you my intentions at the outset, Sir Drake."

He puzzled over that for a moment, then chuckled disbelievingly. "Surely you don't mean to say you had planned a tryst."

She said nothing.

"In Shoreditch?"

He could see the quirk of her lively mouth. "It is a terrible truth, but millers' sons cannot always afford the best of accommodations." She said the words with utter conviction. And suddenly the situation no longer seemed terribly humorous.

"You jest," he said.

"There's no need to make it sound like high treason," she said. Her tone was fraught with laughter. What kind of woman narrowly escaped death or worse and laughed when she spoke of it? Perhaps she *was* lying about her reason for being there, but then what kind of lady would say she had slept with a workingman when she had not?

"I thought you had settled on Lord Milton," he said.

She tilted her head the slightest degree, gave a tiny shrug. "Perhaps I've decided not to settle at all."

He was silent for a moment, then another. Their mounts' hoofbeats clattered on in tandem. It was not easy finding one's way through the mist-shrouded streets, but she seemed to have no trouble.

With some difficulty, he recognized the ale-house that sat at the corner of Warstock and Hutton. She turned her steed toward his rented home with no visible cues. They were only minutes from his house, but in truth, he had no desire to go there despite the pain in sundry parts of his anatomy.

"Aren't you going to see to my wounds, my lady?" he asked.

She glanced at him, brows raised slightly in her mercurial face. "I hardly think that would be proper."

"Proper?" he said, remembering her bare feet, her admitted liaison.

She gave him an arch look.

"I am sore wounded," he said. "Surely that gains me something." His argument was extremely ungentlemanly. The *ton* would call it gauche, he knew, though he understood little of society's upper crust. Still, he found that he failed to care, especially when, after a moment, she turned her mare about and headed back in the direction they had come.

In a matter of minutes, they had arrived at their destination. Dismounting wiped away any lingering feelings of self-satisfaction. Pain struck him like a gong. He swayed against it, head reeling.

"Theatrics, Sir Drake?" she asked, and tied her mare to a hitch near her cobbled walkway.

"'Tis surely a worthy try," he said, and steadying his stance, secured his gelding beside the mare.

She was watching him when he straightened, and he wished, for a moment, that he were a better actor, able to pretend all was well. That he was young and hale and able.

"Come," she said, tone somber.

They walked to her darkened house together. It was no easy task to control his limp, but he almost managed. Still, he doubted she was fooled.

No servants met them at the door. The place was silent and dim but for a fire that flickered from a distant room, casting the vestibule in mottled shadows.

She led him through the echoing foyer to a salon that boasted the fire, and pointed to a brocade chair that stood beside a little table. A small, fat book of poems sat primly upon the oiled oak. "Sit," she ordered, and he did, trying not to wince and failing rather miserably.

She raised a brow and he forced a grin, not adverse to making her believe he still tried to solicit her pity. Indeed, seeing her remove her bonnet and let her chestnut curls trail down her back made him more than willing to play the rogue. Her feet were bare and narrow beneath the hem of her strange black skirt, and the sight of them conjured up unwanted imaginings of more bare skin.

"Perhaps I should spend the night," he said.

She stared at him a breathless moment, then laughed quietly and left the room, but she returned in a minute, carrying a basin and a cloth draped over one slim arm. The firelight gilded her magical features, setting her face aglow and her hair ablaze. It cascaded down her back like molten copper, alive in waves of variegated golds and reds.

Soaking the rag, she wrung it out and stepped up close. Touching it to his ear, she washed it gently, then rinsed the cloth again before carefully probing the wound beside his temple. "The cut is not terribly deep, but it might well become inflamed. You should see a physician."

She was close enough for him to smell her scent. It was strangely calming. Earthy. Friendly. Soothing his aches, easing his memories. But he would be a fool to assume she was a friend. What the hell had she been doing outside Grey's house?

"I've had some contact with doctors," he said, his voice casual. Perhaps he was a better thespian than he knew. "As it turns out, I do not care for them so very much."

"You shouldn't let this go untreated."

"I am told I have a marvelous ability to heal."

"How nice for you." She was scowling at his head. "This may require stitches."

He ignored her statement. "What was his name?" he asked.

"*His?*"

"The lucky lad on Gallows Road?"

"Oh." She smiled a little, a woman of mystery. "A lady of quality doesn't tell."

"I think you may be confused, lass."

"Oh?" She washed again.

"A lady of quality doesn't sleep with millers' sons in a section of town where the majority of the population are cutthroats and thieves."

"Oh yes," she said, looking thoughtful. "That was it."

Her eyes shone like cut emeralds in the wavering firelight. Her lips twitched entrancingly, but he would not be distracted. "So, who was the fortunate fellow?"

"No one with which to concern yourself," she said, but then her gaze fell and her eyes widened as she saw past where his fingers tried to hide his severed breeches. "You were stabbed!"

Damnation! He didn't bother to glance down. "Beautiful and astute," he said.

"Why didn't you tell me?"

"I was trying to be manly."

"Then you were doing a terrible job of it."

He managed a smile. "I've endured worse wounds."

His trousers had been ripped open. Blood soaked the fabric. Perhaps he should have gone straight home, but the chance to be here with her, before the fire, with her fingers soft against his skin, was all but irresistible.

She looked a bit shaken, he noticed, but somehow her worry didn't quite jive with the scene he had witnessed outside Grey's. Aye, perhaps she had been afraid, but she had also been frightfully brave. Of course, one did not preclude the other. He had learned that from Monkey, a pale-faced cabin boy with shaky hands and eyes so wide they swallowed one's soul. A boy too young to leave his mother's side, much less to die on a leaky vessel half a lifetime from home. A boy who should have been climbing trees and teasing apple-cheeked girls, instead of delivering gunpowder to a faulty cannon that would take his life. Damn Fowler for the battle-lusty bastard he was. And damn himself for allowing the bright-eyed Monkey to be drawn into such lunacy.

"You'll have to take them off," she said.

Drake focused on her, drawing himself from the darkling memories. "I beg your pardon."

"Your breeches," she said. "You shall have to remove them."

No. He wouldn't. He raised one brow. "So soon after the miller's son? I am flattered, lass."

"Take them off," she repeated evenly, and left the room.

He leaned his head back against the chair and wondered what the hell he'd stumbled on to. Who was she? Was there truly a miller's son? And why did he find her so ungodly appealing, he wondered, but in a minute she had reappeared with a tray of bottles and bags. She paused in the doorway, eyeing his still-clothed legs. "For a military man, you don't take orders very well."

"Perhaps that is why I never made captain." Or perhaps it was because he had threatened to decapitate Fowler with a boarding axe. Had the crew not intervened, the world would be a better place, but Monkey would still be dead.

"You don't want it to become infected."

"It already has," he said, and put the ragged memories behind him.

She watched him with inquisitive, spring-bright eyes. "What if I promise to sleep with you if you cooperate?"

Despite himself, he felt his interest stir. "Would you?"

Their gazes held. Heat flared between them.

"No," she said.

He couldn't help the smile that tugged at his lips. She was an enigma. But he didn't want an enigma. He had made a vow to himself to find peace and comfort. Somewhere quiet and calm where he would learn to forget. But that was before he'd learned less than three weeks earlier of Sarah's death. "You're making me quite confused," he confessed.

"Good." She gave him a glance from the corner of her eye as she fiddled with the cork on a round, cut-glass bottle. "Take off your breeches."

"No."

She faced him, arms akimbo. "I'll give you the name of the gentleman I was visiting."

"I thought he was a miller's son."

"Perhaps I should have said *gentle man*." She said the words with slow appreciation, fostering thoughts of another's hands against her skin, but he shoved the images aside. Surely he had more important things to consider. His sister was dead, after all. Shouldn't he find out why? Shouldn't he do something worthwhile after his wasted years at sea?

Reaching down, he unbuttoned his breeches. She turned away as he slid them down his legs. The left one was hale, muscular enough. But the right was a twisted branch of agony, an ugly, blighted limb, puckered with scar tissue and torture.

"Good Lord!" she breathed.

He clenched his jaw, then forced himself to relax, to look up, to lean back, as if he were not embarrassed, as if his very life had not been torn from him on that hideous day eight months ago.

"How did you live through that?" she murmured.

He realized he was gripping the chair's arms

and eased up a bit, breathing evenly. "I am extremely strong."

He'd meant it as a jest to lighten the mood, but she barely seemed to notice he had spoken. "The bone was shattered," she whispered.

His throat felt dry. "Yes."

Her eyes looked too large for her winter-white face. "And protruding."

The memories made his stomach lurch. "Yes."

"But they didn't amputate."

They had threatened, had held him down, had touched the knife to his skin. Memories of pain, of terror and nausea and rage exploded in his head. "I may have issued some fairly inventive threats." His tone was marvelously light. "Nevertheless, I believe they would still have amputated had they thought it worth their trouble."

She was scowling. The expression was strangely beautiful.

"I don't believe they expected me to live through the night," he said.

"I'm sorry." Her voice was solemn, quiet, earnest, but he would not let her softness touch the open wound of his mind.

"That they didn't amputate?" he quipped, but she didn't respond. In fact, for one fleeting moment, her eyes seemed to shine with tears. But she turned quickly away.

"I'll just . . . I'll clean the wound. The *fresh* wound," she said.

He watched her, mesmerized, wanting quite desperately to reach out, to touch her tears, to be whole. But perhaps it was too late for that. "I can care for it myself," he said.

"Perhaps," she agreed, and seemed to rally, to become more herself, the spirited, cheeky maid who might very well have stood off the brigands in Miss Anglican's garden. "But I shall do it all the same."

Had he imagined the tears in her eyes? Could he bear to see her cry? He daren't chance it. Better far to make light of it. "Because you lust for me?"

She looked at him again, and he saw the effort she made to return to normal. "Of course."

He smiled. "Now you are pitying me."

"True," she said.

"I don't like to be pitied . . ." He paused. "Unless it will get me into your bed."

The flicker of a smile lifted her heavenly lips.

"Will it?" he asked.

The smile bloomed a little more. "No."

He barely noticed when she touched the rag to his knee.

"So all you offer is the name of the miller's son, then."

She seemed absorbed in her task. "He isn't actually anyone's son."

Against all odds, her touch felt wondrously soothing against his skin. Not like the hands of that bastard barber who had longed to cut him limb from limb. "Isn't that rather unusual?" he asked.

She gave him a scowl, but it only made her more appealing.

"He must be *someone's* son," he explained.

"I meant . . . it is not as if I am robbing the cradle," she said.

"Ahh, an old man, is he?"

"Does it have to be one or the other?"

"No." He watched her steadily, examining every rare feature, every fleeting expression. "It could be me."

"I'll keep that in mind." Her eyes flickered to him and away. "This should be stitched also."

"It will be fine."

She pursed her lips. "It would seem a shame if you died of this." She washed the edges of the wound and glanced toward the puckered scar, tensing a little. "After surviving that."

There was pity on her face. Perhaps, if he

were a proud man, her sympathy would bother him as he had suggested that it did, but in truth, he was touched by her emotion, honored by her worry.

"How are you at stitchery?" he asked.

"My pillows are quite spectacular. The talk of Bloomsbury."

Aye, she was sensitive, but she was also strong. "Think of me as a cushion," he said.

"Dr. Howard is quite good," she said.

He settled his head against the chair's back. "I guarantee I shall never know."

"I would not have taken you for a coward."

Best then that she didn't know the truth; that he had been terrified in every battle, had been sickened at the sight of blood, the screams of the dying. War was no glorious adventure of men. It was horror and sin and waste. Yet perhaps the greatest sin of all was not his own stifling terror, but the fact that he had gained from it. Not only coin and title, but reputation. He could hear the whispers of mothers to their sons as he walked down London's genteel boulevards; *There goes the valiant lieutenant, Jimmy. He fought at the battle of Grand Port. We but pray you will be half so brave.* The words echoed in his ears until he longed to scream at him, to tell them of the dysentery, the debauchery, the dissipation. But he would not, for he *was* a coward. "I wasn't aware that you were considering taking me at all."

She gave him a disapproving glance that made him want rather desperately to kiss her. "Your mind seems to be having some difficulty changing gears, Sir Drake."

Her nose had the tiniest tilt to it. "Not all of us are so lucky as to have just left a lover's bed." Indeed, some of them had given up hope of ever having a lover again. But he felt hope spring to life now. Hope and other things.

"And quite the lover he was," she said.

Her skin was fair and unblemished, looking velvet soft against the fire of her hair. "Are you trying to make me jealous?"

"I'm trying to convince you to give up your nonsensical attempts to seduce me."

"If that was your wish, lass, you shouldn't have brought me here and insisted that I drop my breeches."

"I'll keep that in mind in the future," she said, and turned away, but he caught her arm, breath held at the feel of skin against skin.

"We have a future?" he asked.

Their gazes met. She had ceased to breathe.

Her hair glowed like living flames in the flickering light, and her eyes, bright as fresh-cut jewels, consumed him.

There seemed nothing he could do but pull her down for a kiss.

Chapter 11

His lips were warm and firm, his hand strong and steady as he slipped his fingers into her hair, pulling her down, tugging her closer. And God help her, she responded, reveling in his touch, drowning in his earthy allure. Beneath her palm, his thigh was taut with muscle, and beyond that . . .

Ella came to her senses with a start and pulled rapidly away.

"Sir Drake," she said. Her voice was marvelously steady, while her heart was beating far faster than it had on Gallows Road. "You are wounded."

A corner of his dark devil's mouth twitched. The fingertips of one hand rested on the book of poems that graced the table beside him. *"The greatest bliss is in a kiss—a kiss of love refin'd. When springs the soul without control and blends the bliss with mind."*

She studied him. "Did you do nothing but memorize poetry while aboard ship?"

"I managed a few other things," he said. "But nothing so important as that."

She watched him, wondering. "You are a strange man, sir."

"Strange and wounded," he said. "But I think, perhaps, your love would be the best medicine I could hope for."

His lips were inches from hers, and though she knew far better, she let him kiss her again, if only for a moment.

"A bit early to speak of love, isn't it?" she breathed.

"I was using the term as the revered poets of yore used to—"

"You meant sex."

He paused a second, ran a hand down her arm. "If you insist."

"If I hadn't seen the scar myself I would not have believed you'd been wounded so near . . . where you were," she finished lamely.

His lips quirked the slightest degree. "I am quite an amazing man."

Perhaps he was. Or perhaps he was a liar, a

rogue, a seducer of women. Jasper Reeves had reason to believe Grey was still alive, and she was beginning to think Grey had possessed some sort of power over Sarah. Just as this man had an inexplicable power over her good sense. "Tell me, Sir Drake," she murmured, "why were *you* on Gallows Street at such an unorthodox hour?"

"I believe I told you about my business to the east."

"You could have taken a safer route."

His lips were curved in the vague semblance of a smile, but his eyes smoldered steadily. "But then I couldn't have saved you."

Reaching out, she touched his lips, though she could not have said why. They were smooth and warm, his chin slightly stubbled when she ran her thumb down it. His throat was corded with muscle and sinew, pulsing with life and power. "How did you know I was there?"

"Call it a premonition."

His words tingled through her. "Are you gifted?"

He closed his eyes against her touch, and beneath her fingers it almost felt as if he trembled. "You feel like a gift in my arms," he said, and tugged her gently onto his lap.

She smoothed her hand down his chest, then flicked open his shirt button, because she could, because he certainly wouldn't object. His throat constricted. Beneath her buttocks, his thighs bunched with anticipation. She opened another button. His skin was darkened from years in the sun, his chest as hard and smooth as stone, his entire being mesmerizing.

"*Are* you gifted?" she asked.

He watched her a moment, dark eyes shining. "No, lass," he said. "Just randy."

She stifled a smile and wondered vaguely if he was lying, for she felt something in him, something magical. "You'll never survive the *ton* with that kind of honesty," she said.

"My apologies." He watched her, breath slightly labored, expression intense.

"How badly does your leg hurt?"

"Not at all."

She eased open another button. "You're a terrible liar."

"My apologies again." He watched her with the intensity of a hunting wolf. "I don't mean to rush you, lass, but you've not yet told me the lucky fellow's name."

Beneath her hand, the taut muscles of his chest tightened and shifted as if by magic. A warm tingle shivered through her. She moved her hand the slightest degree. The muscles shifted again. Her lips seemed suddenly rather dry. Things would have been considerably easier if there truly *were* a miller's son.

"Lass," he said, and she came to with a start. "I fear I may be getting blood on your frock."

"Oh! I'm sorry. I . . ." She stood abruptly, but she was still positioned between his legs. "I made you bleed," she said, and turned away.

He caught her fingers in a careful grip. "Wasn't there something you were going to do?" He had covered his wounded limb with the towel. When had he done that? She hadn't even noticed. Perhaps because of his chest. It was all but bare. She had pushed his shirt aside. It was open to his waistband, bare of hair but for a dark, silky band that began below his navel and slipped away to unknown depths. One nipple was exposed, small and erect above the muscled mound of his chest. A scar was sliced diagonally beneath it, and she found that against all kinds of practical logic, she wished to touch it, to run her fingers along its ragged course, to let her fingers stray down the rippling expanse of his abdomen and beyond.

"Lass?"

"I cannot sleep with you," she breathed, snapping her gaze back to his face.

He scowled, but the expression did nothing to make him less desirable. Indeed, if the truth be told, she had never been attracted to the weedy men considered pleasing among the elegant *ton*. She was, and always had been, attracted to power. To the kind of man who would use her and discard her. Who would declare his love in ringing tones, only to take her valuables and leave her bereft and naked, body and soul.

"I meant, I believe you were about to tell me your lover's name," he said.

"Oh. Yes." She caught his gaze with her own, shook off her morose thoughts, and concentrated on the present. Who was this man? Why was he here? "Of course. His name is . . ." But suddenly her mind locked. She had been trained to lie. To fabricate, to build on nothing. She glanced out the window. Tattered moonlight shone on the nodding bloom of a faded rose. "Gardener."

His brows rose. "Gardener."

Holy saints. What was wrong with her? "Yes."

"Might that be his name or his occupation?"

She moved away, stepping from between his legs, putting space between them.

"I believe I told you he was a miller."

"A miller's *son*," he corrected, watching her, drinking her in. It was difficult to breathe. More difficult still to move away. But she managed to put a few feet between them. Though it felt wrong when he was there, within reach, his chest bare, his eyes hypnotic.

"I thought, perhaps, he had defied tradition and put his hand to another profession," he said.

The muscles of his belly were bunched in rows. Her belly looked nothing like that.

"Lass?" he said.

Good Lord. "I didn't think to ask," she said, and turned away, cursing herself. It wasn't as if she'd never seen a naked man before. But he was a different kind of man. Not posh or elegant, but rough-hewn and chiseled. As if he'd been sculpted by the wind, an element of nature. Taking a steadying breath, she selected a needle from her tray.

He was still watching her. She could feel his attention though she didn't turn toward him. "You simply call him Gardener?" he asked.

"In truth . . ." She found a length of sturdy thread but had a bit of trouble managing it with unsteady fingers. "We didn't do a great deal of talking."

Quiet darkened into silence.

"May I inquire about his surname?"

She closed her eyes for a moment and altered her features just a bit. In truth, she had no desire to appear repulsive to him, but she had little choice. Things were moving at a frantic pace, and she had vowed long ago not to lose control again. Not to repeat the mistakes of her past. She knew nothing of him, could not trust him, could not control the feelings that sizzled through her. Hence she looked inside herself and concentrated on homeliness, on dowdiness. In truth she would have to change very little. "I fear I have no way of knowing his surname," she said.

"And this Gardener, he lives on Gallows Road."

"I didn't say that."

"You said he was the reason for your presence there."

"True." She steeled herself and turned toward him.

He settled back in his chair, still watching her, but his expression changed not a whit. "Tell me, lass," he said, "are you trying to fascinate me?"

"No. I'm trying to repel you," she said, and was shocked by the honesty of her own words.

He scowled. "You're not very accomplished."

She couldn't help but laugh, for he was wrong; she was excellent at warding off men. At least she was where most men were concerned. But perhaps he did not fall into that category.

Her hands were not quite steady as she threaded the needle. "Perhaps if I blacken my teeth and neglect to bathe."

"I wouldn't bother," he said, voice low and velvety masculine.

She glanced into his eyes and he stared back, as if she were beautiful, as if she were mesmerizing. What was wrong with him? "This is going to be quite painful," she said, and clearing her throat, managed to pull her gaze away as she approached him.

"A good opportunity to prove my mettle then," he said.

He was arrogant and unperturbed. But he would not be so cocky once the needle bit his flesh. She almost winced at the thought. But the wound needed stitching, and she should be the one to do it, for causing him pain could only improve matters. She stepped between his legs. Her thighs brushed his, and even through the layers of her garments, his nearness made her shiver. Gritting her teeth, she gripped the needle harder, but her hand was still unsteady as she gazed down at his wound. Despite herself, she had no desire to hurt him.

"I've been meaning to ask, lass, have you no servants?"

The lips of the wounds were gaping, making her a bit queasy, which was strange, for she was accustomed to injuries, though they were generally her own. "Of course."

"And where might you keep them?"

"You make it sound as though I store them in the wardrobe with my buttonhooks."

"Do you?"

She shifted her gaze to his, wondering vaguely if he was trying to distract her, trying to make her task easier. "No," she said.

"Where are they, then?"

"Abed, I would suspect."

He considered that for a moment, sensuous lips slightly curved. "I would think a lady of your standing would desire some service."

Perhaps he intended the double entendre. Perhaps not. Either way, his words steeled her resolve. She squatted between his knees, holding her breath as she brushed against his skin. "What I desire is to be left alone."

"Ahh . . ." He sighed. "So you can become promiscuous in peace."

"Just so."

"Which hasn't yet transpired."

Dammit! What had happened to her ability to lie? "Except for Gardener, of course."

"Of course. Are you going to stitch that or not?" he asked.

She refused to look away, to blanch.

"It's going to hurt," she repeated.

"If I pass out will you revive me?"

"I fear I'm fresh out of smelling salts," she said, and poised the needle.

"I'm certain your nakedness would do quite well."

She slanted a glance up at him. "Tell me, Sir Drake, might there be something fundamentally wrong with you?"

"I've been wounded."

"In the head?" she asked, and he laughed.

The sound was pleasant and low. It rumbled through her system like a distant storm, threatening dire consequences if it came too near. And she was too near. Far too near. Steadying herself, she dipped the needle toward his leg.

"What if I scream?" he asked suddenly.

She jumped, then closed her eyes and focused on the task at hand, pressing the needle into his flesh. He didn't so much as flinch.

"If I scream will you soothe me?" he asked.

She didn't glance up. What kind of man didn't flinch? "With nakedness?" she asked.

"I knew from the moment we met that you were a bright lass."

She glanced at his face. Their gazes caught. His lips were still curved into the semblance of a smile. His eyes gleamed in the flickering light. "How are you faring? Truly?"

"If I say it hurts like hell will you take me to your bed?" he rumbled.

She stared at him. Her ministrations didn't seem to bother him in the least. Why? Had his time at sea made him immune to pain? Or did he have some kind of power she did not understand? Who was this man?

"If I say yes will you cease your yammering?" she asked.

"Will it be a lie?"

"Yes?"

"Yes, you'll take me to your bed, or yes, it will be a lie?"

"I believe there may be something terribly wrong with you," she said, and turned back to her task.

"I've been wounded. In your defense," he reminded her.

171

Her stitches were small, even, careful. His leg never moved. "Isn't it rather ungentlemanly for you to remind me?"

"I said I was randy, lass. Not gentlemanly."

"Can't you be both?"

He thought about that for an instant. "I have no reason to think so. Will you sleep with me if I'm impressively brave?"

He *was* impressively brave. It was uncanny. "No."

"Where did Gardener live exactly?"

Was he trying to keep her off balance? Teasing her with his base sensuality, changing the subject, then questioning her? "Why do you wish to know?"

"I'm hoping to learn his secrets."

"Secrets?" She dabbed away a drop of blood with the corner of the towel draped across his lap.

"How he lured you to his bed."

"You are absolutely incorrigible. How did you ever last at sea?"

"I did not spend much time half naked with a beautiful woman between my legs."

She glanced up, but he wasn't laughing. Wasn't mocking her. He still thought her beautiful. That was uncanny too. Unless he was lying. But for what purpose? And how had he known all along that she was a woman? Her spell had been strong. Roth and his nasty cutthroats had believed it from the first moment to the last. "Tell me of yourself," she said.

He remained still for a moment, wordlessly watching her face, as if he were memorizing it, as if he were entranced. "There is little to tell."

And that was strange too. What kind of man didn't wish to speak of himself? Not an innocent one. So who was he? And why had he come to her defense? "Where did you grow up?"

"On the *Serenity.*"

"Aboard ship? Surely you weren't born there."

"I would guess ye might be able to guess from me speech where I was birthed." He had intentionally made his homey burr heavier.

"Ireland," she said.

"County Galway, until the hardy age of nine."

"*Nine.*"

His gaze was dark and steady. "Da thought time at sea would be advantageous for me."

"Why?"

"To make me a man, mayhap."

He was probably telling the truth. Men were, at times, intolerably stupid, after all. "You weren't supposed to be a man," she said. "You were supposed to be nine."

"How unfortunate you weren't there to explain it to Da."

He gave nothing away with his tone, and she wondered what his true feelings were. It was impossible to tell, for she was jabbing him repeatedly with a needle, and thus far he had shown no reaction whatsoever.

"Brothers? Sisters?" she asked.

"I have none."

"You were an only child?"

He was watching her. She could feel it and glanced up at him.

"Why do you ask, lass? Do you wish for children yourself?"

She almost flinched at the question. Could he read her mind? Guess her thoughts? Did he know that the idea had dominated her desires for months on end?

"I'm finished," she said, and dabbed at the wound, ready to stand, but he caught her chin in his hand.

"Do you?" he murmured.

"No," she lied.

His expression was deadly serious. "Good. For you've no need to concern yourself on that account where I am involved."

She couldn't contain her scowl. "You're unable to sire children?"

He was silent for a moment. "So I am told."

174

"By the bastard—" She stopped herself, surprised by her unexpected passion. "By the surgeon who thought you would die before morning?"

He watched her in momentary silence, dark eyes stormy. "My thanks," he said.

"For what?"

"Hating him."

Their gazes met and fused, but she pulled hers away. "You may get dressed," she said, and turned away.

She could tell by the noises behind her that he did just that, but in a moment he spoke again.

"I would know but one thing, lass."

She glanced at him, saw that he was safely dressed.

"What did he do to earn such beauty as yours?"

Ella steadied herself and searched for a coy answer, but the truth came instead. "I am no beauty."

His eyes shone in the firelight. *"Had we but world enough, and time, this coyness, Lady, were no crime."*

She set her medicinal tools aside and looked at him straight on. "Andrew Marvell?"

"My own sentiments, while similar, rarely sound as lyrical." His eyes captured hers. She pulled hers away, feeling fidgety and foolish.

"Here, then," she said, and taking the small volume from the table, handed it to him. "I believe some of his work is in this volume."

He took the book. Their fingers brushed. Feelings washed through her, but she pulled away and cleared her throat.

"Tell me, lass, are all your evenings so entertaining?"

"Indeed not," she said, turning toward the door. "Gardener was my first."

He followed, but even without looking, she could tell that he limped. "I meant the excitement on Gallows Road," he said.

"Oh . . . that . . ." They had reached the foyer. She forced a shiver and turned toward him. "I do appreciate your intervention."

"Do you?" He was standing close enough so that she could smell the rich, male scent of him, almost familiar, almost irresistible.

"Of course."

He shifted a half inch closer. "Enough to—"

"No," she said, and though his lovely mouth quirked up a quarter of an inch, his eyes were deadly earnest.

Opening the door with an unsteady hand, she stepped through. She was an expert at managing people, had been trained to do just that, but she felt strangely unbalanced, as though he were an uncertainty she'd not encountered before. She didn't like uncertainties.

He followed her outside and down the cobbled walk to the hitch where their mounts were tied.

His gelding nickered softly. He put a hand on its neck as she untied her mare, but in that moment he turned toward her and touched her hand.

"Ella."

Feelings sparked off in a thousand errant directions. Their gazes caught and sizzled. Silence echoed in the night.

"You'll make a grand mum, lass," he said.

Did he know her desires? Her plans? she wondered, but she made light of it. "Might you be saying I am old, sir?" she asked.

He stared at her for an instant, then chuckled, low and quiet. Bowing, he mounted his steed with more grace than she would have thought possible, and rode away.

She watched him leave, enjoying the dark, tingling aftermath of his presence, but the fog swallowed him in a moment. And with it came an indefinable feeling, a prickling of the skin, an odd awareness that could neither be fully explained nor understood.

She was being watched.

Chapter 12

Feelings born of instinct and honed by ragged experiences told her to hide, warned her to run before they found her, held her down, probed her mind.

Her hands shook with the need to find a dark place, somewhere secret, somewhere safe, but she forced away the weakness. She would not closet herself away. Not again. No, she would fight. Would use every power in her unearthly arsenal. So she stood very still, letting her senses awaken, letting her mind expand and unfurl until she could pinpoint the location of the interloper, could taste his presence.

He was male. She knew that immediately though she couldn't have said how. He stood behind her and to the left. Some fifteen yards separated them.

And suddenly she wished desperately for a weapon. Something conventional, tangible, not just her own weak abilities, but she forced herself to turn, to remain motionless, to stand her ground. She would not cower again. "Are you going to reveal yourself, or will you hide there like a cur for the entirety of the night?" she asked.

There was a moment of silence before a dim form stepped from the silvery shadows a few strides away. Closer than she thought! Almost upon her. Still, she conjured all her strength, but in that instant, she recognized him.

Jasper. She felt her muscles sag with relief, but she knew far better than to show it. *Never tip your hand.*

"When did you know it was me?" he asked. His voice was steady in the darkness.

Why hadn't she sensed him earlier? Why hadn't she recognized his signature? What was it about Drake that jumbled her senses? She turned away, hiding the tremble in her hands. The mare's reins proved difficult, but she managed to untie them. "You smell of danger and deceit," she said.

"What do you know of him?" he asked, and stepped farther into view, a shadow among shadows.

She led the mare toward the narrow brick

stable. "It's rather unbecoming for you to spy on me. Don't you have minions to do that sort of thing, Jasper?"

"I came on your sister's behalf."

She turned abruptly, heart tripping. "What happened?"

"You don't need—"

"Where is she?" Her heart was hammering loud and hard. "What happened?"

"She's fine. Safe." He scowled, thinking, almost seeming to tense. "Why? Did you sense something?"

She concentrated, but there was nothing there, no pain, no fear, just a smattering of fatigue, of worry. Ella drew a breath, forcing herself to relax. "Why are you here, Jasper?"

"Did you sense something?" he repeated.

She glanced at him as she stepped into the barn. From the farther of the two roomy stalls, Dancer nickered. Silk ignored him. Always aloof. "Is something amiss?" Ella asked.

"No."

Was he lying? Was there fear in his eyes? Could Jasper Reeves feel fear? Could he feel any emotion known to humankind? She turned to face him, fingers stiff against the reins. "Is Maddy in danger?"

Their gazes met. "There is always danger."

Those words were his mantra, had been for as long as Ella could recall, but he had always delivered the caveat with a dispassionate nonchalance. Something was different now.

"She is a Chausette," he said, as if to explain his strangeness. "It is my job to keep her safe."

"Until it is no longer useful to do so." She touched a lantern that hung on a peg set in a heavy timber. It blazed to light, filling the globe with a ball of flame that echoed her emotions. Stupid. She knew better than to allow her feeling free rein, especially when Jasper was near. Speaking a single word, she calmed the flame. The light flickered down grudgingly.

"And what of you?" he asked, shifting his shrewd gaze from the lantern. "Are you well?" He didn't defend himself, didn't explain.

She gritted her teeth against his cool arrogance, then schooled her expression into something more serene and turned toward him. "Of course. I am well and happy."

Silence for a moment, then: "It's not like you to take unnecessary risks, Josette."

Opening Silk's stall door, Ella led the mare inside and turned to remove her tack. Jasper made no move to help with the saddle. "And you see Drake as an unnecessary risk?" she asked.

"You could answer that better than I."

"Yes, I can."

"And?"

"And what?" She was being childish. She knew it.

But he didn't rise to the bait. Never had. "Who is he?"

She shrugged. "He's a military man."

"Whom did he serve under?"

"Leave it be." She said the words abruptly and with more force than she had intended.

He stared at her, eyes flat, face expressionless. "You're losing your objectivity," he said.

"It's none of your concern what I lose."

"We've invested—"

"I know what you've invested in me," she snapped. She also knew he had saved her—from La Hopital, from Verrill, who had taken her whispered admissions and used them against her. *She believes she can become another,* he had told them, tone almost mournful, almost caring. *It breaks my heart to leave her here, but I believe my beloved wife is possessed.* Dr. Frank's eyes had lit with fanatical joy. But Ella pulled her mind from those dark thoughts just as she pulled the saddle from Silk's back. The flame flared inside the lantern globe.

Silence hissed in the little stable for a moment before he spoke again. "I came to tell you that Shaleena will be handling Elizabeth's case."

An imaged flashed in her mind. Darkness. Just darkness, nothing else. For a moment she felt the panic of it, but she pushed it away, calmed herself. "Are you asking for my approval?"

He didn't comment. "I just ask that you be cautious."

"Careful, Reeves," she said, glancing sideways as she slipped the bit from Silk's mouth, "or I'll think you care about something other than the program."

"I believe you know better than that."

Did she? She had thought so, but suddenly she wasn't so sure. Something niggled at her mind.

"What is Maddy working on?"

"You know I can't tell you that." His pat answer.

"I could find out if I wished."

"But why would you wish to?"

She laughed at his tone, ultra controlled. "I'd simply like to see you squirm. Just once."

"You're flip tonight."

"Perhaps I'm just happy. Perhaps you haven't seen me happy before."

There was a pause. "Did Verrill make you happy?"

She turned toward him, temper flaring with the flame. Firelight danced on the rough-timbered walls, setting his face in sharp relief but leaving his thoughts a mystery. Reeves was the master of manipulation. She had learned that early on. "Tell me," she said, "how he died?"

His expression was remote, untouchable. She could change her appearance, but he could hide his very soul. If he had one. "I believe he fell from his horse."

"Which horse?"

"I'm not certain."

She watched him over Silk's glossy back. The mare munched rhythmically at a bundle of golden rye left by Winslow. "If for no other reason, that one statement would tell me you were lying."

He said nothing in his defense. So like him. She felt the anger rise, the anger they had trained out of her. "Why did you kill him?" she asked.

"You're making insupportable assumptions."

"Why—"

"Would you have preferred that he lived, Josette? Would you prefer that he found you? That he told others who you were again? What you were capable of? That you were possessed?"

She felt herself wince.

"He wasn't planning to bring you home, you know. Not while you yet lived. Your inheritance was too great a temptation."

She searched for words, for denials, but there was none.

"There are similarities between him and Drake," he said, voice softening. "Whether you see them or not."

She blinked. "Are you threatening me?" she asked.

He paused for an instant. "No."

Her movements stopped. Silk raised her head. "Are you threatening *him*?" she asked.

There was an eternity of silence. "What do you know of him?"

"Damn you!" she hissed, and he raised his brows the slightest degree, calling attention to her outburst.

"Passion is a conduit for disaster, Josette. You know that."

"What would you know of passion?"

"Nothing." His tone was absolutely level. She could threaten his life and it would not change. Indeed, she could most likely kill him, and make no impression whatsoever. "But I know you were passionate for your late husband."

It was true. She had adored him. Had all but worshipped him. So handsome. So witty. So much in love. "And so you had him killed," she intoned.

Again, he did not deign to defend himself, but there was no need, for she was being unfair. Verrill had not loved her. Indeed, he had loved none but himself. That much he had made ultimately clear. And if he hadn't died . . . then what? Would he have found her? Would he have taken her back . . . to Dr. Frank? A chill coursed through her, but she steeled herself against it.

"Why did you come here, Reeves?"

"As I said, Shaleena has taken the case, but time is running short. I wanted to make certain you've gotten no glimpses into the situation."

He was all business. Talk of death made no impact on him whatsoever.

"No," she said.

He stared at her. His skin was dark, his hair the same. Where did he hail from? What was his history? Perhaps, at one time, she had been infatuated with him. But that was before she had realized he was heartless. Or maybe . . . because of it.

"Nothing?" he asked.

"I told you—"

"We are talking about a child's life," he reminded her. "*I* have no feelings, of course, but I know you would feel badly if you thought you had allowed another to suffer."

She closed her eyes, shutting out the guilt, the horror. "I'm no longer a Chausette," she hissed.

"Her mother hasn't eaten since the girl was—"

"Leave me be!" she snapped, jerking toward him. "Can't you see I'm no longer—" She shook her head. "Leave me be," she repeated.

He nodded slowly. "I'll send Shaleena to the child's room," he said. "Maybe she will discern something," he said, and turned away.

An image flashed in her mind. She squeezed her hands into tightly knotted fists. "Darkness," she said.

He faced her again, silent, eyes gleaming in the uncertain light.

She tried to hold the image at bay, but it came again. Darkness so deep there was nothing. "I see blackness."

"What do you hear?"

She closed her eyes. "Nothing."

"Smells?"

She planned to repeat herself, but she halted, lips parted, breathing through them. "Earth. Soil. It's damp."

Silk nudged her with her nose, pushing her out of the darkness, back into the light. She set a trembling hand on the crest of the mare's sturdy neck, steadying herself.

"I'll tell Shaleena," Reeves said. He was closer now, only a few feet away. Had more time passed than seemed obvious? She could never be certain.

"It may not even be she," Ella warned.

He nodded, giving nothing away, but reached into his pocket and pulled out a handkerchief. "Dry your eyes," he said.

Until that moment she hadn't realized she was crying. She touched it to her face, renewed her composure, and handed back the lace kerchief.

"Keep it," he said, and smiled dryly. "Don't say I never did anything for you."

Chapter 13

Drury Lane was humming with activity. Every gentleman's boots were polished to a ridiculous sheen. Every deb giggled behind her fan, and every chaperone scowled dire consequences at any who would disturb her ward.

High-stepping horses, coats glistening, carried away the phaetons and broughams and vis-a-vis, leaving their illustrious owners behind. Matrons and dowagers gossiped among themselves, dressed in sheer muslins and pale flowing gowns supposedly reminiscent of ancient Roman days.

Ella scanned the crowd. It was all but giddy tonight, geared up for a much-lauded performance of *Hamlet*. As for Ella, she was as carefully groomed as the rest of the *ton*. She had prodded her hair into a relatively becoming style and embellished it with tiny seed pearls. Her high-waisted gown of lawn was embroidered and beribboned. Sage green to bring out the color of her eyes, it flowed from its tiny capped sleeves to her slippers in a cascading shower. The reticule that dangled from her gloved wrist was small and beaded, a silly contraption able to house little more than the requisite handkerchief, although, if rumor were true, the men were more likely to weep than the women; Lenstra, an Italian girl of some fame, was to play Hamlet, after all, and the sight of her supposedly flawless legs in pantaloons was said to move many a man to tears.

Ella didn't particularly care for either women's legs or *Hamlet*, but she would act the part of the smitten patron of the arts. She would laugh when the others laughed, cry when they cried, for she was determined to forget the dark thoughts that had haunted her since the previous night. Her time on Gallows Road had been disturbing enough. Why had Sarah gone there? Why hadn't her potion protected her? And where was the potion now? It would not have been easily destroyed.

Roth's attack had also been troublesome, of course, but not nearly so upsetting as her time with Drake. She could, it seemed, handle violence more easily than desire. Especially the ragged need brought on by the lieutenant's dark presence.

But for now she would forget it all: Roth, Sarah, Jasper, even Drake. Tonight she would be normal.

Ella sat beside Merry May in the box Lord Gershwin kept in his mistress's name. His wife and four children had their own seats across the auditorium and seemed nonplussed by May's presence. Such was the way of the *ton*, too elegant to notice indiscretions . . . unless it suited their moods, which were fickle and wayward and far too mercurial to allow them to sit quietly through a five-hour performance.

No one was more relieved than Ella when the audience was allowed to wander into the lobby during intermission, for the theater was stifling and airless.

"Lady Lanshire."

She turned. Harrison Sutter was making his way through the crowd toward her. "How are you enjoying the play? Lenstra does a dashing Hamlet, doesn't she? It makes one feel rather sentimental, don't you think?"

"Honestly, I couldn't hear her very well over the snoring," Ella said, and he tilted his head at her.

"Don't tell me someone actually fell asleep during her moving performance."

It was then that Ella felt the hot burn of attention focused on her. She glanced to the right and saw Drake watching her. Dark-eyed and silent, he nodded. She returned his brief acknowledgment and turned away, feeling her heart race in her chest. She had searched her soul the night before and found it raw, rubbed bare, worn out. Years of spying and conniving had used her up, and she could do no more. She must, for her own good, for her very *life*, distance herself from those things that stole her peace. From Les Chausettes. From danger. From men who made her hands tremble and her blood run hot. She needed peace, longed for a child, not the foolish longing for a man who would betray her.

She refused to glance toward Drake again. True, she did not know him well. Indeed, she hardly knew him at all, but he shook her to the core. And she could not afford to be shaken. She wanted calm. Needed quiet. Thus she turned to Sutter with a mischievous, if carefully construed, smile.

"Actually, the snores were my own," she said.

Sutter started as if surprised, then laughed. The sound was soothing, his expressions pleasant. She smiled though she still felt Drake's hot attention sear her.

"I am not about to believe such a charming lady as yourself to be guilty of snoring," Sutter said.

Madeline was right; he had a perfect nose. His teeth were nearly as flawless, his fair hair swept back and just graying over his temples. Not a man she would notice at first glance, but he was appealing in an easy way. A mild way. The kind of way that she should find attractive.

"Had I known snoring was a crime, I would have tried to be more stealthy about it," Ella said.

"I take it you don't care for our much lauded Lenstra."

"On the contrary, I'm sure she's quite marvelous," she countered. "I am simply overtired."

"Did you get abed late?"

"I fear I didn't sleep well."

"Anything I can do to help?"

Ella fanned herself, then eyed him over the top of the silly thing's lacy edge. Was he making a proposition? Did she care? He was attractive enough, certainly, but where Drake was dark and alluring and intense—

She halted her wayward thoughts with a silent curse. What was it about Drake that drew her? She did not want dark, alluring, or intense. She wanted pale and average and boring. An easy man. A man like Sutter.

"Might you be able to suggest something to help me sleep?" she asked.

"Apparently nothing so good as a Shakespearean play," he quipped, and she laughed.

Drake's focus sharpened. She could sense his attention like a sunbeam on the back of her neck. Could all but feel his heated thoughts. He wanted her. He'd made no pretense. And his attentions would not be pale or obvious or boring, but as bold and breathtaking as a midnight storm.

"My lady?" Sutter said again.

She drew smoothly back to the conversation, but cursed herself soundly for her straying thoughts. "I'm sorry," she said, and grinned just a little. "I believe I fell asleep for an instant."

He laughed and bowed. "Touché," he said. "As I was saying, they've called for the second act to begin. But here . . ." He handed her a blanket.

She raised her brows.

"I brought it to soften my seat. But perhaps you can make better use of it." He moved away with the flow of the crowd, then grinned over his shoulder. "As a pillow."

The final scene ended. The audience sat in momentary silence, roused themselves, then burst to their feet, applauding wildly. Ella dabbed her damp brow with her handkerchief and rose on the wave though she failed to share their enthusiasm. Surely there was enough sadness in the world without enacting it on the stage. There was loss and loneliness and betrayal, but she clapped with the others, still clutching the handkerchief Jasper had given her on the previous night.

Maybe the acting had been spectacular. Judging from the applause, that was the case, but why did people want to see misery? Surely there was enough to be had in everyday life. Or did these privileged few not feel it? Did they not know the bite of fear? Of hunger? The terror of a mother alone, afraid, clutching her child's night rail, eyes glassy, refusing food, refusing . . .

The musty smell of earth and stale water was overpowering suddenly, filling her nostrils, her head. The darkness was complete, pressing in, blurring her senses. But there was something else. The sound of footsteps. They were coming closer, approaching with slow, heavy tread. She could feel the terror in her very bones. Could . . .

"No!" she rasped, and jerked away in anguish.

"Can you walk?" rumbled a voice.

She glanced up and came to with a start. Sir Drake was holding her elbow in a steady grasp. The musty smell receded slowly. People laughed and gossiped as they streamed out of the theater in confusing waves of every imaginable color. The night was lit with golden orbs that glowed from the street corners. Carriages were jockeying for position, blocking the cobbled length of Catherine Street. A dark brougham stood directly in front of her. She glanced about, searching for her bearings.

"Get in," Drake ordered.

He was standing very close, eyes intense as he stared down at her.

"Where—"

"Get in," he said again. Their gazes clashed.

What had she done? How much did he know? she wondered. She had vowed never to allow another to know of her gifts, her curse. But Drake was already ushering her up through the open door of a rented carriage. She acquiesced like one in a trance, settling onto the padded seat, smoothing her dress primly over her legs, coming gradually back to herself. "I could surely have hired my own cab, sir," she said.

He didn't respond, but watched her with dark, knowing eyes that bored into her very soul.

She refrained from clearing her throat. From fidgeting like a frightened child. "Or are you hoping to take advantage of me?" she asked, trying to act coquettish.

"What happened?" he asked, tone level, eyes steady.

She raised a regal brow at him. "I believe we just saw a play written by Shakespeare and performed with a modicum of talent by an Italian girl with middling legs and—"

"You looked as if you had seen a ghost."

"She's not a ghost!" Ella rasped, remembering the stifling closeness, the smell of decay, a child's boundless terror.

Drake's brows lowered a notch. Ella wanted to close her eyes against her foolishness, to hide beneath the worn leather seat. He hadn't been speaking of the girl named Elizabeth. She did clear her throat now, then chuckled a little, glancing down at her lap and trying hopelessly to hide her panic. Why the visions? Why now? She was done with that. Had put it behind her.

"I didn't think you the kind to believe in hobgoblins and the like," she said, but she felt pale, shaken.

His gaze never strayed. Their knees were all but touching as they faced each other across the brougham. "Are you gifted?" he asked.

"What?" She drew back, filled with terror, with memories too harsh to entertain.

He watched her with darkling, inscrutable eyes. "Are you gifted, lass?"

"I believe I shall get my own cab," she said,

and standing, moved toward the door, but in that second the carriage lurched forward. She bobbled on her feet, almost falling, but he reached out and grabbed her, bearing her onto his lap.

Outside, drivers cursed each other with verve.

Beneath her, Drake's thighs felt hard and ungiving despite his wounds, despite his pain.

"Do you have the gift?" he asked again, close now, his voice little more than a whisper.

"Well . . ." She felt light-headed and cold despite the stifling heat of the theater. "I'm a fair hand at whist and my needlepoint is quite spectacular if I do say so myself."

Quiet settled in, as if they were no longer a part of the world at large, but in their own private bubble, locked away in the semidarkness. "In County Galway there are many with the sight."

"The sight?" She laughed. It sounded maniacal to her own ears. "You think I possess some sort of ungodly power to read minds?"

"Some might call it such," he admitted, but his tone suggested that he was not one of those. "My mother and her kin did not."

Was he lying? Was he hoping to draw her out? To destroy her?

Her hip was pressed snug against his cock. She

could feel its hard length burn through the gauzy fabric of her gown. "I *do* know that you desire me, if that's what you mean," she said. Perhaps she was hoping to distract him, but suddenly she wanted nothing so much as to be held, to lie in his arms and forget all.

His gaze burned her lips. Her breath came in small gasps. For a moment all was still, all was silent, but in the next he slipped his hand behind her neck and pulled her into a kiss. It was neither tender nor uncertain, but hot and demanding, burning with passion and strength and need.

And she answered, barely aware of her actions as she bent one knee and turned in his arms, hugging him with her thighs as she pressed against him.

He growled something low in his throat and yanked down her bodice. It scraped against her aching nipples, but there was no time to think of that, for suddenly the world exploded as he took her in his mouth. She shrieked, arching wildly against him, holding his head to her breast. He strained against the confines of his breeches and suddenly, inexplicably, she could wait no longer. Scrambling backward, she tore at his pants. They opened with irritating slowness, but finally his erection strained forward, hard, ready. He was struggling with her skirts, tugging them up out of the way. They bunched beneath her, but she cared little for their condition. She only wanted to feel, to do, to be lost in the tangible world. A world she could understand. Grabbing his coat in both hands, she yanked herself onto him. He filled her to bursting, thrusting deep with a growl of need so primitive, it was beyond words.

Still, he tried to articulate his question "Are you—"

"Shut up!" she snarled, and jerked against him.

He swore, wrapping his arms about her back, grabbing her shoulders from behind, pulling her onto his straining desire. One breast was bare, its ruddy nub bursting forth, but it didn't matter. Nothing mattered but finding utopia, finding oblivion.

He bucked into her, and she took him, every inch, every spasm, every hard thrust until she shrieked on the summit of release.

He gritted his teeth against the painful pleasure and spilled into her, throbbing, pulsing, shuddering. She collapsed against him with a little shriek, used up, sated, just as she felt the carriage slow. She jerked her head up. They couldn't have arrived already. Couldn't have.

Drake cursed and reached for her, pulling her gown back into place, before reverently covering her breast with one palm for a moment.

"Damn! Dammit." She slid off him, thoughts tumbling dangerously in her head. "My slipper." She was smoothing her hair, tugging at her gown, searching the floor. "Where's my slipper?"

"Ella—" he rasped, but she dared not look at him.

"Just find my shoe."

He turned his head, dazed, then reached behind him to pull her slipper from behind his back. She reached for it, but he held on tight.

Their gazes fused.

"I didn't mean for that to happen," he said.

"Really?" She tried to steady her breath, tugged the shoe from his hand. "Because I did," she said, and tumbled out the door and onto her cobbled walk.

Chapter 14

The streets were dark, but it mattered little. The way to Lavender House was etched in Ella's mind like an old memory, frayed with time and thought and worry. Silk's hooves rang hollowly against the cobbles before coming to a halt in front of the towering manse where her mistress had once lived.

Ella slipped to the ground.

Her feet were bare. The paving stones felt cool and contemplative beneath her soles, as if they waited, pondering. She needed no key to open the door, simply a thought, a motion, and she was in.

No rug lay in the entry, for the inhabitants within wished to hear every sound, to be aware of every movement.

Perhaps the house was silent, but to Ella it

hummed with smoldering thought, with energy. She strode inside. A noise sounded from the parlor. A right turn and a left and she was there. The room was spacious, elegant, twice as long as it was wide, decorated in sea greens and golds. A graceful divan lounged near a window draped in heavy brocade and tassels. Two upholstered arm-chairs faced each other, inviting conversation. The wall coverings were striped with cheery yellow flowers twining in rows.

And two combatants faced each other from the center of the room. Dressed in taut breeches and tunics, they examined each other in silence. One in white, the other in black. Both were lean; both were barefoot. Both were women. Neither turned to face Ella.

"Josette," said the nearer, back still toward her.

"Where is he?" Ella asked.

"Bed," said the other, and without warning soundlessly launched forward, flying through the air at the white fighter. They connected and rolled, spun apart, sprang back to their feet, but Ella had already left.

Grasping her rumpled frock in one hand, she took the stairs two at a time. They creaked be-neath her feet. The second door on the left was closed, but it mattered little. She burst inside.

A splash of light spilled across the bed's lone occupant. Jasper Reeves sat up.

"Damn you," Ella said. Her voice quivered in the darkness.

"Josette." His voice was level, unhurried, unsurprised. He was fully dressed and wide awake with not a hair out of place.

"It's hers, isn't it?" she asked, and threw the crumpled handkerchief in his face.

He wadded it in his fist and swung his feet to the floor. They were bare, the only part of him that suggested less than full readiness. But then he had ever taught them that shoes were uncertain. When in doubt of the surface, bare feet were best. Perhaps he had been ready for a battle. Perhaps he'd anticipated her arrival. The idea did nothing but stoke her anger.

"Where is she?" he asked.

Feelings flared up like fireworks. A child. Freezing, terrified, alone. Just holding the handkerchief had told her that much. Touching it to her face had nearly been her undoing. She should have realized the visions were caused by the hankie. Should have known Jasper would try to use her yet again; she'd not been thinking clearly. "I believe I told you I quit."

He stood up. His clothes looked strangely unwrinkled. His cravat was only slightly askew. "Her mother tells me she would be eight years old on Sunday."

She felt her heart rate slow. Felt her skin go cold. "I can't do it."

His eyes met hers for a lifetime, and then he nodded. "I had to try. The council is applying some pressure. Elizabeth's father is quite high placed."

Elizabeth. Lizzy. She gritted her teeth against the name, but the images, raw as fresh wounds, raged through her nevertheless. Darkness, then a blast of brilliant light. Sun on water perhaps.

"Where is she?" he asked again. His voice was low, hypnotic, pulling her in, rolling her under.

"A river," she said.

"How far from here?"

Trees. A boat. "I don't know."

"Can you see it?"

"No. But I did."

"When?"

She shook her head. It was gone. She felt drained, angry, worn. "Damn you," she said again, but softly now.

"Josette." Madeline rushed up behind her, eyes wide, dark hair tumbling down her back. "What are you doing here?"

"Returning a handkerchief."

"A—" Maddy glanced toward Reeves, and for an instant, if Ella hadn't known better, she would have sworn she saw the flash of regret in his eyes, of guilt and shame and hopeless remorse, but in a moment it was gone, replaced by businesslike implacability.

"Gather the others," he ordered.

Maddy turned toward Ella, but neither spoke. A thought was enough.

"Are you certain?" Madeline whispered.

Ella nodded. They turned away together.

It took only minutes for the coven to be complete. Thirteen women. Warriors of sorts. Ambassadors for a government that did not claim them. Some wore naught but flowing night rails. Two were dressed in breeches. Only Shaleena was naked. But then Shaleena would be, standing tall and alone, apart from the loose circle, breasts outthrust. They were large and round above a narrow waist and full hips.

"This is my project," she said, her voice husky and dramatic in the stillness.

A fire burned in the hearth. Darla fed a handful of meadowsweet to the flames. It flared, casting a blue tint to her silvery hair.

"I believe I've asked you to remain clothed for these sessions," Jasper said.

"*True* witches work sky-clad," Shaleena said.

If he was irritated, Ella couldn't tell. If he was aroused, no one could tell. If he had feelings, none would ever know. When he spoke again, his words were absolutely level.

"You work for the good of the coven," he said. "For the good of Britain, or you work alone."

She stared at him a moment, then sauntered to the center of the circle, hips swaying with provocative exaggeration, but he had already turned away to hand each of the others an item. A doll. A chemise. A hairbrush. They held them in silence, eyes closed, not thinking, merely *being* until one by one, they set their items near Shaleena's feet. To her he gave a scrap of gray linen, two feet long, as wide as her hand. It was knotted some inches from its ragged ends.

"We found this on her father's lawn near the street," Jasper said. "We think it was a blindfold."

Shaleena held it in her hands and flared her nostrils in disdain. "It's been handled since then."

"It's all we've got," Jasper said.

Their gazes met. Shaleena scowled, then tugged the fabric through her fingers. No one spoke. She closed her eyes, then smoothed the cloth across her face. A log popped behind her, but she failed to notice. Indeed, she almost smiled as the others joined hands in a circle around her.

Madeline squeezed Ella's. Support, strength, sisterhood flowed between them. The room was silent but for the crackle of the flames, sparking blue and orange. It flared again and fell, casting light and darkness across solemn faces.

Shaleena began the ancient chant. The words rolled quietly along, rose in volume, fell away. The world went silent, but the room vibrated with power, with energy. Ella felt herself drawn under, as if she were being immersed in warm waves. She could hear, could see, but everything was muffled, altered, distorted.

Finally Shaleena spoke, but her voice was changed, low, raspy with hate, rough with anger. "Ain't so pretty now, are you, girl?"

Feelings flared up, casting Ella into burning white light. "Where am I?" She felt her heart beating heavy and frightened in her narrow chest. Her face felt grubby, tight with grime and tears. Her throat was raw and dry.

"Ain't so sassy neither." The words were a rusty snarl. Shaleena was gone, replaced by another, an image almost indiscernible against the stunning light. Ella blinked, her sight adjusting, but the speaker turned away. He was short, broad, his hair a greasy gray.

"I want to go home," Ella whispered.

"I wanted my boy to come home too, didn't I?" snarled the other. "But he's not coming. Dead." He nodded, voice singsong, eerie. "Died brave they say." His body went still, remembering. "But that does me little good." His voice broke. He reached up to wipe his nose with his sleeve. "But they'll pay now. They'll pay dear."

Ella dug her fingernails into her palms. They were broken and jagged, not unlike her spirit. Her legs felt wooden, her chest compressed. "Please." Her voice was filling with tears. Her throat constricted. "Let me go."

"Shut up," he ordered, and fiddled with something on the scarred table before him. His voice was steady, past mercy, past caring.

"They'll find me," Ella said. Anger swirled up from the bottomless fear. She fisted her tiny hands. Her eyes stung.

But her abductor only chuckled. The sound was gritty.

"You know they'll find me," she said, trying to force strength into her wavering voice, but her tone was high-pitched and panicked. "And then you'll not—" But suddenly he turned. His fist cracked against her temple. Pain and shock exploded in Ella's head. She flew backward, striking the floor. Darkness streamed in, reaching for her, drowning her.

A dozen emotions seared her; a hundred images flowed by on a thousand trilling voices, but finally the voices separated, became clear. They were talking about her. An argument maybe. Ella remained very still, floated in dark water. It lay heavy and deep. Maybe cradling her, maybe pulling her under.

"Jos. Josette." It was Madeline's voice that finally brought Ella to consciousness.

She was lying on the floor, her shoulders bruised against the hardwood. Above her, the ceiling looked shadowed and distant.

"Are you well?"

She didn't try to answer immediately. Five women surrounded her, their faces wreathed in varying degrees of concern. Madeline's eyes looked strained and haunted.

"Jos—"

"I am well," Ella said, and tried to sit.

"No. Wait." Madeline pressed a hand to her shoulder. "Stay for a moment, gather your senses."

She relaxed as requested, not because she wished to, but because she seemed to have little choice.

Jasper appeared in her line of vision, his face as expressionless as a stone. "What's your name?" he asked.

She stared at him. "You're an ass," she said.

From somewhere out of sight, Shaleena laughed. Darla breathed a sigh of relief, and for a moment Ella feared Maddy might cry.

"Let her sit up," Jasper ordered.

They did so. The world blurred around the edges, but Ella remained upright.

"Can you stand?" Maddy asked.

She pushed herself to her feet. Many hands helped her, steadying her, supporting her. It was the way of women.

"How's your head?" Reeves asked.

She didn't answer.

They pointed her toward a nearby chair, but she refused to sit. Instead she turned and faced Jasper, feelings fierce and hot in her soul. "She's still alive."

He made no indication that he had heard her. "Who has her?"

She delayed a moment, letting the feelings wash over her, shifting through the fear, the horror to the practical truth. "A man. Older than you. Virtually the same height."

No one spoke.

"He's hurt," she said, though she felt no mercy for him. "Angry."

"Did you see his face?"

For an instant she felt the sharp strike of pain again, but she ignored it, looked beyond. Still, there was so little. "No."

"Shaleena?" Reeves asked, glancing away.

Ella turned toward the other. Still naked, she stood with her back toward them. The fire limned her curvaceous form as she warmed her hands by the flames, refusing to answer.

"A girl's life is on the line," Reeves reminded her, and she turned, slowly, deliberately. Firelight gleamed on her thighs, her belly.

"Good," she said, and her face was twisted.

Not a breath was released.

"Shaleena!" Jasper said sharply, and suddenly she jerked, blinked, glanced about as she shifted from the trance. They watched her, breath held.

"What did you learn?" Reeves asked.

Her lips curled up a little. "It is rather unpleasant being old," she said, and glanced down at her breasts. "Everything sags."

Reeves's brows lowered. "Try—"

"His son is dead." She narrowed her eyes. "He longs for revenge."

"Why Elizabeth?"

She shrugged.

"Who is he?"

"As you know, I can only see the thoughts present at the time. I didn't happen to be thinking about my name when I struck her." She glanced at Ella, eyes gleaming.

Reeves ignored her attitude, the first-person reference. "Where were you?"

"Home."

"Which is where?"

She shrugged again. Jasper turned to Ella.

She shook her head, squinted, remembering the glare. "It was so bright. I couldn't—"

"You're wrong." Shaleena swaggered toward them, hair gleaming like fire. "Again."

"Shaleena," Jasper warned, but she ignored him.

"There was only the one lantern," she said.

"But it seemed bright to the girl," Jasper said, facing Ella.

She thought back. Terror came again, hollow and consuming. "I hate the dark. You know I hate it," she whispered, and felt her skin crawl, heard the scratchy noises of something nasty and hungry. Something she could not see. Something . . .

Fingers tightened on her arm. She turned her gaze sideways, saw Maddy's worried eyes.

"Josette." Her voice was soft. "You are safe."

Ella nodded, though it wasn't true. She wasn't safe. Never would be.

"The light of one lantern seemed bright to her?" Reeves asked again.

Ella locked her knees, searched for courage. "Blinding."

"Then we shall assume she was kept in the dark until that point."

He was clever that way. Always clever. Thinking. Conniving.

Ella nodded.

"Why?" he asked.

"What?" She tried to marshal her senses, but they were scattered, like swallows in a windstorm.

"Why does he keep her in the dark? Is it solely because it frightens her?"

"I don't . . ." She paused, thoughts scrambling. "I can't tell."

Shaleena shambled into the kitchen.

"You said . . ." He paused, thinking. "'You know they'll find me.' Why did she believe that?"

"I'm not sure."

"Did she recognize him? Does she know him?"

Ella's head was beginning to throb with a precise, piercing cadence. "Maybe. I—"

"Very helpful," Shaleena murmured, returning, apple in hand. Its skin was bloodred, matching her lips. "We now know that the child may or may not know her abductor."

Jasper's jaw tightened, but he moved on. "Where were you?"

She shook her head. She had focused on her abductor, felt the danger there, the evil.

"I told you it was his home," Shaleena said, and took a bite of the apple.

Reeves watched Ella, but she couldn't say whether the other's perceptions were correct.

A drop of juice fell between Shaleena's breasts. She scraped it off with a forefinger. "A hovel," she said, and made a face.

"Where is it?" Reeves asked, facing Shaleena.

She shrugged, took another bite.

"How does it look?"

"I was inside," she reminded him.

"What could you see from where you were standing?"

"The whelp."

"She's unscathed?"

"Scared." She smiled grimly. "Not so terrible brave when wrenched from her mother's arms." There were times after a session such as this, months sometimes, when the core of their borrowed personalities would not leave them.

"She's only a baby," Darla murmured.

But Shaleena only tossed her head. Fear had no meaning for her.

"Was anyone else present?"

She shrugged, shook her head.

"Josette?" he asked.

"I don't believe so," she said.

"What else can you tell me?"

Ella's head felt hot. The world shaky. "She doesn't have much time."

He stared at her a moment, then turned his gaze to the others. "Anyone else?"

"She has a *grande* heart," said Faye. She was the youngest of the coven. The youngest and perhaps the most damaged. "She will fight to survive."

Shaleena snorted, but Darla agreed.

"She will fight so long as she has breath."

Jasper nodded. "Anyone else?"

"It is quiet," Madeline said.

Ella turned toward her, surprised. Maddy's

gifts did not often run toward psychic abilities. Hers were the earthy sort, the kind made of darkness and stealth.

"Where she is held," she intoned. "It is quiet."

Ella swallowed, kept her eyes open to the world, to the horror. "Underground."

"What?" Reeves asked.

"At times I smell earth. Hear footsteps."

"Overhead?"

"I'm not certain. Perhaps."

"Was this encounter current? Just happening?"

Ella shook her head, uncertain. "I can't be sure."

"That's because you've lost your gift," Shaleena said, and sauntering to the nearest chair, sat down, knees apart. "Given it away." She sneered. "The scene happened some time ago."

Reeves's stare was intense. "An hour? A day?"

Shaleena smiled, just a curling of the lips, a darkening of her otherworldly eyes.

He turned toward Ella, but who was she to gainsay? She'd been wrong before. People had suffered. Friends had died.

Reeves scowled. "How much time do we have?"

"Time?" Shaleena blinked coquettishly. "I am

218

flattered, Jasper. But even I cannot determine the number of our days."

"Shaleena," Madeline reprimanded, but the other rose abruptly.

"It's time we move on to other things," she insisted. "More important things."

"What?" Maddy gasped.

"Surely even this motley gaggle has more burning issues than one tattered child."

"This is our mission," Madeline said. "To help. 'Tis the reason Les Chausettes was begun at the start."

"Well, our mission is past."

"What?" Reeves asked.

"She's gone," Shaleena said, and sliced the energized air with the edge of her hand.

Ella felt her skin chill. "No," she said. Shaleena twisted rapidly toward her. Their gazes clashed. "She can't be gone," she whispered.

"People die," Shaleena hissed.

Darla whispered a prayer.

"You're wrong," Ella said, but her voice was weak.

"Truly?" Shaleena asked. "And what makes you think so? Your stellar past? Tell me, Josette, were you jealous of Sarah's talents? Was that what began the trouble?"

A dozen apologies bubbled on Ella's lips. A dozen excuses welled in her consciousness, but Sarah's haunted eyes shone like gemstones in her mind. She had failed, and the girl had paid the price. "I'm sorry," she said simply, and turning silently away, left the house.

Chapter 15

Where the hell was she? Drake wondered. He should never have allowed her to leave his carriage on the previous night. Should have followed her into her house. Should have apologized, pleaded, explained.

But explained what? That he been overcome by her beauty, her charisma? Her inexplicable allure?

Holy God. He had acted like a crazed beast. In light of his past actions he had no right to so much as touch her hand.

He glanced about. Dozens of elegantly garbed people sat about playing whist while scores of others danced in pairs. For a moment he had no idea where he was, whose home he had entered, but he had secured an invitation, had come here, hoping to find her. He'd gone to her house, but a serving woman as old as sin had said she was not at home. He had been tempted to sit on her stoop and wait, but supposedly he was a gentleman, not an animal planning to fall on her like a starving hound.

But the truth was, he could think of little else. She had felt like magic in his hands, in his soul. The moonlight had shafted through the cab's open window and shone on her rapt expression like sunbeam from—

"Sir Drake . . ." He snapped from his reverie, embarrassed by his condition, hard, aching with impatience. "It is very good to see you again."

How much of him? He wanted to glance down, to make sure he was unexposed, but he did not.

"Lady Ballow," he said, and bowed, remembering now that it was her home they currently occupied.

She was middle-aged, carefully groomed, and perfectly able to look down her nose at him despite their height difference. "Not dancing this evening?"

"I fear I am not terribly light on my—" he began, but then he saw her. Like a beacon through the crowd. She was alone, dressed in silken lavender, her hair a chestnut veil down her back, her eyes . . .

"Sir Drake . . ."

"My apologies." He turned back to his tormentor. "What did you say?"

"I was inquiring about your lineage."

He glanced to the side. Her face shone like the sun. Her shoulders were all but bare. Her breasts as pale as moonlight above her silken gown. A gown that could so easily be slipped from her slim, lithe form. He clasped his hands in front of him, taut and uncomfortable.

"Sir Drake." Lady Ballow's tone was becoming testy.

He jerked his thoughts back to their conversation. "My family hails from the green hills of Galway."

"Ahh. An Irishman, are you?"

She was moving through the crowd. "Aye."

"Well . . . if you marry wisely you can yet hope to overcome your heritage."

He could see her from the corner of his eye. She was smiling that smile that made his hands go damp and his tongue stutter. "I can but hope."

"Indeed, my own lineage is not so lofty as one might assume. My mother was naught but a merchant's daughter. Yet the viscount, my dear, departed father, declared, 'She shall be my bride for she is as beautiful as the morning.'"

He turned his attention toward the lady. She had an ungodly long nose and close-set eyes.

He wondered vaguely if it was his duty to say something complimentary, but then Ella laughed, siphoning off his attention. She was speaking to the man with the perfect nose. Sutter.

"My father was a homely man," said Lady Ballow.

Ella laughed again. Drake felt his gut clench. But maybe it was neither love nor lust. Maybe it was uncertainty. After all, he knew so little of her. Who was she? How was she connected to Sarah? What had happened to her after the play? And why, for heaven's sake, hadn't he concentrated on that instead of on her breasts, her skin, the smell . . .

Good God, he was throbbing. What had happened to his control? To his good sense?

"Winny," another woman greeted, joining them. "Sir Drake." He turned his attention toward the newcomer. He had no idea what her name was, but she was tall and broad, with a pair of peacock feathers erupting from her hair at unlikely angles. "Not with Lady Lanshire this evening?"

He felt restless and frustrated. "Is there a reason I should be?" he rumbled.

"Certainly not." She shrugged. "I but saw you

224

mount a carriage together after Shakespeare's *Hamlet* is all. I thought perhaps you were a pair."

No. They weren't a pair. In fact, she'd not said a word to him since the previous night, since he'd held her and kissed her and . . . But no. Her reticence was not the reason they weren't a couple, he reminded himself. 'Twas because he couldn't trust her.

"She was feeling unwell," he said. "I but wanted to make certain she got home safely."

She was dancing now. God, she moved like an angel, as if she floated on clouds, as if she were magic itself.

"Sir Drake?"

He forced himself to turn back to the conversation at hand. To resist grinding his teeth. What did he care if she danced? Everyone danced. Even he danced . . . if she was in the room.

"I beg your pardon," he said.

"I said, I hope all came out well in the end."

She'd felt like heaven. "Yes. She was just a bit light-headed."

"Ahh, well she's such a slim thing. Slight as a willow. Perhaps if she had a bit more flesh like Lady Ballow and myself she would not have that problem."

They laughed. He smiled obligingly. The conversation moved on to wagers and horses and things he could not possibly have cared less about while a woman like Elegance was in the world.

The first strains of a waltz echoed through the ballroom. He saw her again, with a new man now. He stifled his scowl. Her current partner was not tall, but he was commanding. Self-possessed, self-assured. They moved in easy unison, as if they had spent some time together. Who was he? They spun about. His sculpted face showed no emotion, but hers . . . Something sparked in her eyes. Drake felt himself tense.

"They dance well together, don't they?" said Lady Ballow.

He tightened his hands to fists. The music seemed to pound in his head.

"Would you care to know his name?" Lady Ballow asked.

Good God. Was he so obvious? "Who?" he asked.

They smiled pityingly. "Her current partner," said Peacock Feathers.

He felt a sliver of pain slice him at the term. Partner. What did that mean exactly? Had she shared a carriage with this man? Did he, even now, hope to take her there again? "Yes," he said.

"That, my dear sir, is Lord Gallo."

"His father was a member of the House of Lords."

A peer of the realm, then. Not some mongrel whose title had been bestowed on him because he was too slow at tossing his captain into the brine.

"But Gallo doesn't involve himself in politics. Does he, Winny?"

"Oh heavens no. He spends much too much time gadding about for that. Amsterdam, Madrid."

"I believe he spent some time in Copenhagen."

Then why the hell wasn't he there now, Drake wondered. But in that moment the dance ended. Ella turned, granting Drake a glimpse of her face. Her eyes were wide, her face pale. Why? Was she unhappy? Pained? Afraid?

Unexpected emotion sluiced through him like a hot tide.

He had to go to her, to be with her. A hundred reasons for his departure splashed through his mind, but he couldn't seem to formulate any of them. "Excuse me," he rumbled, and waded through the crowd. He kept his gaze on her face. What was she feeling? Anger? Worry? No. Neither. Not quite. Yet there was something. Something not just right. But in a moment he was standing before her. Close enough to smell her earthy scent, to touch her if he could no longer resist.

"Lady Lanshire," he said, and bowed. He tried to make his tone light, as if he had just happened to be wandering past. As if he were just another of the gay throng who had come for a dance and a game of chance, but he could not seem to look away, to so much as glance at the man by her side.

She gave him the briefest smile. "Sir Drake. How are you faring this evening?"

He tried to read her expression. But she gave little away, and that fact above all others grated at him. He wanted nothing more than to learn the truth. To drag it into the open. To learn what she thought, how she felt, who she was. The deepest, truest part of her. To apologize. To explain. To tell her he wasn't an animal. Not usually. But maybe that would be a lie.

"I am well," he said. Was he glaring? He should quit glaring. "And you?"

"Quite well," she said. Her tone was as light as the air, as if their lovemaking on the previous night had meant nothing at all. As if she were not existing only to do it again. "Have you met Lord Gallo?"

Drake turned toward her partner, made some innocuous gesture. They shook hands.

"Good evening," he said, and found he wanted nothing more than to take the other by his well-tailored coat front and heave him from the room. "Might you be Italian?" He forced himself to make small talk. To be civilized. To refrain from violence.

"Spanish by origin, actually."

"Oh?" He wouldn't have cared less if the cool little bastard had traveled directly from the moon. But if he had made Ella unhappy, he would gladly tear him limb from limb. "Where in Spain?"

"Near Malaga, not far from the Aboran Sea. And what of you?"

"Irish," he said, forgetting for a moment to be civil.

"And what brings you to London?"

"The *Sea Witch*," he said, and found he had run out of niceties. "Lady Lanshire, I was wondering if I might have a word."

Her eyes were very large. "I fear Lord Gallo has requested the next dance."

She turned to her would-be partner. Their gazes met, and then he bowed ever so slightly.

"It's quite all right," he said. "I shall be certain to insist on a dance at a later date." Another shallow bow. "Lady Lanshire. Sir Drake." And with that he turned away.

Drake scowled after him. What kind of man would give her up so easily? Who was he? Why was there no passion in his face when he looked at her? Indeed, how could he even force himself to walk away when she was within sight, within reach?

"How is your leg?"

Drake brought his attention to her words with some difficulty. "What?"

"Your leg," she said. "I hope it is healing well."

"Oh." What the hell was wrong with Gallo? Did he not see the magic in her? The magic that *was* her? "It does not hamper me."

"So I remember," she said, and smiling, turned away to stroll into the crowd.

He followed her, remembering too. He was throbbing again, but not his thigh. Her mere presence drove him mad.

"In regard to last night—" he said.

"I hope you weren't planning another tiresome apology," she said, speaking over her nearly bare shoulder.

He had been. He was. "It was wrong of me to . . ." he began, but it had felt so ungodly right. "To take advantage of you."

She paused and smiled the smallest degree, her blush-red lips just curling up at the corners. "That's not quite how I remember it."

"How *do* you remember it?" His voice sounded raspy, desperate. God help him, he didn't understand the ways of the *ton*.

Her eyes shone, but she turned away. "Quite fondly. Still..." She wandered off. He followed, heart pounding with hope. "I fear I mustn't do it again."

Not again. No. Next time he would find a bed, spend the night in poetry and music. Spend a lifetime kissing every hollow, caressing every hillock. "And why is that, lass?"

She raised a perfect brow. "I believe we've discussed this before, sir."

He resisted grinding his teeth. They already ached. "Still planning on attacking some unsuspecting miller's son, are you?"

"I assure you, I shall give him fair warning."

"Why?" He eased his fists open, remembered to be civil, to nod at an elderly couple she greeted with such genteel grace.

"It only seems right," she said.

Dammit to hell. "I meant to say, why him and not me?"

"We've discussed that before also."

"Lady Lanshire," greeted another. Drake turned toward the broadside. The man was tall and thin, with hawkish eyes and a sallow complexion. "You look particularly fetching this evening."

"You are too kind," she said. "Thank you, Lord Shipley."

"Might I ask for this dance to—"

"Nay," Drake rumbled. The denial surprised even himself, for he knew far better. He could feel Ella's gaze on his face. Was she angry? Afraid? Good God, he had no idea. "My apologies," he said, forcing out the nicety and trying a smile. "But the lady has promised this dance to me."

"Oh." Shipley looked at Drake, blinked, backed off a step. "Very well then. Some other time perhaps."

"Certainly," she said.

They watched him leave in unison.

"He may have been my perfect mate," she said.

"Who is Lord Gallo?"

"I believe he is a baron."

"Besides that."

"My lady," slurred a voice.

They turned in unison. Edward Shellum staggered to a halt beside them.

"My lady," he said again, and reaching for her hand, planted a kiss somewhere just short of the elbow. "I believe I remember where I first met you."

"Mr. Shellum." Ella's tone was steady, but there

was something in her eyes. "I believe you might be a bit drunk."

"Me?" He laughed, staggered, ricocheting off her. She tottered sideways. "Jug bitten? Not by half."

"If you'll excuse me . . ." she began, but he grabbed her arm.

"Don't act so high in the instep. I think you might owe me a bit of something."

"Let me go."

Fear. It was fear in her eyes, and suddenly Drake found his hand wrapped around Shellum's upper arm.

"My lady," he rumbled. "If you'll excuse me, I would discuss something with the lad here."

"Certainly," she said.

"Unhand me," Shellum said, but Drake was already dragging him toward the doors. "What do you think—"

"You'll not touch her again," Drake said, coming to an abrupt halt.

Shellum staggered in his wake. "Here now, I'll do whatever—"

Drake tightened his grip, pulled the sot closer, bared his teeth. "You'll not touch her, speak to her, or speak of her unless she initiates the conversation. Do you take my meaning?"

Shellum opened his mouth to object, but then his eyes found Drake's. Their gazes clashed, and then he nodded numbly.

"Good lad," Drake said, and steadying the boy, left him standing alone.

Ella watched him return. He bowed.

"Might I have this dance, my lady?"

She nodded.

Her waist felt small and tight beneath his hand as they took the initial steps. His leg hurt like hell but it hardly mattered; she was in his arms. "Is Gallo a candidate?" he asked as if they'd not been interrupted.

She glanced toward Shellum, who was tottering away. "Gallo?"

"Aye."

"Well . . ." She found her equilibrium with the slightest difficulty. "He *is* Spanish."

They twirled. "I fear I don't understand the reference."

"Foreign men . . . they are reputed to be fabulous lovers."

"Reputed?" Some unregistered emotion sizzled through him. He hoped to God it wasn't relief. "You don't know then?"

She glanced toward Shellum again. "Surely you're not jealous."

"I believe I've told you I hail from County Galway."

She stared at him a moment, then laughed. "That hardly counts as foreign."

She was heaven in his arms. Her head tilted back. Her hair sprayed out in an arc of chestnut waves. "Why not?" he asked.

"Ireland is far too close. Barely a leisurely stroll from my garden gate."

"Perhaps I've not told you that I've spent time in Damascus."

"And?"

"Some might say that makes me Syrian."

"I've spent some time in the kitchen," she said. "The experience hardly makes me a cook."

He tried for more small talk, but there was none. "Are you in love with him?" he asked.

She drew back a bit, pressing her lower regions against his. He refrained from groaning, managed not to snatch her into his arms and carry her to the nearest bed, and boldly resisted passing out. "Lord Gallo?" she asked, sounding surprised.

"Lord Gallo."

"I hardly know the man."

"Hardly know him . . . in a biblical sense or . . ."

She laughed. The song ended, but her laughter

echoed on as bright as daybreak. He was certain, in fact, that the entire crowd stopped to listen.

"Thank you for the dance, Sir Drake. And thank you . . ." She caught his gaze. Something shone in her eyes again. "Thank you," she said, and hurried away.

He watched her go. He should leave her be, of course, should turn away, should be as cool as she. But dammit, he couldn't seem to forget her. She warmed his blood, fired his emotions, made him sizzle with feelings and . . .

And a host of other things he didn't want. He had come to London to relax. To find peace.

But then she laughed. The silvery sound wisped softly across the crowded room, as if she were the only one present, as if he were enchanted, as if she were bewitching his very soul.

But that was absurd. Preposterous.

Peeved with himself, with his foolishness, with his own aching desire, Drake strode from the ballroom and away. The night was quiet around him. He wandered the quiet, lamp-lit streets, trying to drive her from his mind, to exorcise her from his memory, but there was little hope.

For he was bewitched.

Chapter 16

Ella twirled her way through the remainder of the evening, dancing and laughing and flirting, but from the corner of her eye she looked for a tall man with entrancing eyes and magical hands. Hands that soothed, that caressed, that protected. Where was he? Surely he hadn't left, hadn't conceded defeat so easily. Of course she hoped he had. No good could come of their time together. Still, it seemed cowardly of him to give up, and he did not seem to be a coward. He seemed like a battle-hardened warrior of yore, a knight with sword at ready, a man who would fight for what he wanted.

"Who are you looking for?" Merry May asked from behind. Her tone was innocent. Perhaps deceptively so.

Ella gave her a lazy smile over her shoulder. "My next conquest."

"He left," said the other.

Ella raised a brow, took a sip of her blackberry cordial, and turned. Lord Bentley's mistress wore a pearl-encrusted gown of black silk this evening. Her sable hair had been swept up in a bevy of ringlets and garnished with precious gems of every conceivable color. "And to whom might you be referring?"

May was unimpressed. "The man you've been searching for for hours."

"I'm afraid you're beginning to hallucinate. How much punch did you have?"

"Are you saying you're not interested?"

"In whom?"

Merry May smiled, enjoying the sport. "The Irishman."

Ella scowled as if confused, a fine performance on her part. "The what?"

"The imposing gentleman with the midnight eyes and shivery burr."

"I'm afraid I don't know whom you're talking about."

"The fellow who makes women swoon and men snarl."

"You'll have to be more ex—"

"The tall one."

"I really—"

"With the mouthwatering body and the world-is-my-walnut demeanor."

Oh for heaven's sake. "Oh." She tried to make her voice sound bored. But what the hell. Did May have nothing better to do than conjure up ridiculous phraseology? Although, in truth, her mouth did water a little when he was near. "You must be referring to Sir Drake."

May lifted one cynical corner of her cynical mouth. "Yes."

Ella scowled a little, took another sip. "I suppose he is somewhat imposing."

"Imposing." She didn't quite laugh, but she could have just as well. "Is that another word for *delicious*?"

Delicious. A fine choice of words, Ella thought, but continued on as if she hadn't heard. "You know as well as I do that he is the very antithesis of what I'm looking for, May."

"Oh, that's right." She sipped again, eyes laughing over the rim of her crystal cup. "You hope to be bored out of your mind for the rest of your natural life."

"Not bored necessarily. Just . . . content."

"Well, you'd best stay away from Drake then.

He looked as if he might swallow you whole."

The skin at the back of Ella's neck tingled. He did rather give the impression that he could devour her. That he wanted nothing more than to keep her for himself. Safe and adored and admired. And what the hell was that all about? She was hardly the most attractive woman in the room. Indeed, she wasn't even the most attractive woman in the conversation. "But I've no wish to be swallowed at all," she said.

"Then give him to me," May said. "I'm willing to play Jonah to his very large . . . fish."

Ella refrained from bristling. Bristling would be sophomoric, not to mention idiotic. "I'm afraid he's not mine to give," she said, and soothed herself with the knowledge that May was, despite her ragged past and her seemingly mercenary ways, extremely loyal to Lord Gershwin. "Besides, he'd never do for you, May; he most probably couldn't afford to keep you in gowns for a fortnight."

"Lucky for me, I would rather be out of them where he is concerned," she said, but just then Gershwin came strolling up.

He bowed. May nodded. Ella curtsied.

"I'm not interrupting anything. I hope."

"Nothing of import," Ella said, but May disagreed.

"On the contrary," she said. "I was just saying how delectable Lady Lanshire's latest conquest is."

"Sir Drake?" Gershwin said.

"Do you know him?" May asked.

"No," Gershwin said. "But he is devilishly intriguing. Were I you, I'd certainly be interested."

May tilted her head. "Tell me, my lord, is there any hope of ever making you jealous?"

A moment of intimate quiet passed between them. "I am jealous every minute you're not in my arms," he said, and she smiled as he led her to the dance floor.

Ella watched them go, feeling that foolishly familiar ache to belong, to have someone. And though she fought against it, she found she could no longer enjoy the festivities. Hence she left shortly after, but when she reached her own front door, she was not prepared to go inside.

Sighing, she paced restlessly through her garden to the pond near the far wall. It was a fine night. Moonlight frosted the water, gilding each tiny ripple with gold. A bench was nestled beneath an arbor bursting with velveteen blossoms. Kicking off her slippers, she sat down, barely noticing the fragrant blooms, the chunky moon, the lulling sounds of the night as she stripped off her pale gloves and laid them one atop the other on the armrest.

Why had Drake left? Or, more aptly, why did she care? Or, still more to the point, why had he been interested at the outset? She was no great beauty, no beguiling enchantress . . . at least not without her—

"Are you a witch?"

"Lud!" She jerked to her feet, heart pumping madly as she searched the shadows.

She found the intruder seated on a rock not thirty yards away.

Drake. His hair shone blue-black in the moonlight, the dark planes of his face sculpted by shadow and silvery light.

How the hell could she have missed him? He wasn't a small man. He rose to his feet, as slow and steady as the tide. His coat was gone, and his shirt shone starkly white in the darkness.

"I did not mean to scare you," he said.

"Then you shouldn't hide in my garden like some rabid vermin," she countered. He had, in fact, frightened her, and fear made her testy.

His eyes shone in the moonlight, as if he understood her mood and found it naught but amusing, but instead of approaching, he leaned his back against a spreading chestnut and studied her. "I fear I may not be cut out for balls and soirees and the mincing finery of the elegant *ton*."

She watched him, felt her pounding heartbeat quiet.

"Strange," he mused. "All the years at sea . . . countless months with nothing but waves and wind while I dreamed of home and hearth. But now, after all this time . . . maybe I'm suited for little else."

She felt for him suddenly; his voice was melancholy, and his face, etched as it was in moonlight, looked haunted and noble and . . . But wait a damned minute. What the hell was his haunted, noble face doing in her garden?

"So you decided to stalk me?" she asked.

He thought for a second. "I don't believe you could call it stalking since I arrived here first." He took a step toward her. She backed away.

"If I scream my servants will arrive in a heartbeat," she said.

He stopped and gave her a quizzical glance, identifiable even in the darkness. His eyes were slightly narrowed, his broad neck bent just so, as if he endeavored to understand her. "Are you certain you even have servants?" he asked.

"Of course I have servants. I'm a countess and

quite wealthy." The fear was gone, but the testiness remained.

"These servants, are they less than a hundred years of age?"

"Y . . ." She paused. He had rolled his sleeves away from his hands. They too were sun-darkened, long-fingered, tapered. She remembered those hands on her skin. But who was he really? "I'm quite certain Cecelia is. I'm not entirely sure about Amherst," she said.

He laughed with his eyes and glanced again at the moonlight on the water. "When I was a lad I would oft sneak off to the millpond. Mum worried. But I could swim like a selkie."

She considered that for a moment, but the thought of his hands on her skin kept distracting her, making her honest. "I cannot imagine you as a boy."

"No?" He glanced at her. "I was quite adorable."

"Were you?"

"'Tis what my mum said."

"Well . . . mothers don't lie."

"No indeed," he agreed, and picking up a stone, tossed it into the water. Pearlescent rings shimmered from the point of impact, widening. "She was the one who taught me to swim. Said that she foresaw a specialness in me and wished to keep me safe."

"Really?" A specialness. What did that mean? Was *he* a witch? Is that how he had seen through her guise on Gallows Road? she wondered, but knew better than to ask.

"Said she hadn't suffered the pangs of child-birth only to see me drowned in yon stinky bog."

"A practical woman," she said, then: "Why are you here?"

"Do you swim, lass?"

He glanced at her again, and though she did her best to hold on to the testiness, she felt it slipping away beneath his moonlit gaze. "I see now that my upbringing had its shortcoming," she said.

"You don't swim?"

"In truth, Drake, there's little reason for ladies of quality to be floundering about in—"

"But there might be every reason for *you* to learn the skill."

"Very amusing."

"You should learn," he said.

"Why?"

"So you don't drown in yon stinky bog."

"Ahh. Well . . . as a general rule, I stay out of bogs of all sorts. Stinky and otherwise."

He tossed another stone. Water echoed out. "'Tis hot," he said.

She scowled at him. "I noticed that, at times, there is no connection whatsoever between your current topic and your next," she said.

"'Tis hot. The water's cool," he explained. "I could teach you."

"To swim."

"Aye."

"It doesn't seem quite . . ." She glanced at the water. And although it was tempting to think of the cool waves easing up her limbs, she had no intention of making him privy to that temptation. Or to the fact that she too could swim like a selkie. "Proper."

"Not so proper as seducing an unsuspecting miller's son, of course."

She thought about that for a moment. "Perhaps that wasn't so much proper as . . . practical."

"If you're looking for practicality . . ." He raised a hand, indicating himself. "I am not only practical but accessible."

"I'll keep it in mind."

"As will I, apparently," he said, and there was something almost self-reproachful in his tone.

Ella canted her head, studying him. "Might you be admitting that you're smitten, Sir Drake?"

"Tell me, lass, does *smitten* have the same meaning as *randy* in the vernacular of the *ton*?" he asked, and strode toward her.

Perhaps she should have been frightened, or at least offended, but she couldn't quite resist laughing. "Yes, in fact, I think it might."

"Then the answer is yes," he said, and caught her with his smoldering gaze. "But I am still sorry."

"About . . ."

"A carriage was not the proper place," he said. "'Twas not right of me."

But it had seemed right, actually. Breathtakingly right. Her hands felt shaky at the thought of it, her chest too tight. But she would not be so foolish again. This was not the man for her. "And a garden?" she asked.

He turned his head, ruggedly beautiful in the gilding moonlight, his expression wry, his eyes self-deprecating. "All but perfect."

She laughed and shook her head. "I rarely make the same mistake twice, Sir Drake."

"'Tis just the reason I did not suggest a carriage ride."

At first glance, one didn't see the wit, the raw, dry humor of him, for he looked stern and ungiving, but it was there, just beneath the surface, waiting. His own brand of earthly magic. "I don't see how a garden would be much of an improvement."

"What of—"

"Or a kitchen, a stable, or a belfry." But all three sounded exciting, among the crockery, the harnesses, the . . . whatever the hell they kept in a belfry.

"I could do better," he murmured, low-voiced, and the promise shivered over her skin like a caress.

"I doubt it," she breathed, and felt his attention home in, sharp and focused. She amended her statement immediately. "Because you shan't ever get the chance."

"Because of the miller's son?"

She managed a sigh. "I fear he is hopelessly alluring."

"Is he?"

He was very close now, all but touching her, searing the torrid memories in her head. "Like a Greek statue."

"Hard of head and mostly naked?"

"All naked in my dreams." She sighed again, then worried she had overplayed her hand.

A half smile played with his fairy-god lips. They were the only part of him that looked soft.

"Tell me truly, lass, how do you keep the men from you?"

She raised her brows. "In all honesty, sir, most aren't as tenacious as you."

"That cannot be possible."

She glanced about as if searching the foliage for intruders. "Are there others hidden hither and yon?"

"There are not," he said.

She laughed. "Don't tell me you checked."

"As you wish." His tone was dutiful.

"You checked?"

"Yes."

She raised a brow, thinking. Who was this man? "Why?"

He stared at her as if she must know the answer, then: "Because you are you. Because you are entrancing," he said.

Well, yes, she was, if she wished to be. If she used her powers, if she made an effort. But she hadn't. Not with him. Indeed, the opposite was true. So why was he here?

"I am hardly entrancing," she said.

He watched her a moment longer, then reached out with slow deliberation and touched her face. Feelings shivered down her neck, tingled in her nipples, zipped away to her stomach. "In truth, lass, you are the most alluring woman I have yet to meet."

His fingers felt like gossamer waves against her skin, but she steeled herself against his touch. "Just how long exactly *were* you at sea, sir?"

He didn't smile, didn't allow her to lighten the mood. "A lifetime," he said.

"Perhaps then . . ." she began, but in that moment he tilted his head down and kissed her. Feelings stormed in like midnight clouds, stealing her breath, scattering her thoughts.

"Sir Drake," she said, pressing a hand gently to his chest and feeling her heart hammer hopelessly, helplessly, against her ribs. "Surely there are other woman you could seduce."

"I too would have thought that to be true," he said, and trailed the flats of his nails down her throat. She tried to suppress the shiver. "But since I met you . . ." He scowled, let his voice fade away as if he had lost his line of thought, as if she were all-consuming. "What kind of magic do you possess?"

For a moment her breath caught in her throat. What did he know? What did he suspect? she wondered frantically, but she hammered down the fear. His words were nothing more than the ploy of a desperate man. He had admitted himself that he was randy. "Surely you don't believe in such nonsense," she said.

He skimmed his hand over her shoulder and down her bare arm. "What nonsense is that then, lass?"

"Spells and curses and all that foolishness."

"You think magic foolish?" he asked, and lifting her hand, kissed her palm.

Feelings trembled like a rising chant through her, but she forced herself to speak. "Yes," she said. "I do."

"Then you've not lived in the green hills of me homeland," he murmured, "where the wee folk frolic like lambkins upon the hillocks."

She stared at him, trying to ignore the shivery rise of hair at the back of her neck. Trying to ignore how his eyes shone like moonlight on water and his voice was made of music and promises. "I never imagined you as a poet, Drake," she said.

"I never imagined you at all," he said, and kissed her again.

Her heart beat slow and heavy. Through the frail silk of her lavender gown, his legs felt granite-hard against hers. And above that his desire seemed just as firm, long and ready and eager.

"This is . . ." She pushed him away with her hand to his chest, meaning to retreat. But the muscle beneath her palm felt so ridiculously intriguing, she found she could not quite leave him. "This is a bad idea."

He watched her, dark eyes entrancing. "Are you certain, lass?"

She almost failed to speak. "Yes."

"'Tis not my fault, you ken, that my father was a merchant."

She tilted her head in question.

"Had I foreseen the future I would have insisted that he become a miller."

She laughed. "'Tis not the occupation that I find so hopelessly alluring."

"Then there is hope?"

She forced herself to sober. "You shouldn't have come here. 'Tis not right." And yet it felt right, right and real and filled to the brim with promise. "It's . . . disturbing."

He skimmed his thumb over her bottom lip. She refused to shiver. "I admit, lass, that it disturbs the hell out of me."

She scowled, trying to listen to his words, not simply stare at his mouth. Trying to decipher his meaning, not imagine him nude. That was rude.

"I'm a practical man, lass," he rumbled. "I do what I must. What I should."

"And what should you do?" she murmured.

He paused for a second, watching her. "I should get gone from here. Should put you far behind me. But I canna seem to manage it." His burr was particularly heavy tonight. "Might you guess how spooky you are?"

"I am not spooky."

"Why can I think of naught but our time in the carriage?"

"Because you're a man?" she guessed, but indeed, she had thought of little else herself. Beneath her fingers, his skin felt warm and firm. Muscles played enticingly. Through the fabric of his shirt, his nipple felt rigid and demanding. What would it feel like to pull it into her mouth? To make him mad for the feel of her?

"I am ever so pleased that you noticed," he said.

"It was hard to ignore."

"It is hard again," he said, and she felt herself blush, which was strange, for although she had not seen it all, she had seen a great deal.

"Have you no shame?" she asked.

"Very little where you're concerned." He

skimmed his thumb across her palm. "Perhaps you should remove your gown."

"What?" She drew back with a little hiss of surprise.

He caressed her face with his gentle fingertips. "You are hot," he whispered.

He was right. She felt feverish, but *his* skin felt just as warm. "As are you."

"'Tis not healthful to overheat."

"How true," she murmured, and found with some surprise that her fingers had already begun releasing the wooden buttons of his shirt. He closed his eyes and let her have her way. Perhaps she felt him shiver, and perhaps it was that shiver that made her lean forward with aching anticipation and kiss his chest. He rasped something indiscernible between his teeth, but she could not be distracted. Pulling his shirt from his breeches, she rested her hand on his abdomen. It was like velvet on steel. Sunlight on marble. She moved her fingers sideways, dipped her thumb into his navel. He jerked his head back but said nothing. Not moving away, not rushing her. And perhaps it was that shivering patience that made her touch her lips to his nipple just as she had imagined. The muscles jerked tight beneath her hand, but he remained as he was, breath quickening. She slipped her hand upward, felt the full, heavy muscle against her palm, and sucked the nipple into her mouth.

"Holy God, woman!" he rasped, and gripped an overhead branch in one powerful hand. She drew back a fraction of an inch, body aching for release, and lapped her tongue across the erect nubbin.

Then everything happened in a blur. His belt buckle fell open. His erection throbbed against her palm. He moaned deep in his throat, and then she kissed him, crashing her mouth against his with insane ferocity.

And suddenly she was clinging to him, straddling him. His back was against the chestnut's smooth trunk. He gripped her bottom in steely fingers and plunged into her. She threw back her head at the first thrust, rocked to her core, and he plunged again. The rhythm was erratic. The footing was uncertain, but she didn't care, couldn't care. She clung to the rigid muscles of his shoulders, striving, pumping, until he growled his release and shuddered against her.

She gasped at the summit of her own climax, then fell, sated and sweaty, against his chest.

He staggered, threatening to fall, and she unhooked her legs, sliding her feet to the ground.

"Lass," he murmured, but in that second she heard a rustle of leaves to the left.

She jerked in that direction.

An intruder. Near the gate.

"Quiet," she warned, and grasping the hem of her gown in one hand, bent to lift a rock from the ground.

Chapter 17

Was someone watching them? Spying on them? Drake dragged himself out of the euphoric maelstrom, trying to marshal his senses. But in that instant, he realized Ella was slipping off toward the noise.

Without thought, he stepped up behind her and snatched her back. She turned toward him with a silent snarl, and for one wild moment, he thought she might strike him. Their gazes caught, flashed.

"Stay put," he ordered, and securing his breeches, stepped forward. Beneath the shadow of a trio of oaks, the night was as dark as black velvet. Off to the left, leaves rustled. Drake jerked in that direction, only to see a hare skitter into a tangle of foliage. The scent of lavender filled the air.

"Just a coney," Ella murmured, and he turned, peeved to find her directly behind him.

"Did I not tell you to stay put?"

Some indefinable expression shot across her delectable features and was gone, replaced by the glimmer of a smile. "I am ever so impressed by your gallantry, Sir Drake. But I truly don't believe there is any need for you to protect me from the fierce, feral bunnies that invade my garden."

He let out his breath and ran his fingers through his hair. What the hell had he been thinking? He had vowed to woo her, to be patient, charming, not take her like a deer in rut. "It sounded bigger."

She smiled. "A *large* feral bunny."

Perhaps he should be able to laugh at himself, but he'd been an idiot. Again. Letting her seduce him. Letting her . . . But who the hell was he fooling? He was the one to blame. The one to come here, unable to stay away, to endure being without her.

"I am sorry," he said, but was he really? Or would he do it again a thousand times, given the chance? "I did not mean to . . ." He paused, struggling to untangle his thoughts.

"Which makes me wonder what it would be like if you meant to," she mused.

He watched her, breath slowing, then cupped her chin with his hand and gazed into her eyes. They shone in the moonlight, telling secrets and lies. But neither changed the fact that he could not resist her. Their lips met with hot tenderness. He kissed her, slowly, deliberately, letting her fill his senses. "'Twould be like that," he whispered finally.

She blinked her magical eyes. "Impressive."

Watching her, he traced her ear with his thumb, then slid his hand lower, feeling the hollow of her throat where her heart thrummed hard in the delicate shallows.

"And this." His kissed that hollow, felt her life beat against his lips.

Her eyes had fallen closed, but her lips were parted the slightest degree, showing the glimmer of pearlescent teeth. "Oh."

"And this," he said, and kissed the edge of her angel's mouth.

"I see." She sounded breathless, and somehow that sound was nearly his undoing.

"I would spend the night worshipping you by moonlight," he whispered, "would watch the morning sun light your face, and use the day to memorize every breathtaking detail of you." He trailed the tips of his fingers down her sternum, then tripped sideways, trilling along the edge of her bodice. She shivered beneath his touch.

"'Tis lucky indeed that you don't mean to, then," she said, and lifted her gaze to his.

"And why is that, lass?"

"Because I might feel the need to do this," she said, and rising on her toes, kissed him with mind-numbing intensity.

"Holy God," he murmured.

"Or this," she said, and slipping both hands up his torso with bold intimacy, stroked her palms down his arms, plowing his shirt aside. It fluttered to the ground behind him. Her hands made a slow caress down his biceps, then dropped to trace a languid path along the quivering muscles of his abdomen. He let his eyes fall closed to the shuddering beauty of it, and stood before her, entranced by the feelings.

"Which would be most embarrassing," he said.

"Wouldn't it just?" she quipped, and spreading her fingers, ran her hands up his torso so that her thumbs brushed his nipples in tantalizing unison.

He gritted his teeth against the sensation, but there was no stopping the shiver. "Lass," he said, and framing her face with both hands, kissed her with trembling passion. "I would do things far better the next time," he breathed.

"There shan't be a next time," she whispered, but he skimmed his hands down her shoulders, pushing the tiny sleeves away. The bodice dropped lower, baring the high curves of paradise, and there was nothing he could do but kiss the taut mounds that lay pearly and perfect above the lace.

She rasped a breath between her teeth. He kissed her shoulder. She tilted her head to the side, allowing him further access. And he took it, caressing the sharp blade of her collarbone, the tiny hollow above, moving just so to push her hair aside and lay a row of kisses along her satiny neck.

"You're not my sort," she insisted, but he stepped behind her to discover the row of buttons that ran straight and true down her spine. The first of them was little more than a tiny pearl between his fingers, but surely if he could scale the rigging in gale-force winds, he could manage one wee button. It opened with some difficulty, baring a small vee of her back. He placed a kiss there.

"Then there is no harm in this," he said, and released another tiny sphere.

Her head was turned to the side, her profile perfect, limned by the moonlight, caressed by the night. Her lips were slightly parted and her eyes almost closed, heavy lashes sleepy over passion-rich eyes.

The buttons fell open one after the other, trailing down the long, graceful sweep to her waist. The hooks on her petticoat did the same until nothing hid the smooth length of her back from his sight. He kissed his way down the bumpy column of her spine to the edge of her gown, but she had caught it before it fell and held it tight to her bosom. He tugged it lower and kissed her at the crease of her buttocks. She was holding her breath, just as she was holding her garments. He kissed her again, lower still, and this time when he tugged, she let the clothing fall, trilling over her willowy frame to slip with a languishing sigh to the cobblestones. Fabric pooled at her feet, baring the sweet curve of her buttocks, the endless length of her legs. He eased one worshipping hand down the curve of her waist, then squatted to kiss her where his hand had been. She trembled, rasping something, but he was too immersed to discern her words. Smoothing his palm over one buttock, he rained kisses down the center of her being, over the crest of her trembling behind and down, where her cheeks met below. Holding a thigh in each hand now, he urged her legs apart. They separated slowly, and he eased between them, lapping gently.

She gasped and jerked away, stumbling on her garments as she spun toward him. He rose quickly, wanting to save her, but she had found her balance and stood before him, legs slightly spread, eyes wide.

And there was nothing he could do but stare. Nothing but absorb the sight of her there, caressed by the night, loved by the moonlight.

"Lass . . ." he breathed, drinking her in. "It cannot be that you do not believe in magic. For you are the very essence of it, made flesh and whole before me blessed eyes."

He took a step toward her, but she grasped his arms. Her eyes were desperate pools of uncertainty as she held him there. Their gazes caught and fused. He saw the desire warring with the discipline, the need pitted against the logic, but suddenly her hands were on his belt, tearing it open.

His air left him in a rush. "Listen, lass," he rasped. "I would be slow about it this time if . . ." he began, but she was already pushing down his breeches. He clumsily toed off his boots in unison with his pants. In a moment he was as naked as she. She stared down at his erection, hard and ready, then lifted her smoky eyes to his. His throat closed up with hope and lust and aching desire.

"You must not look at me like that, lass, or . . ."

She stepped toward him. "Or what?"

"Or I will forget my mission."

She stopped, nearly pressed up against him. "You have a mission?"

He scowled. "To be slow about this."

"Ahh," she said, and reaching out, wrapped her hand around him. He gritted a moan. She kissed him. "Perhaps slow is overrated."

"Nay. Nay, 'tis not."

She tightened her hand. "Perhaps fast is far superior."

He steeled himself against the pleasant torture and felt himself weaken. "I imagine that might be possible."

She kissed his chin, loosed her grip, and slipped her palm down his throbbing cock to the hot, loose sac of his balls. She squeezed gently, and he threatened explosion.

"Perhaps slow is impossible," she breathed, and in that moment he crushed his lips to hers. Fire burned between them. She pushed against him, hot and firm and wet against his aching desire.

He pressed her against a tree. She arched back, but reality struck him suddenly, and he broke away, breathing hard.

"Holy God, lass, I will not make that mistake again."

"Mistake?" she queried.

"To rush the magic."

"I don't believe—"

"But I do," he said, and turning quickly, gathered up their clothes. When he straightened, she was staring at him, eyes wide as twin moons. Was there anger there? Was there frustration? Dare he hope there was disappointment?

Nearly smiling, he spread their garments on a mossy stretch of lawn beneath the oaks, then raised his hand for hers.

Understanding lit her eyes. She took a step forward, and he clasped her fingers in his, drawing her onto the makeshift mattress. Beneath their feet, their bed was springy and alive. She faced him in the moonlight, and he kissed her.

"Slowly," he murmured.

"If we must," she whispered, and the real magic began when they slipped down onto their garments.

She was like sunlight in his hands, like dreams and hopes and happiness. He kissed every inch of her, her face, her neck, her breasts, the firm hollow of her belly. And down, lower, until she writhed beneath him. Until there was no longer any question of waiting. Until she tugged him up and arched against him, hot and wet and demanding, pulling him in, swallowing him whole, squeezing around him.

He groaned at the ecstasy of it, caught in her eyes, in her heated embrace as she rocked against him.

There was no longer any hope of delaying. She arched her head back. A shaft of moonlight sliced between them, gilding her breasts, making his cock ache with need.

The tempo increased, driving them on, pushing them higher. Her nipples thrust toward the sky, rigid and ruddy. She clawed at his back and climbed, squeezing him between her knees until he released with a growl and a shudder, almost drowning her shriek as she jerked against him one last time.

Spent and breathless, he collapsed, rolling to his side, careful not to crush her. Her hair felt damp and soft and cool beneath his shoulder. Her face shone with perspiration. Their hearts thundered along in unison.

But her eyes were closed. Almost as if she were

denying the magic, as if she were hiding. As if she were ashamed.

Worry crowded in. "Ella?" he whispered, and touched her face.

She lifted her lids, found his face, eyes dark magic in the moonlight.

"Are ye well?" he murmured, and she smiled.

"Perhaps slow is not so terrible either," she breathed.

He pressed the backs of his fingers to her cheek. "You are hot."

"Don't be absurd." Her chest rose and fell in the moonlight, nipples dark against her ivory skin. "Ladies of quality do not get hot."

"You're sweating."

She gave him a glance from the corner of her eye. "Ladies of quality do not—"

"Come," he said, and rose with an effort. She glanced up, and for a moment he feared she would refuse, but when he reached for her, she took his hand and stood beside him.

It was only a short way to the silvery pool. The grasses felt coarse against his feet, the cobblestones rough, and the water, when they stepped into it, was as soft and cool as satin on his skin. He moved deeper, and she came along slowly, like a doe just testing the depths, every step careful until the waves lapped over the silky curls between her trim thighs. She shivered, and he drew her into the shelter of his arms, kissing her, because she was magic, because he couldn't resist. Then they ventured deeper, letting the silken waves lap at their bellies, their ribs.

"Relax," he murmured finally, and folded his arm across her back for support.

"This is madness," she said, but he shook his head.

"This is magic. Trust me, lass," he said, and she did, easing back onto the waves, breasts pale and lovely in the glistening moonlight, hair framing her entrancing form, seal-soft as it flicked against his arm, his chest, his belly.

It was no great hardship to teach her to float, to turn in the water like a selkie, to swim, not well, but a little until he could no longer resist lifting her into the shelter of his arms and kissing her again, sweet curves slippery-soft against his body.

She shivered against him, skin cool against his.

"Are you chilled?" he asked.

"No."

"Liar," he said, and carried her back to their nest. She dropped her feet to the earth, and he kissed her slowly, thoroughly. Trapped by the sight of her, the feel of her, he lowered himself to their garments and pulled her down beside him, where they sat facing each other. He couldn't help but ease his hand down the curving waves of her, across the valley of her waist to the swell of her hip. She shivered, but from desire or cold, he could not tell.

Reaching for his shirt, he dried her face, her breasts, the length of her legs.

His erection pulsed between them, and he found, despite everything, that he wanted her again. "My apologies," he whispered.

Her eyes were enormous in the moonlight. "I think I can forgive you," she murmured, and kissed him.

He touched her face when she drew back. "Perhaps . . ." He paused, knowing he should not speak, should not interrupt the enchantment. "Perhaps you could forget the miller's son . . . if only for a spell."

"Drake—" she began, but he touched a finger to her lips, shushing her, not wanting to hear, to know, to feel the magic crumble beneath him. He trailed his finger lower, loosing her mouth.

"How long have you been widowed, lass?"

"More than ten years. We were not wed long

before he was . . ." She paused, glanced down. "Before he was taken from me."

He nodded. "And you yet miss him?"

Her eyes were troubled, showing a dozen expressions he could not guess. "Why do you ask?"

He studied her, trying to understand. "Why else would you not marry again?"

She glanced away for an instant, as if wishing suddenly to be elsewhere, then lowered her gaze to their clothing. "Perhaps I simply enjoy my freedom. Is that so difficult to believe?"

He studied her, trying to understand. "Aye," he said. "It is."

She raised her gaze with a snap.

"Forgive me, lass," he said, "but you do not seem to detest the act of . . ." He couldn't quite find a suitable word for the wonder they had shared. "The union between a man and a woman," he ended poorly.

She blinked.

"Do you?" he asked.

She shook her head.

"So I must assume you enjoyed the same . . ." He found it difficult to force out the words, to think of her with another. "With him."

She was watching him, eyes wide and enticing in the moonlight.

"Did you not?" he asked.

She shifted her gaze downward. "Yes, of course."

He swallowed the jealousy, knowing it was foolish, trite, childish. "Then why have you not married again?"

She glanced toward him again. "Do you think it enough?"

He shook his head, uncertain of her meaning.

"This." She swept a hand toward the trees, toward the pond. "That we have just done. Is it so important? Important enough to spend the rest of your—"

"Aye."

She laughed a little at his intensity, touched his face. "In truth," she said. "He was not . . ." She paused, seemingly searching for words.

"Was not what?"

"He did not do it nearly so well as you," she breathed, and kissed him. The caress was as sweet as a promise, and when she touched his chest, he nearly pressed her back onto the grass, but he found, to his surprise, that he wanted more than the heated rush of her closing around him.

"But you were happy?" he asked, ignoring the aching crush of a jealousy he would not admit. "With him?"

271

"Yes, of course. Why would I not be? He was a count. And handsome. Everyone agreed."

Was there something in her voice? A bitterness maybe? Or did she but miss her late husband and feel the sting of his loss, even now, moments after lying in Drake's arms.

"Is that it then?" The idea scorched him, but he pushed aside the ache, for he would know the truth. "Was he so wondrous that you can find none to replace him?"

Placing a hand on his chest, she slipped her fingers downward. He closed his eyes to the caress. "I'm not certain," she said. "Let us try again so that I might better assess."

Her fingers closed over his hardness and he shivered, but he caught her hand, pulled it gently away.

"I would know, lass," he said, and kissing her fingers, held her gaze. Still, she hesitated for a moment before speaking.

"As I said, he was a count."

"I have known several counts," he said. "Some were decent men. Some were . . ." He thought of the words slung about aboard ship. "Not," he finished lamely.

Her lips quirked up for an instant. "He wooed me," she said. "Brought me flowers. Sang me ballads."

He concentrated on resisting the scowl. If a

272

tune could be shoved into a sea trunk, he could, perhaps, manage to carry it. "And the singing . . . that is important to you?"

She watched him so closely, it felt as if she were inside his very soul. "At the time, perhaps."

"No more?"

"My mother died when we were yet young. Perhaps I needed . . ." She shrugged. "Tenderness. Or what passed for the same."

What did that mean? he wondered, but another thought struck him. "*We?*" he asked.

Emotion shone in her eyes for an instant, then flashed away. "I had a brother," she said.

"You have not mentioned him," he said, watching her face, trying rather desperately to read her expression. "He is gone also?"

"As is my father."

"So you were alone in the world."

"Yes. Or at least, I felt that way. And Verrill . . ." Her tone was steady. "He was very thoughtful."

"And a count."

She gave him a nod. "But he was not wealthy."

Pieces of the puzzle slipped quietly into place. "And you were."

She sat very still, very straight. "Perhaps my father was . . . was not the best of parents, but he used his money wisely."

"And you had no relatives with whom to share the wealth."

She seemed stiff, but when she spoke, her tone was steady. "I was well set after my husband's death."

The picture seemed clear suddenly; she did not avoid marriage because her own had been so marvelous, but because it had been so dreadful. "I am sorry," he said, and watched her. There was hurt, almost hidden, in her eyes, but it did nothing to diminish her beauty. "That he mistreated you."

She started the slightest degree. "I did not say that he did."

He remained silent, thinking, then: "How did he die, lass?"

She fiddled with a fold of fabric beneath her. "'Twas a hunting accident. He fell . . . from his horse."

He touched her face, because he could not help himself. "Then he is twice cursed."

She gave him a quizzical glance, her eyes very bright.

"He could neither ride nor appreciate the miracle of you."

She exhaled softly. As if she'd been holding her breath. "On the contrary, sir, he was an excellent horseman."

He scooped his hand down her shoulder. "I am sorry," he murmured again. Her gaze met his, drawing him in, pulling him closer. He kissed her.

And then there was no stopping. No way to resist. They made love one last time, slowly now, breathlessly, meeting, joining, reveling in the slow burn until they fell into bliss and she was nestled in his arms, sated and warm.

He watched her sleep for nearly an hour, marveling at the mystery of her, the beauty, the strength. But finally she shivered, trembling in her slumber, and he woke her gently. Her eyes were sleepy when she sat up, and he could not help but kiss her again. Slipping her gown over her head, he escorted her down the curving footpath. Beneath the sweet-smelling arbor, they kissed again, before turning the corner and strolling to the arched front door.

One last kiss, one more caress, and he forced himself to leave.

Chapter 18

Ella watched Drake disappear into the shadows. Her feet were bare, her gown askew, but it mattered little. Nothing mattered. Nothing but the magical memory of his hands on her skin, the musical feel of her name on his lips.

She smiled dreamily, then chided herself for her girlishness, but she could not quite contain her smile as she turned toward the door. It was then that the familiar sensations struck her. Familiar, but not quite so.

She turned, searching the shadows. "Madeline?" she called softly.

There was a moment's delay, a heartbeat of silence before Jasper Reeves stepped from the darkness.

"What are you doing here? Where's Maddy?" she breathed.

He gave her a strange glance. "I believe she remains at Lavender House."

She searched the darkness behind him. "Are you certain? I thought . . ."

He was watching her, and she realized suddenly that she should not have admitted she had mistaken his presence for her sister's. Admitting a weakness was a veritable sin amid Les Chausettes.

"I worry about her," she finished lamely.

"She is safe," he said, but his voice sounded strange, almost as if he felt some sort of emotion.

"Then why have you come?" she asked, and found that she was angry again, fidgety, even before she remembered the noise in the garden. The memory struck her hard. Had he been there? Had he seen her with Drake? Dear Lord, had he been watching her? Watching *them*? The idea made her feel a little sick somehow. As if her father had seen her naked. "How long have you been here?"

"I only just arrived. Why?" Was he telling the truth? His face was shadowed, but it hardly mattered. Jasper gave nothing away. Still, she passed her hand over a nearby lantern and watched a pale flame flicker to life behind the rounded globe.

Reeves stared at the tiny flame, then shifted his gaze to her. "There is reason to believe Grey has . . . powers."

She felt her heart stutter. "What?"

"Grey," he repeated. "The man who seduced Sarah. Who caused her death."

"I know who Grey is." But she had been temporarily distracted, as if her time with Drake had wiped all problems from her mind. She took a deep breath, trying to clear her mind. "What kind of powers?"

He shook his head.

"Magical powers?" Perhaps it was what she believed herself, but she had never put a word to it. Never allowed herself. She paced the narrow footpath restlessly. "You think Sarah was hexed?"

"Perhaps," he said. Cautious. Always cautious.

"No." She twisted her hands. "She was young. True. But she was intelligent. And strong. Stronger than you know."

"As are you."

She stumbled to a halt.

"And yet you believed every word that fell from his tongue," he added.

"Who are you talking about?" she whispered.

Silence lay between them, then: "Your husband," he said. "Of course."

She drew a careful breath. "He wasn't magical," she said. "That you can believe." In fact he was evil. Evil and conniving and ungodly cruel. He had pretended love, and she had bared her soul to him. Had told him secrets she had shared with none but her sister—that she was gifted, that she could adopt others' features, could mold her own. He had been skeptical at first, then fascinated. But never horrified. Never scandalized. Not until the day Dr. Frank had arrived from La Hopital. The day he had proclaimed her to be mad, possessed by demons, a danger to herself and others.

"Rosamond went through the ashes at the house on Gallows Road. She felt a whisper of something."

Rosamond could feel things others could not. In that regard, she was the most gifted of the thirteen. But Ella refused to believe.

"Sarah would have left a residue. Perhaps it was her gift that Rosa felt."

"She couldn't breathe. I had to take her from the house. To get her outside."

Ella tightened her fists, loosened them. "She sensed evil." It wasn't a question. She knew each of her sisters well. Had catalogued their gifts in her mind. Priscilla could judge the truth in a speaker's words. Beatrice had an unearthly affinity for the beasts of the field. And Rosamond could feel the emotions left behind after a person's departure.

"What do you know of Drake?" Reeves asked.

Ella jerked at the question. "What?"

His expression was implacable. "Sir Drake," he said. "I was told you have been seen—"

"That's ridiculous." She was pacing again.

He watched her in silence. "Many things are."

"He didn't know Sarah."

"Are you certain of that?"

"Yes." But why had he been on Gallows Road in the small hours of the morning?

"So you feel no power in him?"

She stared at him, saying nothing, for Drake *did* have a power. An incredible, bone-tingling magic. The kind that drew her to him. That made her ride by his town house when she hoped none would see. But he was not evil. She was certain of it. "No," she said, but Reeves refused to turn away from her direct stare. Their gazes clashed. He could not read her mind, she reminded herself. Had never been able to. Though at times she had felt differently.

"Are you in love with him?" he asked.

Her heart jolted at the question, but she kept her voice steady. "I would have you remember that I am no longer in your employ, Reeves," she said. "Neither am I a child. Indeed, what I think or feel or do is entirely—"

"You're a Chausette. It is my duty—"

"I'm not a Chausette!" she rasped, feeling breathless. Worn out. "Can't you understand that?"

"You cannot leave the coven. Not truly."

"Well, I *have* left."

"You . . ." he began, then paused, took a moment, began again. "I would ask a favor."

"What?" She didn't try to hide her surprise. There would be no point. Reeves never asked favors.

"I want you to try again to find Elizabeth."

She cringed. The name scorched her. "I can't. I—"

"Lady Redcomb wishes to take over the project."

His voice was level, his body still, but there was something in the way he said the words. Something odd. Ella closed her mouth. Watched him. "And?"

He fisted one hand, then let it relax, still watching her. "She doesn't have your abilities," he said.

She drew a deep breath, steadied herself. "Flattery, Jasper?"

"Truth." He said the single word with such unbiased certainty that she paused.

He pressed on. "I took the information you had gleaned to my superiors."

She nodded. It was little enough. An old man. A hovel. The smell of earth and stale water. It could be anywhere on the isle. Or off, come to that. But she didn't think so. Though she didn't know why.

"They are looking into recent deaths of young men between the ages of eighteen and twenty-nine in an effort to find the culprit."

"And?"

"There are too many. They'll find nothing in time. Shaleena is right. The girl will—"

"Don't!" Visions of Sarah flashed through her mind. Dead eyes, lax hands, hopelessness. "Can't you see I'm tired of your manipulations? Weary of your—"

"Maddy could die."

"What?" she rasped.

He drew a breath, remained silent for a heartbeat. "Lady Redcomb," he corrected. "She isn't strong enough for this task."

"Shaleena is the one who—"

"Shaleena believes the girl's cause is lost."

Anger flared up like fireworks. "And beneath her?"

He didn't answer. "Lady Redcomb wishes to go to the mother. To link with her."

She felt herself pale. Connecting with the child's personal items had been difficult enough, but then Ella had felt only a portion of the girl's fear, the girl's pain. Linking in person with the mother . . . The agony would be unbearable and possibly eternal.

"I refused to let her go," Reeves said. "But she's been strange lately. Belligerent. I—"

"Very well," she said, and closed her eyes for an instant.

He remained silent, speechless. Perhaps for the first time in the entirety of their relationship. "You'll do it?"

"Yes."

"Do you want a full coven?" he asked.

"No." She steeled herself. "I too want an audience with her mother."

Quiet shuffled in. "I know you're strong, Josette," he said. "But I can't allow—"

"The child will die," she said. "As will the mother."

"The mother's in no danger despite the earl's—" He stopped himself.

"The earl's what?" she asked.

"The mother is safe," he said.

And she almost smiled. "Sometimes you are a tremendous fool, Reeves."

He scowled the slightest degree.

"She's not eating," Ella said. "Nor will she."

"You know that?"

No. Yes. Maybe. "Not today. Not ever."

For a moment she almost thought she heard him curse. It would be yet another first. "You cannot tell her you're a witch," he said, and she laughed, despite herself, despite the frustration and the dread and the aching terror.

"Do you think I've learned nothing from my marriage, Reeves?"

He watched her in silence, then: "When do you wish an audience with Elizabeth's mother?"

She tugged her mind from thoughts of Drake. It shouldn't have been so difficult. "I already agreed to do it," she said. "There is no reason to continue not to use her name."

"When?" he asked.

Pain flashed through her mind. Worry. She glanced toward the weakling flame that flickered above the candle. It was little larger than a pea. "First light," she said. "As soon as I've rested. Who is she?"

"I cannot tell you that."

She lifted her chin, managed a smile. "Do you want her to die?"

He hesitated for a moment. "Mary Pendell."

It took her a moment to place the woman's common name, but when she did, she caught her breath. "Elizabeth is the earl's daughter."

He didn't respond.

"The Earl of Moore? Your superior?"

"What would make you think so?"

She would have laughed had things not seemed so dire. "I'm a witch, Reeves. Not an imbecile," she said.

For a moment she almost thought he smiled.

"Wait here," she said, and entering the house, climbed the stairs to her bedroom. The potion she'd made was in a bottle on her mantel. In a moment she was back outside.

"Give this to Madeline," she said finally, and handed it to Reeves.

He took it without a word, scowling a little as he closed his fingers around the fine cut glass and nodding.

She turned away, but his words stopped her.

"Be careful," he said.

She glanced over her shoulder. "Of what?"

"I'm not certain. Things are not exactly what they seem. The earl is . . ." His scowl deepened. "Don't trust anyone."

"Have I ever?"

He narrowed his eyes. "Perhaps you've changed," he said, and she knew he was referring to Drake, to her dreamy expressions, to her ridiculous happiness. "Be careful," he said, and disappeared into the night.

Chapter 19

Reeves was wrong, Ella told herself. Drake was only a man. A man who happened to find her irresistible, who could not bear to think of her with another, who wanted her for himself.

But maybe the same could have been said of Grey. There was no reason to believe he hadn't cared for Sarah. Hadn't been enamored with her even. But he had also taken her away, altered her somehow, or so she guessed. He had made her think of nothing but him. Isolated her. Women's strength came through interaction, through sharing, through numbers. Perhaps some men instinctively knew that.

Ella paced the length of her bedchamber. It seemed small suddenly. Tight. Airless.

She wished she had never left the garden. Had

stayed in Drake's arms forever. In his thoughts. In ecstasy where—

What was wrong with her? She paced again. This wasn't like her. She knew better. Far better, than to allow herself to be captivated by any man. A man who would pretend to care. Would use her. Take what was hers. Lock her away where there was no air. No freedom. Where men probed at her mind and . . .

But Drake would never do that. He had felt the sting of betrayal himself when his father had sent him to sea. He had endured intolerable pain, and it had made him stronger, kinder. She felt it in him. She couldn't be wrong.

Her skin tingled where he'd last touched her. Her ears burned where he had whispered heated words. He thought her beautiful. She stepped in front of her mirror. Her image stared back. Tall. Pale. Plain.

So what did he see in her? And why? How had he known she was a woman when they'd met on Gallows Road? What had he been doing there? And what of the night at the theater? After she had taken the girl's handkerchief she had been all but paralyzed by the harsh strike of the unwanted visions. Most men would have been frightened or at least shocked by her behavior. But not Drake.

He had acted almost as if she were normal. As if he expected her to act in just such a manner. Why?

Did he know she was a witch? Her heart clenched up tight. Had he known all along?

Her image stared back, plain and unexciting.

But perhaps he simply saw her differently. There was no reason to believe there was anything sinister involved. He would have no way of knowing she was anything other than what she seemed. Her paranoia was all foolishness. Foolishness fostered by Jasper Reeves, who wanted nothing more than to convince her to return to the coven. Hadn't he repeatedly proven that he would do everything possible to protect the program?

Drake was just what he seemed. Nothing more. Nothing less. A beautiful man, wounded in battle. Not just his body, but his mind, his heart, his poet's soul.

But in that second she remembered a fragment of a conversation she'd shared with Sarah. *He's so kind, so lovely, and when he touches me, my very being sings for the joy of living.*

She too had been inspired to sing. And she was not the singing sort. Not since La Hopital at any rate. Not since they had stolen her soul. Her hope. Her unborn child.

Worry gnawed at her, but she slipped out of her gown and into her night rail, then crawled into bed, refusing to think. Cecelia had changed the bed linens. They smelled of the posies she'd wrapped in a scrap of fabric and left on the pillow. Ella drank in the scent, exhaled carefully, shut off her shrieking mind, and refused to dream.

"No!" Ella screamed. It was dark. Too close. No air. No room. She was going to die. Alone.

"My lady! My lady."

She awoke with a start, heart pounding, lungs gasping for breath. She was in her own room, in her own house. All was well. All was . . . But then the images stormed in.

"Cecelia." She grasped the old woman's voluminous gown in clawed fingers. The other's eyes looked round and white with terror. "Have Winslow saddle Silk."

"Now, my lady?"

A haunted, tearstained face stared up at her. "Immediately," she ordered.

"Very well." The old lady nodded uncertainly, as one does to the frightened and insane. "I shall tell him you'll be needing an escort to—"

"No!" she insisted. "No escort." She was already

on her feet, flinging her night rail aside, forgetting modesty.

"But a lady of quality—"

"Doesn't live here," Ella said, and dragged her gown over bare skin. "Go now," she ordered, and Cecelia rushed from the room.

Ella was astride within minutes, racing down the darkened streets. Dawn was yet hours away. The night was black, the air still. Mist swirled in, hiding all, but she dared not slow down.

The Earl of Moore's London estate was a sprawling manse of stone and mortar. The driveway was cobbled. Silk's shod hooves beat a staccato tattoo against the stones. Sparks scattered as she skidded to a halt. A dog barked, but Ella didn't stop, didn't hesitate. Dropping the mare's reins, she raced up the walkway and tore open the heavy timber door.

A servant in a billowing nightshirt stepped into the hall ahead of her. Candlelight wobbled across his terror-pale face. "Who are you? What do you want?"

"Where is your lady ?"

"Leave here."

Ella realized suddenly that he held a poker in his left hand. He hoisted it in a brave show of intent, but his arm shook.

"Where is Lady Moore?" she asked again.

"I shall call the watch if you don't leave this house at—" he began, but she was already yelling.

"Mary!"

"Madame—"

"Lady Moore!" Ella screamed again, but in that moment a woman lurched into the room.

"Have you found her?" Her cheeks were sunken, her eyes dark, haunted, well beyond any emotion but dread. "Do you know where she is?"

"Lady Moore."

"Is she dead?" Her voice was no more than a rough whisper, her skin pale as ashes around her burning eyes.

"I've come to help," Ella said, "but you must calm yourself."

The noblewoman stood, feet bare, legs braced as if for a blow. "Is my baby dead?"

"No." The word came unbidden. "No. Not yet."

"Not yet." She tried to stumble forward, to grasp Ella's hand, but her knees buckled, spilling her to the floor. Her braid, long and dark and frayed, toppled over her bony shoulder. "Not yet. Not yet." She was chanting, rocking.

"My lady." Ella hurried forward, knelt beside her, took her hand, but all she could feel was the terror, the emptiness, the hopeless despair. "We might yet save her, but I need your help."

"Help." She was still swaying, like a wounded animal, like a mourning mother. "Help."

Reaching out, Ella grasped her chin and drew the other's head up so that their gazes met. "Cease," she demanded.

The swaying stopped. Her mouth dropped open a fraction of an inch.

"Where is she?" Ella asked.

"I don't know." She shook her head. "You think I know?" Her eyes were streaked with red, dry of tears. The swaying began anew.

"She said, 'They will find me.'"

Lady Moore had gone perfectly still.

"She said you would find her," Ella repeated.

"Who said?" she rasped.

"Think," Ella ordered. "Who would wish her harm? Who would wish to—"

"What the devil goes on here?" demanded a gruff voice.

Ella didn't glance up, but remained as she was, focused, concentrating every fiber on the moment at hand. "I can find her," Ella said. "I can find your Lizzy. But time is short."

"Who are you? What do you want?" asked the earl from behind.

"I want to help," Ella said, and squeezed the woman's hand, trying to mesh their minds, to reach out. "I *can* help. But you have to help *me*. A man has your daughter. He's old, bent, angry. You know him."

The woman shook her head.

"Who is he?" Ella asked, opening her mind, her soul.

The other's lips moved. Ella leaned in, breath held, reaching for the images, the feelings, the signs. A face nearly appeared; weathered skin, gray hair.

"Brooks!" raged the earl. "For God's sake, get this woman out of here!"

Ella closed her eyes. Saw a hooked nose, a—

But suddenly hands grabbed her shoulders, pulled her away. The forming image twisted wildly.

"Wait. Wait!" she ordered, but she was yanked free of the mother's hands and spun about.

And there he stood. The man in the image. The man with the graying hair, the angry eyes, the hooked nose.

Ella froze. "What have you done?" she gritted.

"What in God's name are you talking about?" demanded Moore. "Robby, fetch the constable. Brooks, take her away."

From the darkness of Ella's mind a little girl sobbed, but the sound was quiet, her strength almost gone. "Where did you put her?" Ella whispered.

The earl stared, fear and rage and horror all congealing on his craggy face.

His wife shot her gaze from one to the other and scrambled raggedly to her feet. "What's happening?" she demanded. "Edgar, what—"

"He took her," Ella said. "Put her in a hole. Is—" But the image in her mind shifted suddenly, changed, sharpened.

She stumbled back, weakened.

"What are you talking about?" screamed the lady, and grabbed Ella's hand. "What do you know?"

Brooks was trying to drag her away, but the mother held her with ferocious strength, her fingers sharp as claws against her wrist. "What has he done?"

Ella shook her head. "Not him. Not . . ." The images came again, spurred by the mother's hands on her arms. "Same face." She jerked her gaze to the father's. "But . . . different. Older. Wounded." The sensations trammeled her. She put her hand to her head. "Don't hurt me," she whispered. "Why would you hurt me, Bicky?"

Lady Moore stumbled back as if struck. "Bixby," she whispered.

"What are you saying?" demanded her husband, but his voice had gone hollow.

"His brother." Lady Moore swayed. "Lord Bixby."

Ella jerked at the name. Jerked with pain, with knowledge. "Where is he?"

"This is madness," insisted the earl. "Mary, return to your bed. You're in no condition to—"

"Henry died," Ella intoned. Her voice was not her own. Neither was the knowledge of the boy's death.

"Because of Edgar," hissed his wife, but her gaze never left Ella's. "Because of my husband."

"I didn't start the war. It wasn't my fault," protested the earl. But they barely heard him.

"Find her," whispered the lady.

"Have you any idea what this will do to my reputation, Mary?" rumbled the earl. "To *your* reputation?"

"Where is he?" Ella asked.

"His estate is—"

"No! No. A hovel. A . . ." Ella searched for the images. "A scarred table. A—"

"The old stable," rasped the mother. "Behind Riverbend. It's falling down. Crumbling. We . . ." Her nails cut into Ella's skin. "Is she there? Is she—"

"A well." Ella could see crumbling stones erupting from an unkempt lawn. Could feel the damp cold. "Is there an old well?"

"Good God," said the husband, and striding up, tore Ella away. The pieced images shattered.

The earl's fingers were hard about Ella's arm, but she straightened, herself once again. "Leave me be," she said, "or as God is my witness, you will die where you stand."

The man's eyes widened, he too straightened, their gazes met, and then he dropped his hands.

She held his gaze with her own, hard and ungiving. "Does your brother's estate have an old well?"

"No." He shook his head.

"Yes it does!" insisted his wife. "Behind the house. Near the river."

"Mary . . ." warned the earl, but Ella snapped her gaze to the girl's mother. Hope had sprung like lightning into her tortured eyes.

"What road?" Ella asked.

"Asp. The white house by the river."

Ella turned toward the earl. "Contact Jasper Reeves. Tell him where I've gone."

"I know no Jasper—"

"Get him," she ordered, "Or spend the rest of your life enduring your wife's hatred, and your own consuming guilt."

Chapter 20

The road sped beneath Silk's galloping hooves. Houses trailed past like fleeing ghosts. A white manse loomed in the darkness. Ella reined Silk onto the lane and galloped up the incline, over the lawn, past the house.

Time was short. Nay, it was up. The well. Where was the well? She searched the darkness, and there, almost hidden by shadows and brush, she saw a tumble of stone.

"Lizzy!" she screamed the girl's name as she leaped from Silk's back. "Lizzy!" Timbers covered the top of the well. She braced her feet and dragged the first aside, yelling again.

But she heard nothing. She screamed again, panting, struggling against the rough-hewn planks. They were as heavy as death, dragging at her shoulders.

"Elizabeth! I'm coming." One more board and she would be able to squeeze through.

"Your mother waits. Don't give up. Don't let them win," she implored, and then she heard a faint mewl from below. "Dear God," she breathed, and yanked at the plank. But suddenly the world exploded against her head. She stumbled sideways, tumbling to the earth, striking the well with her shoulder. Darkness splashed in, but from the corner of her eye she saw another movement. She jerked away.

A board flew past her head and thundered against the stones.

"Who the devil are you?" growled her attacker.

She watched him groggily, trying to concentrate on the hatred, the agony, the power she had seen in the image. But her ear was bleeding, her head swimming.

Even in the darkness she could see the resemblance between the brothers, though Bixby was older, worn, seething with pain and anger.

"I know she's down there," Ella said, but her voice was barely audible.

"She's paying," he growled, and took a step toward her.

Ella managed to shimmy up the stone wall behind her, to gain her feet, but the world was heaving beneath her. She widened her stance, narrowed her eyes. "It's not her fault."

He shook his head. "I never said it was." He was drawing the board back again, over his shoulder, like a cricket player at bat.

"Then let her go." She shifted carefully away from the well, almost falling, catching her balance. Her head was pounding, obscuring her sight, muffling her thoughts. "Before it's too late."

He laughed. The sound shivered across her skin. "It's already too late," he said, and then he leaped.

She tried to escape, but her limbs wouldn't quite obey. Pain smashed across her spine. She crumpled to the earth.

"No." She rolled to her back, finding him through the haze of pain. "No. Not too late." She was panting, barely able to force the words past her straining lungs. "She's still alive."

"And you think nothing else matters?"

She tried to scoot backward on her hands and feet, but her legs tangled with her gown. He stalked her. "No. No." She shook her head. The movement was too much, almost spilling her into oblivion. But there were images in the abyss. Names, faces. "Henry mattered," she gasped.

He paused for a moment, seeming to fall into another place for a moment, then: "My Henry. He had his mother's eyes. But my hands. Big." He nodded. "Strong. And smart. Just the thing for the academy."

She nodded, managed to scoot back a few bare inches. Unconsciousness hovered, threatened, but she would remain lucid. If only for a few more minutes. "He *was* smart," she whispered.

"Brave as a Viking. My brother said he'd be safe. An officer." He nodded. "They care for their officers."

"Brave," she agreed foggily.

"He's dead," Bixby screamed, and swung. She rolled, but not fast enough. Agony struck her arm. Still, she made it to her feet, and he was off balance from the swing, leaning in, bending forward. She stumbled in close and brought her knee up under his face. It connected with flesh. Cartilage crunched. He screamed and stumbled backward, but she was beyond mercy now and driven by desperation. Swinging around, she delivered a kick to the head. He reeled sideways, fell, and lay still.

Ella staggered to the well. "Lizzy! Elizabeth!"

There was no answer. Lurching to where Silk watched from the lawn, she tried to unbuckle the reins from the bit, but her right hand refused to move, forcing her to use her teeth. She wrenched the leather from the metal, smearing blood across her gown.

But a noise from behind startled her. She spun about. A horse flew at her. An apparition in white jumped toward her.

"Where is she?"

Not a ghost. Not Bixby. But Lady Moore, still dressed in her night rail, hair wild around her tragic face. She'd taken no time for clothes or saddle or thought, driven only by terror.

Ella managed a nod toward the well.

"Lizzy!" she yelled, and threw herself toward the well.

"Wait." Ella grabbed the woman's wrist with her good hand and spun her about. "Reins . . ." It was impossible to breathe, to remain erect. "Not long enough."

The eyes haunted her even in the darkness.

"It'll do you no good to die with her," Ella said.

"You're wrong," said the other, and ripping free, scrambled over the crumbled lip of the well.

Ella pressed her arm to her ribs, holding down the pain. "She doesn't want to die," she whispered, and the woman stopped, eyes wild in the dark halo of her hair.

"What do I do?"

"Get your reins, your leathers, whatever you have," Ella ordered, and steadied herself against the stone.

The woman was gone in an instant, back in little longer. Her fingers fumbled against the leather, but in a moment she had them secured to Ella's, then she was gone, scrambling over the edge of the well in a second, holding the reins in white, knobby knuckles, shimmying down.

"Careful. Be—" Ella began, but she was already alone.

The world grew misty around the edges, but a weak croak from below brought her to.

"Baby. My baby," she crooned, voice softening. "Lizzy. It's Mama. It's me. Come to take you home." There was the sound of sobbing, then louder, desperate with terror, with a pain so deep it hurt to hear it: "Help us! Help us!"

Ella turned mistily, stared blurrily into the depths. "Can you tie the rein around her?"

Water splashed from below. "No." Another sob. "No. It's too short."

"Boost her up." The world was spinning slowly right, then left, like a toy on a street. "Tie it around her."

There was another splash. A muffled whimper. "I can't. I'm not—"

"Then she dies," Ella stated, and gritted her teeth against the knife of pain that sawed her arm.

There was silence, the sound of stumbling through water, of falling, of labored breathing.

"Pull." The voice from below was desperate, breathless, filled with doing and hope and life. "Pull her up."

"God help me," Ella murmured, and gritting her teeth, pulled with every fiber in her being. Lady Moore pushed from below. But lucidness was fading, blurring, darkening. Ella shook her head, wrapped the rein about her wrist, and staggered backward.

The girl inched upward. Almost there. Almost. But suddenly pain swung out of nowhere. She screamed as it struck her shoulder.

"Get away!" roared Bixby. Blood covered his face. "Get away!" he shrieked, and struck again. Pain blasted her arm. She was slammed sideways, propelled by the force of the blow and the weight of the dangling girl. Her head struck the stones. There was a shriek from below. But it was faint, as if it came from leagues away. As if it didn't matter. Reality faded. Dimly she saw the old man draw his weapon back, but suddenly he was snatched away. There was a scuffle of noise, then silence.

"Josette. Josette."

She opened her eyes to Madeline's face. It was pale with worry, wide-eyed with fear.

"You shouldn't have come alone," Maddy reprimanded. "I told him not to let you."

"Where's the girl?" Jasper's voice was rough, concise.

Ella nodded toward the well, where her arm was stretched up and away by the girl's weight.

"Dear Lord," Maddy gasped. "She's got it tied to her wrist."

For a moment Ella almost thought she heard Jasper curse, but it was probably the pain, probably the thrumming in her head.

"Give me a hand," he ordered.

"Hold on, love. Hold on," Maddy said, then stood.

The rest was a blur. The reins tightened against the numbness of her arm, but in a moment the girl was pulled over the lip of the well and deposited on the grass.

"Is she breathing?" Ella asked, teeth gritted against the pain as Maddy struggled with the knot.

"Just," said Reeves.

"Mother . . ." Ella breathed, and managed to draw her arm to her chest, to cradle it against her body. Fireworks were exploding inside. "Down there."

Jasper untied the girl, tossed down the leather, shouted into the well, but Ella didn't hear the words, didn't listen.

Upon the grass, the girl looked tiny and hopeless, feet bare and faintly blue in the predawn light, wet hair swept away from pale, shiny skin.

"Cold," Ella murmured.

Maddy scrambled out of her jacket and draped it over her, but Ella shook her head. "The child."

Madeline winced, turned, wrapped the garment around the girl's shoulders, and then the mother was scrambling over the side.

"Lizzy. My Lizzy." She wrapped the child in her arms, dragged her into her lap. The narrow form lay limp and silent, her stillness damning all. "Baby," the mother whispered, and swept a shaky hand across her daughter's sunken cheek.

Mourning silence answered.

Ella's throat was tight, burning, blaming, choking her.

"Don't leave me. Please." Lady Moore was rocking, swaying back and forth, hunched over her daughter's flaccid body. "Take me with you. I can't live. Can't live without—"

But in that moment the girl's eyes opened, wet lashes sweeping up like a sleepwalker's. "Mama," she murmured, and the woman began to cry, bent over her child, weeping and praying in incoherent sobs.

Hot tears slipped silently down Ella's cheeks. She leaned her head back against the stones. They felt coarse, but wondrously cool against her skull.

So this was it then, she thought. Her reason for being, for existing, for being born.

"Get out of here." Jasper ordered, but his voice was distant, and in truth, she wasn't sure whom he spoke to.

"She's wounded," Madeline said. Her voice was low, gritty with emotion.

"This wasn't the proper task for you."

"And it was right for *her*?" Maddy asked. "Look at her. She could have been killed."

"But she wasn't," Reeves said, and then Ella fell, slipping quietly into the darkness.

Chapter 21

Despite the fact that he had learned his social mores amid brigands and buccaneers, Drake knew he should not have come so early to Berryhill. He had, after all, seen Ella just hours before. Seen her, touched her, loved her. Which was precisely why he was there, standing on her stoop while impatience pounded him like a wild tide; he could not stay away. Could not think of anything but how she had looked, felt, smelled. Even in his sleep, he had dreamed of her. And so he had come, her thick anthology of poems in his hand, waiting breathlessly to see her again. The heralded lieutenant, wanting nothing more than to hold her swan-soft hand, to listen to the music of her voice as she read sonnets in the sparkling morning light.

He would have laughed had he not been so pathetic.

The footsteps he could hear shambling through the vestibule were as slow as good tidings. The door opened with creaky weariness, and a face appeared, as old as death itself. Ella had been kind to assume Amherst had not yet reached his hundredth year.

"Good day," Drake said, stomping down his impatience and trying, rather hopelessly, to remember something about congeniality. If he wasn't mistaken, it did not involve scowling. "You must be Amherst."

The old man stared at him with rheumy eyes, then nodded once. "Yes, sir." The motion nearly sent him toppling down the steps. "That I am, sir."

"I was hoping to give my regards to Lady Lanshire."

No comment.

Drake reminded himself not to grit his teeth. "Might she be at home?"

"Yes, sir." There seemed to be a lifelong pause between each word. "She is, sir."

"I wish to see her." *And touch her and hear her magical laughter ring like silvery bells . . .* Holy God, he was acting like an idiot. "If she's available."

310

The old man blinked. Or perhaps he fell asleep for a moment. "And whom shall I say is calling, sir?"

"Drake." He gritted his teeth. "Sir Drake."

Another slow nod, then: "I am sorry, sir."

Drake waited for him to continue, but he had either finished his thought or, possibly, died.

"For what do you—" Drake began, but Amherst seemed to bump back to life finally.

"My lady will not be . . . accepting visitors this day."

Why the hell not? "Why?"

"I beg your pardon, sir."

Drake bit back a scowl. "I hope she is not feeling unwell."

Amherst nodded, a mannerism he seemed to use for every occasion. "I fear she is feeling unwell," he echoed.

Drake stared at him. That was impossible. Ella had looked all but perfect on the previous night, as lovely as a sonnet, as healthy as a summer rose. So why would she be refusing visitors? Or was it just him she avoided? Perhaps she was regretting their time together. But that hardly seemed possible, for it had been spectacular, breathtaking, magical. Indeed, he could think of nothing but the sound of her sighs, the feel of her skin. Not finances. Not pain. Not even Sarah. "That cannot be," he said. "She was in perfect health last . . ." He paused a fraction of a second, rather belatedly remembering diplomacy. "Last evening, at Lady Ballow's, she seemed perfectly well."

The old man nodded. Drake considered shaking him.

"What happened?"

"I fear she took a spill . . ."

"What the devil—"

"From her horse."

What the hell kind of lunacy was this? Drake had seen her just hours before. Had kissed her beneath the arbor, had escorted her safely to her door. No harm could have befallen her, unless it had happened under her very roof.

For a moment he was tempted almost beyond control to shake the truth from the old man, but they were no longer on the high seas. Here in London they were civilized, or so it was said.

"How unfortunate," Drake said. "She must have fallen on her way home."

The old man's gaze never flickered. "Yes, sir."

Lies. Why the lies? "It is nothing serious, I hope," he said, remembering to be subtle, to be civil, when both instinct and training demanded that he be anything but.

"I fear her arm has been dislodged from its socket."

Dislodged! How? Why? It was all Drake could do not to toss the old man out of the way and leap up the stairs to see her for himself. To make sure she was well. To hold her in his arms. To demand answers.

"There are also . . ."

Drake gritted his teeth against the old servant's halting speech.

"Some scrapes and bruising, but the doctor assures us . . . she will mend in time."

What could have happened? Surely her staff hadn't harmed her. She was not exactly Amazonian, but she was no wilting violet either. He had known that ever since the first night in Miss Anglican's garden. Indeed, he had suspected things were not as they seemed, that she had somehow bested the thieves herself. But perhaps the truth was more sinister. Perhaps she was one of them, their leader, able to send them running . . .

But that was ridiculous. She was naught but beauty and grace and . . .

What about the night on Gallows Road, though? Maybe she had never been in real danger there. Maybe she would have done just as well without him.

And since she had been wandering the streets then, there was no reason to believe she hadn't done so again on the previous night. But where? And why?

"I wish to see her," Drake said.

"I fear the doctor insists . . ." Amherst nodded as if his statement were already complete. "That she rest."

For a moment Drake again considered tossing the old man aside, but damaging a man in his second century didn't seem quite right . . . even to him. "Of course," he said, and shoved the narrow book back into his breast pocket where he kept it. "Well, tell her I called."

"Certainly, sir."

Drake turned away, every muscle tense, mind thrumming. Things were not what they seemed. That much was certain. And some unknown sense he had never quite acknowledged made him feel the situation was somehow connected with Sarah.

Mounting his gelding, he turned toward Hawkspur. He had been avoiding his inherited estate and the raw feelings it evoked since his return to London, but he could do so no more. The journey went quickly, for his mind was busy, spinning away at a thousand worries. Grosvenor Street had changed little since his last visit.

Memories assailed him as he tied his mount and walked up the paved path to the towering house built of Cotswold stone. How long had it been since he'd traversed that winding walkway? Years certainly. More than a decade since his father's blatant attempt to impress him with his newfound wealth and frilly daughter, since they had shared harsh words and harsher silences.

Drake winced at the worsening pain in his leg. He had been too careless with it last night, but it had seemed of little import then. Strange how the pain seemed to lessen when she was near. When she touched . . .

Growling silently at his thoughts, Drake drove her image from his mind and knocked at the broad, weathered planks of the front door.

A woman answered on his third rap. She was young and pert with a turned-up freckled nose. Her face was round and her body plump. He didn't recognize her, but neither did she identify him. And he would just as soon keep it that way. For there were things he would understand. Things that might well make themselves clear only if he pretended to be that which he was not.

"Good day," he said, and gave the girl a smile.

He wasn't good at smiles. Had not been for many years. And yet Ella made him want to be, to laugh, to break out in song. "My name is William Tye. I'm an acquaintance of your mistress."

The girl's eyes grew wide and she seemed to pale a bit, but she said nothing for a moment. He filled the silence.

"And who might you be?"

"My name is Julia, sir."

"Might your mistress be about, Julia?" he asked, carefully keeping his tone light, his face smiling. "I've been abroad for some months and only just returned last night. Hence I thought I might pop round and give my regards to Miss—"

"I'm so sorry, sir," she interrupted, and indeed, she did look unhappy. "You mustn't have heard."

He dropped the jovial expression gratefully. "Heard what?"

"Me mistress she's . . . well, she died, sir, some six weeks back."

"Died!" he hissed, and perhaps his performance was more accomplished than he realized, because she winced as if struck.

"I'm so sorry, sir, I didn't realize you were . . . That is to say, we thought all her friends knowed . . . knew. And . . ." She paused, seeming to assess the situation. "P'raps you should come in for a spell. Sit down. Have a bit of tea."

He nodded and followed her inside. She led him past a marble bust of Mozart. It had been one of his father's most treasured possessions. Sarah had become an accomplished pianist, he'd been told. At the same age Drake had learned to avoid the captain's fists.

He passed the parlor to his right. He had sat there a lifetime ago while his father had displayed his wealth. Had sat there and silently damned the old man for a hundred offenses: his blustery arrogance, his wife's untimely death, the forced exile of his only son while he gloated over his spindly daughter like a pedigreed pet. But Sarah had never seemed to share his animosity. Bright-eyed and soft-smiled, she had, from the first moment he saw her at three years of age, seemed to adore him inexplicably. He had resented even that.

The pert-nosed maid indicated an upholstered divan, then clasped her hands nervously. "If you'll but sit tight I shall fetch some tea and biscuits. Or would you prefer something stronger? 'Tis a bit early, I know, but you look a mite . . . well, a mite winded."

"Please don't bother yourself," he said. "But

if it wouldn't be too much trouble, perhaps you could sit." He indicated the ornate silver-shot chair across from him. His father had purchased it while on a tour of the continent. Drake had been battling a storm in the Caspian Sea at the same time. They had lost two men and most of their supplies. Monkey had proven to be indispensable as a rodent catcher, and cooked rat had become a mainstay. "Tell me what happened."

She glanced toward the kitchen, as if wishing to be elsewhere, but she finally acquiesced, perching on the edge of the cushion and staring at him with sad, limpid eyes.

"I'm sorry, sir, but what was your name again?"

"William," he said. Lying did not come easily to him, but Sarah was dead and he would know why. That much he owed her for kinship alone. And perhaps far more for the childish animosity he had maintained despite her adoration. "William Tye."

"And . . . I don't mean to be presumptuous, good sir. But how did you know my mistress?"

How much did this girl know of his sister? Enough to realize Sarah had known no one by the name of William Tye? Enough to know he was lying? "We were friends," he said, and almost wished it had been true, for regardless of his own aloof detachment, she had shown him nothing but kindness. "In truth, I was something of an admirer." Another lie, of course. He had resented her from the moment he'd learned of her existence. She had killed his mother, after all, and still hadn't had the good grace to be anything like her. Where Kiara Donovan had been bright and earthy and lively, Sarah had been shy and soft-spoken. Yet she had been the apple of their father's eye. He'd shown her off like so much newly acquired furniture, even though she had looked reedy and pale the last time he'd seen her, barely eight years of age, eyes wide as moons above her ridiculously frilly frock. "She always seemed so kind."

The trace of a watery smile touched the maid's lips. "She was that," she said. "Always thoughtful. Until . . ." But she stopped, glanced toward the kitchen again. "Are you certain I can't get you no tea?"

"Until what?" he pressed, careful to keep his voice even.

"Until recent," she said, and worried at her lower lip.

What the hell did that mean? "Might I ask how she died?"

"In a fire. At . . . at a friend's house. 'Twas a terrible tragedy."

"A fire?" He allowed himself to scowl.

She did the same. "I'm sorry."

"What friend?"

She hesitated just a moment before she spoke. "Mr. Grey." Her voice was small, her mouth pursed with something. Disapproval? Sadness? Had she and Sarah been friends? Or as good of friends as their social circumstances allowed? "Mr. Timothy Grey."

"You don't like him?" he asked.

She clasped her hands carefully in her lap. "It would be wrong of me to say as much, sir. 'Specially since he passed on too."

"In the fire?"

"Yes, sir."

Something about her tone intrigued him. "You didn't approve of him."

She glanced up, eyes wide. He tried another smile, reminded himself to relax.

"I was her friend," he said, voice quiet, inviting trust. "As were you, I think."

Her eyes brightened again, fat tears threatening to spill over the precipice of her lids. "Miss Sarah, she was teaching me to talk proper. The master, he didn't want to hire me on 'cuz . . . *because* I hadn't been trained as no chambermaid."

He waited, letting her talk.

"I was only a housemaid before I come here and that don't pay near so well, but Miss Sarah asked her father to take me on. Said I was bright and I could learn."

"And he listened to her?" Even though he hadn't so much as considered allowing Drake a few more months at home, even at half her age.

"The master . . ." She shook her head and sniffled a little. "He was terrible proud of Miss Sarah. Said she could find herself a peer of the realm if she set her cap for one."

Emotion burned Drake's soul. He refused to believe it was jealousy. For surely he was well past that foolishness. Good God, he was a grown man.

"Perhaps I have no right to ask," he said. "But I would appreciate any information you can give me. This Grey . . . what kind of man was he?"

"Truth to tell . . ." She paused, scowled. "I never did meet him."

"He didn't call at the house?"

She shook her head.

"Then how did you know of him?"

"She spoke of him some. In private like."

Why in private? "She didn't tell the others?"

She shook her head. "She thought Finny would disapprove."

"Finny?"

"The head woman. The master hired her some years back, and she took it upon herself to look after Miss Sarah, 'specially after the master's death. Maybe I should have told her of Grey. Maybe . . ." Another shake. "But Miss Sarah, she seemed so happy."

He contained a wince. "He made her happy?"

Her expression was troubled. "At the outset leastways."

"But something changed?"

"She just . . . She just faded like. Slow. Bit by bit, so to speak. I worried. We all did, but there didn't seem to be nothing we could do. Then when she said she was going to live with her cousins in the country, I thought sure that would be the best thing for her. Get her away."

Perhaps their father's distant "cousin" Hannah and her well-mannered brood could have given Sarah the sense of kinship she needed, that Drake had neglected to supply. And perhaps that kinship would have set her straight. But she had never arrived at the sprawling estate just outside

Huntingdon. That much he knew. He glanced out the window, wishing for second chances that were never to be.

"Had her brother been attending her as he should this would never have happened," she said.

Guilt spurred Drake, raking his soul. He turned back toward her. "And perhaps you should have informed the others of this Grey."

The girl's face seemed to crumple in on itself. Her eyes filled with tears, and her slim hands shook.

"I'm sorry," he said, and let the guilt claw his viscera at will. She was right, of course. If he had been a decent guardian . . . a decent brother . . . she would yet be alive. Still smiling her shy smile. Still sending him gifts and notes and pressed wild-flowers. Just before the battle of Grand Port, he had received her last package. She worried for his well-being, she said, and kept him in her prayers. He wished to God now that he could have said the same. "That was cruel of me." Enough pain had been caused. Enough time wasted. "It was not your place to care for her."

"No." Her voice was soft. Her lips trembled a little. "'Tis true. I should not have kept secrets. I should have told Finny everything."

He felt a cool draft of premonition whisper over his skin. "Everything?"

She twisted her hands. "There was a lady too."

The house felt rather airless suddenly. "What's that?"

"Miss Sarah, she had herself a female friend she called Lady L."

Ella's face flashed unbidden in his mind. He waited, not breathing.

"Miss Sarah would oft visit Lady Harting for the day, but I'm—"

"Harting?"

"An elderly acquaintance. They become friends some time back." She worried at her lip again. "But I suspect now that Miss Sarah never stayed long after the old lady's nap."

"What did she do after her departure?"

She scowled a little, as if she might have already said too much. "I'm not certain."

"Do you think this lady was somehow connected to Mr. Grey?"

"Lady Harting?"

"No, Lady L."

"Oh. I don't know," she said, but her expression suggested that she had suspicions that made her cringe.

"Yet you think so. Why?"

For a moment he thought she would deny it, but she didn't. "Just a feeling, I suspect. After seeing Lady L, Miss Sarah sometimes acted . . ." She paused, shrugged.

"What?"

"Kind of sly like about it."

"Sly?"

"Like she was doing something she oughtn't."

He'd been holding his breath, he realized, and let it out slowly. "This lady, how did she look?"

"She never come here to Hawkspur, but once I went along with Teeter to fetch her from Lady Harting's."

"And?"

"She was just saying good-bye to a lady on a horse. Someone I hadn't never seen before."

He wanted to hurry her along, demand answers to questions that were, as of yet, unformed, but he nodded instead. "And what was the significance of that, do you think?"

She shrugged. "I don't know. Maybe there wasn't none."

He held his hand open in his lap, but his heart rapped urgently against the book of poems still kept in his pocket. "But you believe differently."

"Well, I didn't think much of it at the time. But later I got to thinking that it was almost as if the lady didn't want to let herself be seen."

"But you did see her," he prompted.

"Well, that's the funny part. I did . . ." She scowled, thinking back. "But I didn't."

"I'm afraid I don't understand."

"It was like there weren't nothing . . . *wasn't anything* . . . to notice about her."

He relaxed a bit. The stranger was certainly not Ella then. The mystery woman was someone else. Someone unknown. For no one could forget the sunshine that was Lady Lanshire. Still, he persisted, for he would learn all he could.

"Can you tell me anything about her? Outstanding features? The color of her hair?"

She shook her head. "Brownish, I guess," she said, making a face.

Not chestnut. Not the color of living flame. Of life itself. "Did Sarah ever say Grey and this Lady L were friends?"

She shook her head. "She didn't much talk of her at all."

"Were Grey and the lady ever together?"

"Not that I know of."

"Do you know where she lived? Why she spent

time with my—" He stopped himself, a word from giving himself away. "Sarah."

"I'm truly sorry, Mr. Tye," she murmured, and he realized in that instant that she thought he had referred to the deceased as "my Sarah." There was pity in her eyes. Pity for a love lost. When in truth he had never loved his sister at all. Had never forgiven her for being the child his father had cared about. The child his mother had died for. "But there ain't much I can tell you."

He nodded. "No." He forced a smile. "'Tis I who should apologize. I did not mean to press you."

"We all miss her something fierce," she said, voice still softened by a Cockney accent.

"I'm glad she had you to befriend her," he said, and that much was true. Perhaps life here at Hawkspur had not been everything he thought it to be. At least Drake had had his mother's soft burr to sing him to sleep each night for nine years. That, and the tears in her eyes when she'd hugged him at the pier. Him standing in his scratchy suit, unable to say good-bye lest he burst into tears and shame himself beyond redemption. But he would never forget her face, her magical Irish eyes, her love, which would be his, she promised, to the grave and beyond.

But did she still love him? Or did she blame

him for coming so late to Sarah's defense? Was she ashamed? Or did she understand his weaknesses. His childish jealousy?

"Miss Sarah had many a good friend," Julia said.

But one of them had killed her, Drake thought. He was sure of it, felt it instinctually . . . in his deep, as his mother had said. *Listen to the deep of you, laddie. For that be where the truth lives.* "Are you certain there is nothing more you can tell me of this mystery lady?" he asked, forcing out the words.

She shook her head. "My apologies."

He nodded, rose to his feet, and took her hand in his. "Thank you," he said, and bowing, turned to leave, but she stopped him in an instant.

"She was tall," she said.

He swiveled slowly back, heart performing a dirge in his chest. "What?"

"The lady," she said, scowling at her thoughts. "She looked fair tall. And slim. Not plump like me."

He felt the world go pale, but it was foolishness. Ella was blameless in Sarah's death. 'Twas what "the deep of him" said. Surely London was filled to brimming with tall, slight women.

"And she had her a fine mare," Julia added.

The world slowed. "Oh?"

The girl nodded. "Miss Sarah, she had her an eye for horses. Taught me a bit. The lady's steed looked to have some barb breeding. Refined like, with a dish to the face, and dark all over, but for four long, matching stockings."

Chapter 22

Ella was gifted. Just as Sarah had been. Drake was certain of it, though he wasn't sure how or why. Perhaps he had enough of his mother in him to sense what others didn't.

Wandering the darkened streets of London, Drake pored over his agony. Maybe he had always felt a strangeness in Sarah, and maybe it had made her existence more difficult. Maybe she had felt alone, isolated. Just as he had been.

Or perhaps he was entirely wrong. Either way, he would learn the truth of her death.

Why had she died? Was it an accident as all said, or was it more heinous than that? And how was Lady Lanshire involved?

It was well past noon when he sat in a wooden straight-backed chair in the public offices of Southwark.

"Sir Drake." Constable Redding entered the room. His dark blue coat was secured with gold buttons, and his cone-shaped hat sat low above no-nonsense eyes. "What can I do for you?"

"I was hoping you could tell me more about my sister's death," Drake said.

Redding seated himself behind a battered oaken desk. "As I told you before, there was little to determine. I fear your sister succumbed to an unfortunate fire."

"You said the residence was owned by a Mr. Grey."

"That is correct."

"When did the fire start?"

The constable shuffled his feet, leaned back in his chair. "Sometime during the night. I would have to consult my records to ascertain the date."

"What time did the fire brigade arrive?"

Redding shifted his gaze toward the door, much as the chambermaid had only hours before. "As close as I can figure it was shortly before dawn. As you know, a gaffer from across the lane saw the flames and sent his grandson running in—"

"So you're saying my sister had spent the night with this Grey." Drake saw no reason to soften his tone as he had earlier in the day.

Redding glanced uncomfortably toward the floor. "I don't mean to make any trouble for you, sir. I'm certain your sister was a fine young woman."

Drake ignored the implication. Sarah was dead. It was his fault. Her reputation was the least of his worries. "But that's what you suspect. That she had spent the night, maybe several nights, with Grey."

The constable caught Drake's gaze and gave a single nod.

Anger rippled through him, hot and searing, but he kept it at bay. "Have you asked yourself why?"

"I beg your pardon."

"Have you asked yourself why she was there?"

Redding pursed his lips. "I know her death came as a shock to you, sir. A young woman like that, and from a good family. But fires aren't unusual in Bermondsey. What with the docks and the shoddy housing and—"

"So as long as the death happens in a poor part of town, you're willing to look the other way."

Redding's face turned ruddy beneath the conical cap. "I'm sorry for your loss, but your sister . . ." His voice trailed away.

"My sister what?" Drake asked.

Their gazes caught and ground. "Well, she made her own choices, didn't she?"

Silence pulsed in the room. "Perhaps," Drake said, and stood up, heading toward the door. Toward air.

"She didn't have to do none of those things," Redding said.

Drake stopped, gut clenched. "What things?" he asked.

Redding stood. He shifted his gaze toward the door again. "Well . . . I'm certain she was a fine, upstanding young miss."

"What things?" Drake repeated, and took a step toward the constable.

The other's expression darkened. "The old jeweler on Bond Street thinks she come into his shop the day before the fire."

Wild thoughts scrambled through Drake's head. "And?"

"He was missing a couple of fancy cap pins when she left."

Three days passed. Drake hadn't seen Ella since the night in her garden, that night of sterling ecstasy. But he blocked that from his mind. His sister was dead. Indeed, she had been abducted and tortured. Perhaps not physically, but mentally, emotionally. He was sure of it. Something had happened to her. Something had taken over her mind, had convinced her to leave her home, to forsake both her upbringing and her morals. Indeed, he was half certain the same was happening to him, for it took all his self-control to stay away from Berryhill, to force himself to delve into Sarah's death, into Sarah's life. Nevertheless, he had done just that. But there was little to be learned.

All reports indicated that she had been healthy, and if not happy, at least content. But something had changed. Or someone had changed her.

"Sir Drake," said Merry May. He turned his head, coming back to himself, once again hearing the buzz and hum of the crowd that washed around him like brightly colored waves about an immovable boulder. "I didn't realize you were a fan of the turf."

Behind her, horses were being paraded to the post, shod hooves dancing, shiny manes shaking. "I am told one cannot miss the Two Thousand Guineas," he said. That was indeed what he had been told. Thus he had come, planning to learn what he could about a man named Grey. About a girl with overlarge eyes who had never ceased to send him little gifts accompanied by anecdotes of everyday life, regardless how he failed to reciprocate. But he had seen Ella's mare tied amid the melee that surrounded the track and could think of nothing but the fact that she was there, that she was close.

"'Tis all but a national holiday," May agreed.

He managed a smile despite his darkling thoughts. "And who are you backing, if I may ask?"

"Me?" She jerked slightly as if startled. "Gamble? Oh heavens no. I'll not put my hard-earned coin down on some hapless nag likely to fail in the final furlong."

"I take it you're not an avid horsewoman."

"One might say as much."

"So you don't ride?"

"Very little. And after what happened to Lady Lanshire, I may never do so again."

Raising the goblet of champagne he'd purchased from one of the nearby marquees, he took a sip and wished to hell he had a pint of rum instead. Old habits, even those one eschews, died hard, it seemed. He nodded to a passing pair of dowagers dressed in bonnets the size of small sloops, and walking gowns that brushed the earth like street sweepers behind them. He had no idea who they were. Neither did he care, so long as he appeared nonchalant. "What *did* happen exactly?" he asked.

She gave him a surprised glance from beneath raised brows. "You mean to say, you haven't heard?"

"Just the barest details," he said. "I've been rather busy." Busy trying to keep himself from her, trying to forget how she felt in his arms. Busy trying to delve into the mystery of Sarah's death instead of daydreaming about Ella's eyes and lips and skin like a knobby-kneed lad in short breeches.

May watched him closely, as if she might ascertain things she should not know. "I had hoped *you* would be able to enlighten *me*."

"And I thought sure you would have spoken to her." He took another sip of fine French grape. It tasted like vinegar. Damned Frenchmen.

"Oh, I spoke to her," May said. "As much good as it did me."

Near the turf track, a booming voice called the start. A dozen horses thundered from their starting positions, but he failed to care.

"What do you mean?" he asked.

"She merely said that she fell from her horse."

The same story he had been told, then. "But?"

She gave him a glance from the corner of her

whimsical eyes. "Have you not seen her ride, Sir Drake?"

He had, of course. Had in fact *felt* her ride. In more ways than one, he thought, then was forced to wrestle his wild memories back into submission lest he careen into another far-flung fantasy that involved her and him and an utter lack of clothing. "Perhaps her mare stumbled," he said. "It must have been quite dark after the soiree."

She canted her head slightly, watching him. "Yes, perhaps the darkness made her tumble from her mount."

He ignored her facetious tone, wondering what she knew. What she suspected. "London's ladies are certainly having their share of trouble of late," he said.

The crowd was screaming. A thousand raucous voices cheering for a dozen frantic steeds.

"How do you mean?" May asked.

"I heard a young woman was killed in a fire not so many weeks past." Off to his right, a small boy with a grimy face pressed between a gaggle of young toffs and came out on the far side just tucking something into his ragged jacket. Drake caught his eye for an instant before the grubby urchin nipped into the crowd and was gone.

"Oh yes." She shook her head. "Miss Donovan."

Her eyes shadowed at the memory. "A terrible tragedy."

Was there subterfuge there, or was he looking to find fault where there was none? "Did you know her well?"

"No." She sipped from her own cup. "She was younger than I. Don't ask by how much," she added quickly. "And seemed to have different friends."

He nodded, took a drink of gall, judging every nuance. "Visiting a friend, wasn't she?" he asked.

Perhaps a bit of skepticism shone on her face, but if so, she hid it well. "I believe I did hear something to that effect."

"Was the friend hurt, do you know?"

May canted her head. "She was a bit young for you, wasn't she, sir?"

He raised a brow. The crowd roared.

"Why else the interest?" she asked.

"I thought the *ton* survived on gossip alone."

She laughed. "That may well be true, but I fear I wasn't in her immediate circle."

"Who was?"

She shook her head.

"I heard she was an accomplished equestrian," he said. "Did she ride with others?" This mincing charade was driving him mad. He longed to be

338

direct. To demand answers: Had she known Lady Lanshire? Had they been friends? Acquaintances? Adversaries?

"Most probably. Hyde is all but murderous of an afternoon what with the hordes of riders and drivers. Lady Lanshire being as bad as any."

He felt his heart lurch at the sound of her name, but kept his voice steady. "She likes her steeds too, I hear. Might the two have known each other? Met in Hyde or elsewhere?"

"It's possible," she said, then glanced over his shoulder. "But you may as well ask her yourself, for it appears as if the doctor couldn't keep her abed on race day." She lifted her hand in greeting. Drake turned.

And she was there, amid the milling crowd. But if the truth be known, it seemed as if the crowd was no more. As if she stood alone in gleaming singularity. She wore a gown of daffodil yellow and carried a frilly parasol. Her hair had been done up in green ribbons that matched the cloth which crossed her chest and held her injured arm in place.

Their gazes met, and though he knew he was weak, he felt himself pulled across the distance, drawn toward her as if he were steel to her magnet. Or maybe it was vice versa.

"Sir Drake," she said. Her voice was cool.

"Lady Lanshire," he responded, but he wanted nothing more than to pull her into his arms, to feel her body against his. And suddenly it seemed as if his suspicions of her were beyond ridiculous. Beyond belief. Standing there in her daffodil gown and mint sling, she looked as fresh and innocent as a spring blossom. As young as hope.

He longed to taste the scent of her. To feel her name on his lips, to read her sonnets in the shade of a spreading oak, and take her into his trembling soul.

But it was all foolishness. She was no innocent. He knew it. Felt it in his very core. She had been on Gallows Road for no apparent reason, had been inside Grey's house. Why? And why had her servants lied about her injury? "I heard you were wounded," he said.

"This?" She lifted her bandaged arm slightly. "No. I just longed to wear a sling and draw the fleeting attention of the illustrious *ton*."

Her eyes were as wide as a babe's. Her smile was as bright as sunlight, and he longed to hold her, to shake her and protect her and hear her sigh against his skin. "How did it happen?"

She glanced at him askance. "You do not believe I simply wished to be noticed?"

In truth, he longed to believe every foolish syllable that slipped from her irresistible lips, but he could ill afford to. "How could any fail to notice you?" he asked.

She was silent for a moment and he almost winced, for his tone was entirely wrong, too adoring, too smitten. Too honest.

Their gazes held for an instant, and then she laughed, almost as if it were an afterthought. As if it were forced. "Flattery, Sir Drake?" she said.

He stifled explanations, apologies, quivering pleas. "What happened?" he asked again.

"This? 'Twas nothing but a silly accident. I fear I fell from my horse."

"I was with you," he reminded her and took a wee step closer, because he was weak, because he could not help himself. "Saw you safely to your door."

She raised her gaze to his, her eyes filled with laughter, with challenge. "But it was such a lovely night. I decided on a ride."

"After . . ." Memories of their time together stormed through his mind, leaving him momentarily breathless. "In the dark?"

"Quite."

"Where to?"

She glanced at the parasol she held in one hand,

then lifted her eyes to give him a coquettish glance through her lashes. "Surely you're not jealous."

She was drawing him in. He could feel the inexorable tug at his very soul. "Should I be?"

"Absolutely not," she said, and smiled. "You knew at the outset that I had no intentions of being either monogamous or serious."

He felt his stomach twist. Was she implying that she had gone to another man? Could it be true? The idea threw him off balance, tilting him toward insanity. "Ahh, of course." He kept his tone carefully light. "The irresistible miller's son."

"Just so."

"I suspect . . ." he began, but suddenly a thought gnawed at him. He felt his skin go cold, felt his expression freeze. "Was it he?" he asked.

"I fear I've no idea what you're talking about," she said, and turned dismissively toward the track.

But he grabbed her hale arm, turning her back toward him. "Did he do this to you?"

Her irresistible lips had parted ever so slightly. "Whatever are you talking about?"

His words were pulled from between gritted teeth. "Did he hurt you?"

She blinked, face flushed, eyes devouring her magical face. "Would you care?" she breathed.

More than he could bear. More than he could admit, even to himself. The idea gnawed at him. Consumed him. His teeth hurt with his anger. "Give me his name," he said.

She laughed, but the sound was breathless. "Why ever would I do that?" she asked.

He held her gaze, unable to look away, to release her. "So that I might kill him."

Her brows lowered a fraction of an inch over her intoxicating eyes. "Tell me, sir, are you always so prone to violence?"

"What happened?" he asked.

Her lips parted again as if she wished to say something she would not, then: "'Twas a fall," she said flatly. "Nothing more."

"Do you care for him?" The words came out unbidden.

"Who?"

"The miller's son." His voice sounded guttural, like a part of the earth, as base as any drunken captain he had ever despised. "Do you care so much for him that you would protect him even after this? Would lie for him?"

She stared at him, unspeaking for a moment, expression unreadable. Then she reached up and touched his face with blistering tenderness. The feel of skin against skin was almost his undoing.

Her velvet gaze seared him. "I swear to you, he did me no harm," she vowed.

He tried to resist her, to remember why he had come, but her touch was magic, and he found that his eyes had fallen closed beneath her silken caress. "Come to my bed," he said, and opened his eyes.

She smiled a little. "I cannot."

He wasn't above begging, above groveling. Indeed, perhaps there was nothing he would not do, and in that moment he thought he saw a bit of his own insanity in her eyes. But she was stronger.

"I cannot," she repeated, and drawing away, stepped quickly into the boisterous crowd.

It took every grain of his self-control to remain where he was. Indeed, he managed to turn away, but leaving her behind felt like hell had come to greet him. He tried to remember Sarah, to recall why he had come. For justice. For revenge. Lady Lanshire was somehow involved with his sister's death. He knew it, but every time his mind bent toward her, his thoughts slipped away. He could think of nothing but how she felt beneath him, around him.

Nevertheless, he spent the day trying to learn what he could of Grey, of Sarah, but he found that he was ever searching for her. Hopelessly scanning the crowd until he felt he would go mad with the loss of her.

Afternoon waned. Evening set in, and still he knew nothing. Nothing but the fact that he was obsessed.

Grinding his teeth, he left the track behind and headed for his mount, but the mob had begun to disband, making the journey difficult, and when he passed a scarlet marquee, he realized with jolting clarity that his feet had brought him to Ella's mare. Even in the deepening darkness, he recognized the dark barb, felt himself drawn toward it, reeled in, and then he heard her mistress's laughter. Or maybe he only felt it in his soul, for he was bewitched. He had heard of such things in his homeland. Had never doubted that this magic existed. But he had not thought that it would capture him. And yet when he saw Ella there in the darkness, standing beneath a leaning oak, half hidden behind a hansom cab, he could not despise her. Even though she was with another.

Her back was to him. The shadows were deep. Yet he recognized her, her laughter, her essence, her dark draw on the very core of him. He felt it in the deepest part of him.

Passing on the far side of a bevy of departing

carriages, he eased closer until naught but a single mount separated him from them.

"Mr. Sutter," she was saying. "I think this is highly improper."

"Surely you are quite wrong." The bastard she was with was leaning toward her, his mouth inches from her ear. "'Tis our duty as members of the rollicking *ton* to be quite scandalous."

"Is it?"

"Certainly," he said, and kissed her neck.

She tilted her head back and moaned. And it was that sound, that tiny sighing noise that made Drake wish to commit murder. To tear Harrison Sutter limb from limb before dragging Ella to the darkest part of the world and making her his alone.

Indeed, he stepped forward to do just that, but reason found him, stopped him. He closed his eyes against the insanity, clenched his hands into fists, and turned silently into the night.

Chapter 23

Ella felt Drake leave, felt her gut twist with agony as he turned away. Was that how he had made Sarah feel? Had she given him her soul, only to have it torn and shredded? Had she felt as if her very heart was clawed from her chest only to be used and sacrificed?

After her battle with Bixby, Ella had been abed for some days, had been afforded long hours with naught but her thoughts to keep her company. Yet she had been obsessed with memories of him. His touch, his voice, his scent.

It was that obsession that made her realize the truth; he had bewitched her, just as he had bewitched Sarah.

"My lady?"

She turned back toward Sutter, barely able to see him for the strength of Drake's presence. He had been so close. Wanting her, calling to her with his dark, unmistakable allure. But she would not succumb. Not now that she recognized him for what he was.

"Yes?" she murmured, and searched the shadows past Sutter's shoulder. Perhaps he wasn't truly gone. Perhaps he would yet come for her, take her, force her to be his alone.

"Then let's away," Sutter said.

She focused. What had she said to him exactly? What had she implied while Drake stood just out of reach? Things she did not mean, that much was certain. But she would not be used again. Would not be cheated and wounded and left alone to struggle with demons she could not defeat. She would wrest herself from Drake's dark spell no matter what the cost.

Still, it was wrong to hurt another to do so. And she could not mend wrong with wrong. Sutter was a good man, a gentle soul. And if she did not love him, did not yearn for him, was that so bad? She had told herself, told others, that that was what she longed for. That that was just the kind of man she hoped would sire her child.

"Mr. Sutter," she said softly, but he interrupted her with a finger on her lips.

"Shh, my love. Not here. Come home with me.

We shall speak there. We shall read poetry by the fire and share a thousand thoughts."

Thoughts. Gentleness. It should be what she wanted. Indeed, she had been certain that she longed for just that, but now . . . "Is that what you want from me? Poetry?"

"Wordsworth is calling," he said, skimming his knuckles across her cheek. "And if there is more . . ." He cupped her face with his palm. It felt soft and gentle against her skin. "Then so be it," he whispered, but she felt nothing. Nothing but impatience, but regret. Did that mean she was ruined for other men? That she would never be satisfied without Drake's hands on her, without his dark magic whispering in her ear? Would she never learn? Was she doomed to repeat her sins, her foolishness?

She winced at the hot memories. "Harrison," she began, but he ran his hand down her throat.

She shivered, but not from anticipation.

"You're cold."

"No," she said. "I—"

But he was already removing his jacket, curling it around her shoulders, pulling it snug across her breasts. The warmth from his body surrounded her. Maybe she was wrong. This was what she wanted, after all. What she had wanted all along.

A lover who would not wound her. Who would give her the child she longed for without making demands on her.

"Come home with me," he whispered again.

The image of a fire filled her head. Of poetry and candlelight and security.

"I fear it wouldn't be right."

"Right?"

She forced a smile. "What would our friends think if I left with you?"

"I would not smear your reputation," he said. "We shall travel separately."

"'Tis good of you to concern yourself with my character, but—"

"Come with me," he whispered again.

"I cannot."

"Then I shall come to you."

She paused. She would be safe in her own home, but did she want him there?

"You ride ahead," he murmured. "I shall wait, say my good-byes. None need know that we are together."

She opened her mouth to speak, but he spoke first.

"None need know," he repeated.

And she nodded. In an instant, she found herself beside her mount. She was astride before she remembered his jacket and drew it from her arms, but he placed a hand on hers.

"No, please, keep it, my love. Keep it, until you are in my arms."

She acquiesced.

"Go now," he said, and she did.

Beyond Haymarket, the cobblestones clicked beneath Silk's hooves. Firelight flickered in Ella's head. Poetry felt soothing in her brain. But suddenly Drake's face was there, filling her mind, taking her thoughts, warming her limbs. She shrugged out of Sutter's jacket.

If Drake intended her harm, why hadn't he tried to coerce her into going with him? Why had he not insisted? In truth, he had never been anything but kind, protective. Never overpowering or overbearing. Not tonight. Not ever.

But perhaps that meant nothing. Perhaps he knew his influence over her. Perhaps he was simply biding his time, knowing she would come to him. Perhaps he was simply . . . She shook her head, driving the thoughts from her mind and urging Silk onward. But suddenly Drake's town house appeared in the darkness before her, as if it were at the end of every path, as if it could not be avoided. In a moment she had dismounted. She was at his door in an instant, but there was no reason to knock, for it opened as if by magic. And he was there.

Then she was in his arms, crushed against his chest. His lips felt hot and firm against hers. He lifted her into his arms, carried her up the stairs to his bedchamber.

The door closed, but she failed to notice. She was caught in his eyes, in his embrace. His bed was broad and curtained. Moonlight splashed across his mesmerizing face. The bedsheets felt cool against her back. Then he was kissing her lips with slow, burning passion and she was lost, floundering until she no longer wished to escape.

She was sinking in the warmth of his touch, the strength of his allure, embedded in it, immersed in it. She reached for his buttons with her uninjured arm and they peeled away, revealing smooth sheets of sun-darkened skin over glorious, shifting muscle.

Yes, she was powerful. But he was stronger, irresistible. She smoothed her palm over his chest. He closed his eyes, trembling at her touch, and it was that movement, that shiver of weakness that thrilled her, for even with all his strength, he wanted her.

"Drake." She touched his cheek. His hands were dark magic, holding her to him. She was lost.

That much she knew, but she would not hide from it. She would know the truth, hear it said out loud. "I know—"

"I am in love with you," he said, and kissed her again, then found her eyes. "Though I have tried to be otherwise."

She studied him from inches away, heart pounding with hope. But she had been wounded to her very soul, and that wound would not heal quickly. "There is no reason to lie," she said, her voice soft in the darkness. "I cannot resist you. Little matter how you feel."

His face was dispassionate, as though he fought to hold his emotions at bay, but his eyes were burning. "I love you. God save me, but I do. I know you are . . ." A muscle jumped in his jaw. "I know you are not what you say you are. That you are more than you admit, and yet I can think of nothing else. Whatever you have done, whatever you will do—" he began, but in that moment she kissed him, for it was true. All true. She had not bewitched him. As much as she had tried to deceive him, she had been unable. From the first he had seen her honestly. And yet he loved her. Perhaps it was because he too was gifted in some almost imperceptible way. But whatever the reason, it was right. It was good.

Their joining was magical. No misgivings. No uncertainty. They were one. Their gazes never separated. Not even in the final moments when she crested the wave and rode to ecstasy. He shuddered against her and she collapsed to her side, breathing hard, wrapping her good arm around him.

She loved him. His strength, his face, his scent, his—

But suddenly she froze, trying not to think, yet her mind was scrambling over the bumpy past to days of worry and hope and fear for a young girl, a fledgling witch to whom she had given a gift, a scent, a potion that would keep her safe.

Jerking her gaze from Drake's, Ella scanned the room. And there on the mantel, she saw the small amber bottle she had given Sarah.

Chapter 24

"**W**here did you get the cologne?" Ella's voice sounded hollow, as if it came from a great distance, as if it were not her own. She sat up, gown wrinkled about her waist, chilled, scared.

Drake turned, glancing toward the mantel, toward the bottle, and suddenly the warmth was gone from his face. His expression was tense, his eyes guilty. "It was given to me."

She was frozen in place, playing a scenario back through her mind. Sarah, face somber as she took the bottle in her hand, vowing to use it, to keep it safe. "She would not have given it away," Ella intoned.

Drake rose to his feet. He looked beautiful, beautiful and powerful, but his expression changed, flashing to anger, to hatred. "What do you know of her?" he asked.

Ella stood up, trembling. "Sarah." She whispered the name like a prayer. "She was my friend."

"So that's how you snared her," he said, and grasped her arm. "With that potion? With that scent?"

"What are you talking about?"

"Just as you snared me. So I can think of nothing else." He shook her. "Can dream of nothing else."

He seemed very large suddenly; tall, terrifying. "Who are you?" she whispered, though she knew the answer.

"I've told myself her death was my fault. Caused by my jealousy. My pettiness. But it was you . . ." He gritted his teeth as though he couldn't go on, but rage and terror and sorrow were brewing in Ella's soul.

She caught him with her gaze, lowered her voice. "Set me free," she ordered, but he only tightened his fingers on her arm.

"You cannot hold me," she intoned, but she was wrong. He had a power she couldn't bend with her mind, couldn't break with her will. "Let me go."

"Who are you?" he gritted, shaking her. "Tell me—"

And in that instant she saw Verrill, saw his

rage, his cruelty. An incantation formed in her mind, boiling up, consuming her. She thrust it at him. Her spell was nothing but a puff of air. Still, he staggered backward, stumbling into the bed frame, his injured leg giving way beneath him.

She stepped toward him, wanting to help, to soothe, but he struggled to his feet, eyes ablaze with anger, with hatred. And she fled, flying down the hall, leaping through the door, throwing herself into the saddle. Silk's galloping hooves echoing against his voice as he called her name. But she didn't stop.

He had Sarah's scent. Had stolen it. But that was the least of the things he had taken from her. He had stolen her gift, her power, her very life.

Once again Ella had allowed herself to be duped. She'd been drawn in by a power she didn't understand, couldn't contain. Yes she was strong, yes she was trained, but it was nothing compared to the earth-shattering feelings he'd conjured in her soul.

Tears streamed down her face, obscuring her vision. She slowed Silk to a walk, leaned over her crest, crying. He was a warlock, a killer. And she had loved him. Had wanted him. Still wanted him, if the truth be told.

But she could not . . . would not succumb to

his dark allure. Would not make the same mistake again. For she had suffered that route, that pretend love.

He had seemed so right for her. But Verrill had seemed right too. So kind, so loving, when in reality he had been the personification of evil. Just as Drake was.

She had thought they shared a bond. Had thought they had both suffered and overcome and had become better for the experience. She winced at the memory of the puckered scars on his thigh. How had he survived such a hideous injury? How but by—

It was then that the truth struck; 'twas not his own power that had saved him from such a grievous injury. It was magic. *Her* magic. He had taken the potion she had given Sarah. Had used it for himself. How powerful he must be to make the essence his own; it was formulated for Sarah alone, or for one very much like her. A sister perhaps or . . .

She straightened, realizing suddenly that Silk had stopped.

In her mind, Drake stared at her, echoing the glance of another. Of Sarah. The eye color was different, but the rest was the same, somber, intelligent, moving.

Ella's mind soared away, remembering Sarah's words of her brother, Thomas, a military man. A handsome man. A serious man, a poet in his heart, she had said. And wounded. But he had a good soul. She was certain of it, and one day they would be friends.

Drake had her potion, Ella realized dazedly. Not because he had stolen it. But because Sarah had given it to him, to keep him safe, to keep him whole.

"Thomas," she whispered, and prepared to turn Silk around, only to realize she had done so long ago.

Drake was not the evil warlock who had drawn Sarah into a life of crime and eventual death. He was her brother. Her guardian. Ella was certain of it suddenly.

Silk's hooves clattered against the cobblestones. Lantern light slashed across the street, leaving them more in darkness than light, but she did not slow the mare's pace.

They slid to a skittering halt in front of his door. Throwing herself from the saddle, Ella flew up the steps and burst inside. And he was there, dressed in trousers and coat, black hair tousled, dark eyes troubled.

"I didn't mean to harm her," she rasped, tears burning her throat.

"Ella—"

"But she was entranced. She came at me. I tried to stop her without hurting her. But she struck her head."

"Leave," he said, face ashen. "Get out."

Sorrow squeezed her heart. Guilt clawed at her, but she pressed on. "I tried to keep her safe. Truly I did. But—"

"Get out!" he ordered, but she shook her head. And in that moment Harrison Sutter stepped into view.

Ella started, then froze, for the pistol he held steady in his hand was pointed directly at Drake's heart.

"It's no use," Sutter said, tone level, eyes steady. "Our Ella is not easily dissuaded once she sets her course. Are you, Ella?"

"Grey," she said, and felt the truth of her words singe her soul.

He smiled, still looking harmless, kind. "At your service, my lady. Or shall I call you Josette?"

"Why?" It was the only word she could force from between frozen lips.

He shrugged. "Because I can, I suppose. I learned that some time ago. In Madrid, actually."

"You killed Leila," she hissed, but he laughed.

"No, my dear. I did not kill her. In actuality I

seem to have convinced her to kill herself. At the time I was as surprised as any by my powers of persuasion."

"Why? She—"

"I believe she was to meet with a friend of ours. A woman you so charmingly call Vision. A woman who would have told her of Napoleon's intentions to invade Spain." He canted his head. "France was willing to pay rather handsomely to keep that information quiet, and I was just then beginning to realize the power I have over a very select group of people."

She felt breathless, lost, floundering in a sea of regret. "You're a warlock."

"Warlock." He considered that with a smile. "The word has negative connotations, I fear. But yes, I suppose that is indeed what I am."

Ella shook her head, trying to understand, to think. "Why Sarah?"

He opened his mouth, but Drake spoke first. "Because he's a coward."

They turned toward him.

"Too weak to challenge someone older." Drake said. "Someone stronger."

The two men stared at each other. "I hate to disagree," Grey countered, "but as you can see, I am challenging *you* this very minute. You . . ."

361

He glanced toward Ella without moving his weapon the smallest degree. "And your beloved here."

"Let her go," Drake said, voice steady, eyes the same, steady and low and unmoved. "I'm Sarah's brother. I'm the one to be concerned with."

"Do you think so?" Sutter asked.

"Yes." The edge of a dark smile curved Drake's lips. "In fact I do. For I'm the one who is about to kill you."

For an instant, fear shown in Grey's eyes, but then he laughed. "Funny thing though. I seem to be the only one holding a gun."

"Then you'd best shoot me now," Drake said. "Before I—"

"It's me you want," Ella rasped.

They glanced toward her and she nodded, rushing on. "It's why you came to London, isn't it, Sutter?"

Grey stared at her an instant, then nodded admiringly. "Tell me, my dear, can you read minds too, as well as your other talents?"

"There's no need to read your mind," she said. "For I can feel your evil. You came here for me. That I know. But why?"

"As it happens I make a very good living convincing witches to do my bidding." He laughed.

"That sounds rather diabolical, doesn't it. Indeed, I—"

"Sarah was naught but goodness," Drake countered. "She was gifted, yes, but she was not a witch."

Grey stared at him, eyes shining, and tsked. "I suspect it is the older brother's place to declare his sister's innocence, is it not?"

"She *was* an innocent," Drake said.

"Perhaps when I met her," Sutter said, and brightened his grin. "But I felt her fledgling powers from the first. And I knew, *knew* she would be of use."

"Then why kill her?" Drake hissed.

"Kill her?" Surprise showed on his mild features. "I did no such thing. Nor did I intend to. Not for some time at any rate. Until she could be replaced by someone better, someone more powerful. I knew another would come along, for you see, witches are attracted to their own kind." He smiled fondly. "In actuality, Sir Drake, it was your beloved here who killed her. Just as she was trying to explain to you."

Drake turned toward her. Ella met his gaze like a blow.

"It's true." She could stop the words no more than she could stop the beating of her heart. "I killed her," she said, and dragged her attention back to Grey. "You and I will work well together, Sutter."

He lifted a brow. "I believe we will. As soon as we are rid of your beloved here."

"He is not my beloved."

He smiled a little. "Even better then," he said, and raised the short muzzle.

Panic burned her like acid, but she struggled to keep her tone steady, almost bored when next she spoke. "But I'll not risk another death."

"Some risk is necessary." Grey thumbed back the hammer.

"They'll hear the shot," she said. He looked at her again. "If you kill him, they'll hear the shot. Tie him up instead. Leave him here. I'll go with you. Anywhere you like."

"Oh my dear," Grey said, and shook his head sadly. "Is this what you've been reduced to? Groveling? For him?" Moving to the right, he circled Drake, putting them both in his line of fire. "Is that what love has brought you to?"

She curled her lips in the semblance of a dark smile. "I believe I have already told you that I don't love him."

"But you lie."

"No—"

"You lie," he repeated evenly. "Would you like to know how I came to realize that?"

She opened her mouth to speak but he was already continuing.

"It's because I have no power over you. I gave you every opportunity to become enamored with me. Gave you a blanket. Gave you the very coat off my back."

Drake scowled.

"Ahh, so your beloved doesn't know," Grey said, and smiled fondly at Ella. "You see it's like this. I have some kind of . . ." He shrugged, looking modest. "I won't say unique . . . but *unusual*. I have an unusual *something* that draws gifted women to me. And Josette here, well . . . she is unusually tactile. Able to sense things through touch. Hence I gave her certain items that had been in my possession for some time. That I had had against my skin. A blanket. My coat. I worried, of course, that she would be able to sense my true intentions, but I kept my thoughts well disciplined when I was in possession of them . . ." He shrugged. "I thought only of her, of how I would love her, would cherish her."

Drake's gaze was absolutely steady on Grey, never faltering, never turning.

"But our Josette didn't seem to return my affection. The items I gave her should have brought her quickly to my side. But . . ." He turned back toward Ella. "But you returned to him instead of coming to me." He shook his head, disappointed. "Therefore, he must die. It's for your own good, really. Surely you don't want to become just another woman, just another wife, bobbling about a moldering estate with his baby on your hip."

The image was clear in her mind. The child had a chubby fist wrapped in her gown and was leaning back, laughing as they twirled about. His hair was chestnut hued, but his eyes were the dark, entrancing magic of Drake's.

"With me you will become even more powerful," Grey said.

She stowed the image jealously away, for Drake and his child were indeed what she wanted. What she had wanted all along. "Stealing trinkets from old men on Bond Street?" she asked.

"Sarah was a weakling," he said. "She was capable of no more. But with you . . ." He shook his head. "Who knows what powers we can defeat?" His voice rose dramatically. "What principalities we can tumble."

"None," she said, tone as steady as the floor beneath her bare feet. "Not if you harm him."

But Grey only smiled.

"We shall see," he said, and aimed.

Ella cast her spell quickly, but fatigue made it weak. Terror made it unsteady. Still, the force of it knocked Grey sideways. But he found his balance and raised the gun. It was then that Drake attacked, spurting across the room to strike Grey in the chest with his shoulder. They crashed to the floor.

The pistol roared like a cannon. Drake jerked. Blood flowed between them.

Ella screamed, frozen in horror. But Drake was still alive, still coherent, gripping the gun in both hands.

The two struggled madly for it, writhing on the floor, the pistol frozen between them, but finally it moved, grinding inexorably toward Grey's head until it was pressed against his ear.

"For the women I love," Drake gritted, and pulled the trigger.

The gun bellowed. Grey jerked. His eyes went wide, and then he lay still, staring at the ceiling in horror and disbelief.

"Drake!" Ella scrambled to him, turned him onto his back. "Drake." His eyes were closed, his body limp. "No! No." She bent over him, kneeling. "I didn't mean to hurt you. Not you!" She rocked back and forth, aching, crying. "Not Sarah. Please. God please."

"You're a witch," he whispered.

She gasped, jerked her gaze to his face. His eyes were open, his expression placid.

"You're alive," she rasped.

He didn't bother to agree. "You're a witch," he repeated.

"Just lie still. I'll fetch help." She lifted his head to scoot out from underneath, but he caught her hand.

"As was my sister."

"Drake." Guilt and shame and terror seared her, burned her like a fire. "Please, let me get a doctor to—"

"When you tell me the truth."

She caught his gaze, held it, forced herself to accept, to admit. "Yes," she said.

He nodded, considered, blew out a breath. "I'll not see a doctor," he said.

"But . . . You promised."

"I lied," he said, and grimacing, pushed his hand beneath his coat to pull out her fat compilation of poems. A bullet had furrowed a diagonal path through the pages and become lodged in the back cover. A trace of blood was smeared across the spine. "I meant to return this."

"Keep it," she said, and kissed him.

Chapter 25

Their marriage was a private ceremony held in the untamed gardens of Lavender House. It was attended by witches and friends and one rather ponderous miller's son, who happened, by wildest coincidence, to be the estate's new gardener. Madeline came alone, seeming quiet and reserved. For reasons unexplained, she had left the coven and Jasper Reeves's dubious protection, but Ella put Reeves's strange behavior and her sister's unusual melancholy out of her mind. Maddy was safe. Drake was whole, and she was completely and desperately in love.

Two months later little had changed.

Ella sat in bed at Berryhill with Drake's head cradled on her lap.

"Can I assume you've gotten over your infatuation with the miller's son?" he asked.

She smiled and swept the dark hair back from his forehead. Was it as noble and handsome as it seemed, or was she, after all, entranced? "I don't think it would be very considerate of me to disregard him out of hand merely because he's a few pounds overweight."

"Pounds?" Drake questioned.

"Stones," she corrected, and winced a little at the memory. Perhaps she should have chosen another if she had hoped to make Drake jealous. "Not to mention the lacking teeth."

He watched her, expression somber.

"The baldness. The height." She sighed. "Or lack thereof."

"You are the most beautiful woman I have ever seen," he said.

She raised a brow and traced a forefinger along his jaw. "Tell me, sir, have you always been cursed with such poor eyesight?"

His dark eyes shone in the firelight. "I believe, in fact, that I was entirely blind until the moment I saw you across Miss Anglican's dance floor."

She watched him, memorizing every detail of his face. "I should have known you at the outset," she said. "You have Sarah in your eyes. But I couldn't seem to see it. Tell me, sir, have you always been so gifted that you could turn aside others' magic?"

"Sarah was the special one. I was not gifted," he said. "Not until you." Lifting her hand, he kissed her knuckles. "I am sorry I lied. Sorry I wasn't here to protect her, to—" he began, but she shushed him.

"Your duty was elsewhere."

"I wish it were as simple as that," he said. "I wish I had felt some sort of loyalty to king and country. But the truth is—"

"You resented her." She tilted her head, willing away his pain. "Resented her pampered life, your father's love, while you were wounded in a seemingly hopeless war."

His dark brows lowered. She skimmed her newly ringed finger along a furrow.

"I'm sorry," he said again, and she smiled.

"She forgave you."

His gaze bored into hers. "How do you know?"

"Because I am a witch," she said, and smiled again. "But mostly because I was her friend. She loved you. Bore no ill will. Or she would not have sent you the potion."

"Which saved my life."

"While you saved my soul. I love you," she said.

The glimmer of a smile lifted his lips. He was

naked. The tail end of a sheet trailed lazily across one lean hip, hiding his damaged thigh, but baring his scars.

"And I you," he said.

Leaning down, she kissed him. "I can tell."

He slipped his hand behind her neck. "Can you?"

"Why else would you give me such a wonderful gift?"

He canted his head, studying her. Truth to tell, he wasn't the romantic sort. Not the kind to shower her with gifts. Oh, he'd bought her riding gloves of kid leather a few days past as well as the dressing gown that she still half wore. And just yesterday he'd found a book of poetry by Jane Winscom. It lay open beside the bed, but truth to tell, it was more beneficial for him than her. She seemed to find elegies strangely erotic.

"What gift is that?" he asked.

She smiled again, secret and happy, and skimmed her hand over the gauzy fabric beneath his head.

"The gown is hardly new. I bought that—" he began, and froze. The world limped along. He sat up slowly, carefully, never losing eye contact. Bracing on one arm upon the mattress, he leaned across her body and stared into her eyes.

"Ella—" he began, but words failed him.

Nevertheless, she answered. "Yes," she said.

"Are you—"

"Yes."

"The doctor said I would not—"

"The doctor was wrong . . . again."

"But how—"

"The usual manner, I believe."

He felt breathless, lost, thrilled beyond words. New life, new hope, new chances to make things right, to start fresh, to love. Reaching out, he skimmed his hand behind her neck and caught her gaze. "It's not the miller's son's, is it?" he asked.

And she laughed.

Next month, don't miss these exciting new love stories only from **Avon Books**

In Bed With the Devil by Lorraine Heath

An Avon Romantic Treasure

Lucian Langdon, Earl of Claybourne, is thought by many to be beyond redemption—a fact that makes him perfect for Lady Catherine Mabry. She needs a man of his reputation to take down her vicious uncle. But the more she gets to know Lucian, the more she realizes that what she asks of him will destroy the man she's come to love.

A Match Made in Hell by Terri Garey

An Avon Contemporary Romance

Nicki Styx is slowly adjusting to her new life as guidance counselor to the dead. Things are going well, until the devil himself makes an appearance—and it's Nicki he's got his eye on. And there's no escaping the devil, especially when he's after your soul.

Let the Night Begin by Kathryn Smith

An Avon Romance

Years ago, Reign turned his wife Olivia into a vampire—without her consent. Enraged, she left him, swearing never to return. But revenge proved too sweet to resist. When an enemy turns out to be more dangerous than either of them suspects, Olivia and Reign are forced to trust each other—and the love they once shared.

Lessons From a Courtesan by Jenna Petersen

An Avon Romance

Victoria and Justin Talbot were happy to part ways after their forced marriage. But to rescue a friend, Victoria must return to London, this time disguised as a courtesan. Her new "profession" enrages Justin—but seeing her again makes him realize that, despite their rocky beginning, their love was meant to be.

AVON

978-0-06-133535-8

978-0-06-144589-7

978-0-06-137452-4

978-0-06-415218-5

978-0-06-116142-1

978-0-06-143857-8